Shadows of BRIERLEY

A Far Horizon

VOLUME TWO

Shadows *of* BRIERLEY

A Far Horizon

VOLUME TWO

a novel

ANITA STANSFIELD

Covenant Communications, Inc.

Cover: *Peony* © Daniel F. Gerhartz. For more information go to www.danielgerhartz.com.

Cover design copyright © 2011 by Covenant Communications, Inc.

Published by Covenant Communications, Inc.
American Fork, Utah

Printed in the United States of America
First Printing: May 2011

17 16 15 14 13 12 11   10 9 8 7 6 5 4 3 2 1

ISBN-13: 978-1-60861-315-1

Chapter One
Leaving Brierley

Scotland—1839

Ian MacBrier helped strap the final piece of luggage onto the top of the carriage and jumped down. Heavy skies were growing heavier; dark clouds were getting darker. Ian wondered for a moment if they should postpone their journey another day with the hope of better weather. But he knew that rain could persist for days, and prolonging the inevitable would only prolong the heartbreak of unavoidable good-byes. He gave the servants some instructions and went inside the magnificent house called Brierley, trying not to think of how he would likely never see it again after today.

Ian hurried up the stairs where he found his wife and her sister rechecking the last few items they were packing into satchels they would carry with them throughout the journey. His sister-in-law Bethia didn't acknowledge his entrance into the room, but that was normal. For the majority of the time, Bethia existed more inside of her own mind than she did in the real world where most people existed. Ian had helped care for Bethia enough that he was accustomed to her strangeness, and he could generally calm her down if the people existing only in her imagination did something to upset her. But it was Wren who could handle Bethia better than anyone. The sisters were inseparable. Ian had been well aware when he'd married Wren that he would also take on the responsibility of her sister. And he was fine with that. There was no woman in the world like Wren. He would have done anything—would *do* anything—to have her in his life. And today, Wren was willing to leave everything behind to begin an unpredictable and likely harrowing journey to unknown places for reasons that were based far more in faith than on any rationale of practicality.

Wren smiled at Ian and set aside her packing to embrace him, as if she sensed his unrest and hoped to buffer it. When it proved successful, he held her tighter, then longer when he didn't want to let go. With the exception of his knowledge of God's place in his life, Wren *was* his life. She was his strength, as vital as the blood that coursed through his veins. They were utterly inseparable. He felt certain if they even attempted to exist apart from one another, they would both be too heartbroken to function. And now they would be leaving here together for reasons that were complicated at best, and far from easy in any respect. But they both knew it was the right thing to do. They'd both experienced an undeniable, personal witness that this was the course God wanted them to take. Their experiences had been completely independent of each other, but the path before them had been made equally clear. There were reasons they needed to remove Bethia from this place; with her fragile mental condition and in her present circumstances, it would be impossible to keep her in this community and keep her safe. But Ian's need to protect Bethia was only a portion of his motivation for leaving the home of his youth. He'd been born with a bizarre sense of wanderlust that had brought much grief to him and his loved ones. Only recently had he come to understand that God had planted such feelings in his heart in order to prepare him for this step in his life. Leaving was the only thing he could do in order to remain at peace with himself.

"We should go," he said to Wren, forcing himself away from the sanctity of her embrace. Rain started pelting the windows with a startling intensity. A quick glance at his wife revealed the concern in her expression.

"A little while longer won't hurt," she said as if she could fully sense his reluctance to take this final step. "Perhaps if we wait, the weather will clear, or—"

"You know as well as I that the rain is more likely to persist than not," he said. "We just need to go. It *will* hurt to put it off. Every hour we delay will only make it more painful." He cleared his throat as if it could clear away the hovering fear he had of the doors of Brierley closing behind him.

"Are ye worried, Ian," Wren asked, "about leaving all of this behind?"

He looked at his wife and chuckled, glad to find that the question contained some humor that somewhat abated his present emotions. "If you're implying that I can't live without the comforts of Brierley, then you have a very short memory, my love. I lived very well without them while I wandered the streets of London."

"I know, Ian. And ye lived very well without them when ye married me and lived in our tiny house behind the tailor shop. I know all of that, and that's not what I mean." She touched his face with gentle fingers. "I mean leaving yer family, the safety and security of yer home."

Ian looked down and blinked hard to hold back the burning in his eyes. "I will miss my family very much," he said, "as I know you will. But delaying the inevitable will not help the matter. Tell me what I can do to help you so that we can be on our way."

"There's nothing more t' do, Ian," she said and glanced discreetly at her sister. In a softer voice she added, "She'll keep refolding her things for as long as we're here. We can be ready in a few minutes."

"And Shona?" he asked in reference to the sweet little maid who had taken so thoroughly to Bethia—and Bethia to her—that they couldn't even consider leaving without at least asking Shona to go with them. She had been so eager to come along that it had strengthened Ian's resolve in believing this was their destiny. Shona had no family to speak of, no life in Scotland that she would regret leaving behind. And her being with Ian and his family as they traveled would make everything easier for Bethia *and* for Wren—which of course would make the journey easier for him. What did he know about seeing to a woman's needs? But Shona was gifted about such things. She was reliable and devoted, and Ian had thanked God more than once for making it possible for her to join them as they embarked into an unknown future.

"She's ready and waiting," Wren said.

"Let's go then," Ian said with firm resolve.

Wren touched his face and smiled; courage filled her countenance. "We know this is the right thing, my love. God will be with us. He will surely comfort our sorrow."

Ian nodded but couldn't speak.

Ten minutes later they were standing in the hall near the door, surrounded by family members with whom they'd already shared multiple good-byes. The last few days had been laced with mention of the last time they would all be together for this or for that. At times they'd been able to make jokes about the pending departure of Ian and his family, and the way Ian's brother Donnan would remain at Brierley and become the Earl of Brierley at whatever point their father left this world. At other times, tears couldn't be held back, especially by Ian's parents. Ian had done well at holding back his own tears, although he felt certain that a good cry would be in order over such an event. It was little different from a death, he believed. He'd lost his brother James and his best friend Greer to death. Both events had been tragic, and he'd grieved deeply. Leaving Brierley felt akin to that in some ways. But his grief over leaving did not negate even slightly the absolute faith he had in his charted course. Just as he knew that Greer and James were gone, he knew that this journey to America with his wife and his sister-in-law was in God's hands, not his own, and there was nothing he could do or say to change it.

Unable to bear the agony, Ian opened the door and stepped out, urging the women closer to the carriage. Because of the rain, the family all followed under the shelter of umbrellas, and he watched through a haze while final good-byes were shared. He helped Bethia, Wren, and Shona into the carriage and watched his brother guide his own family back into the house. Donnan glanced back once to share a final, steady gaze with Ian before he disappeared, then Ian turned to face his parents.

"Ian." Anya took his face into her hands. "Oh, my sweet Ian." He knew his mother's reluctance to let him go was understandable, but it was still making this harder. "How I wish there was something I could say to make you change your mind."

"We've already talked about this, Mother, and—"

"I know," she said, fresh tears accumulating in her eyes. "I understand, Ian; I do. I respect you for this decision . . . even though it breaks my heart. I just want you to know that . . . you will always be in my heart. And God willing, we may yet see each other again before this life is done."

"God willing," Ian repeated, knowing it was the best answer he could give. He was putting his life into God's hands, and it would only be by His will that such a reunion might take place one day. For all he knew, for all that any of them knew, he would never again return to the shores of Scotland. America was so very far away, and the land itself so enormous. The future was completely uncertain and subject to circumstances that Ian could never imagine.

Anya took hold of Ian for one last embrace. They held to each other tightly until he feared she would never let go; he had to initiate the separation or stand there forever. He gently did so and heard her sob. He looked into her eyes once more and glanced toward his father, recalling with clarity the firm, emotional embrace they'd shared only moments ago. Then he stepped into the carriage before he could have even a moment longer to think about what this meant or to prolong this agony any further.

Once inside the carriage, Ian took a deep breath. He exchanged a long, steady gaze with Wren, who was sitting next to him. He glanced across the way at his sister-in-law, who was sitting next to Shona. She was a little more tall and plump than either Bethia or Wren, who were both of average height and build for a woman. Shona's hair was a medium brown, a shade somewhere between Bethia's blonde and Wren's nearly black tresses. All three women wore their hair up and pinned to the back of their heads in a similar fashion.

Bethia was absently gazing out the window in a way that was typical for her. She unconsciously rubbed her hand over her rounded belly, and Ian felt a pang of fear in wondering how he would manage such a journey with two pregnant women. He reminded himself for the thousandth time that he knew God would be with them, and the carriage jolted forward. Ian turned abruptly to look out the back window of the carriage, catching a glimpse of his parents huddled close together beneath an umbrella. He watched them, expecting to see them go inside, but they didn't. As the carriage rolled farther away, the view of the splendid structure called Brierley broadened. He absorbed it into his memory until the carriage took a turn and he could no longer see the house *or* his parents. He turned to look at Wren and held her gaze until they both felt compelled to look out the windows at their sides, taking in the beauty of the lush, green Scottish countryside as it was being bathed in a continual downpour.

When they had traveled far enough to get beyond the familiar landscape of the valley where they'd both been raised, Ian lost his fascination with the scenery. Wren continued to take in the view. She'd never traveled more than a few miles from her home. But Ian had seen it all before, and the memories associated with leaving his home previously were not necessarily pleasant. He'd come back with the firm declaration and belief that his wanderlust had been cured. He'd married Wren and made every effort to settle down and be content. But the compelling need to leave his home, strengthened by the undeniable witness that God had a greater plan for him and his family, had gradually integrated into the necessity of removing his family from this place for the sake of keeping Bethia safe.

They traveled steadily through the day, stopping only when absolutely necessary. The darkness of late evening had completely overtaken them before they stopped for the night. The driver would get a good night's sleep and go back to Brierley where he was employed. From here, Ian would arrange for their travel to continue to Liverpool in a hired coach. The inn where they stayed was less than adequate in his opinion, but it was the only place available in the middle of nowhere. He had stayed in far worse places in the past during his years of wandering, but he wanted the women to be completely comfortable and safe. They had a hearty meal, which they opted to eat in their rooms when it became obvious that Bethia seemed unsettled by the noisy crowd. Her reluctance to be left alone at all in such strange surroundings enhanced Ian's gratitude for Shona being with them. This way, one of the women could always be with Bethia, and Ian could have time alone with his wife without worrying about the well-being of his sister-in-law.

Rain battered the roof of the inn all through the night; however, Ian slept tolerably well in spite of it and was pleased to discover at breakfast that the women had also slept well. Bethia was more calm than on the previous evening and seemed more engaged in the adventure of going to America.

Once they were on their way again, Bethia said, "I think Greer would have very much liked t' be with us on our journey."

"Perhaps he is," Wren said, and Ian cast a subtle glare at her. He knew she meant that Greer might well be with them in spirit; since they both believed that spirits lived on after death, it was not difficult to imagine. But he also knew that Bethia often suffered severe delusions, and he didn't want to encourage her to think that her deceased husband might *actually* be among them.

"He's dead, Wren," Bethia said firmly, as if her sister might not have known.

Ian felt relief over Bethia's clear perception of reality in that regard, but the comment still rankled him. Greer had not been dead very many months, and the means by which they'd lost him were shrouded by a mist of horror in Ian's memory. The strangeness of his tragic death was overshadowed by the fact that prior to the unlikely accident that had left him with an infected wound that took his life, everyone who knew him had believed he'd died years earlier in a fire. Everyone except for Bethia. Greer had been secretly living in the cellar of their home, interacting with his wife, relying on the illness of her mind to make everyone else believe that her talking about him was just a product of her imagination. Now they knew that Greer had been alive during that time. But since there *were* people existing only in Bethia's mind, it was difficult even now for Ian to sort out Bethia's perceptions from what was real. Mentally he knew the difference, but sometimes an emotional part of him had trouble with the fact that he'd lost his best friend to death—twice. And the deception and strangeness surrounding the memories always left him uneasy. The one thing he knew for certain was that Greer was indeed dead. Ian himself had helped bury Greer's body secretly in the woods. With the community already believing he was dead, there could be no public explanation of his dying again without bringing to light the reality of Bethia's state of mind. Wren had feared for years that people might not understand, and that Bethia might be forced to live in some horrible asylum. *That* fear had not come to fruition. But when Bethia's pregnancy had become obvious, and no one knew that her husband had actually been alive, it had quickly become evident that she could never live peacefully in the community. She was surrounded by people who didn't understand, and some who were spewing out harsh judgment and shunning her to the point of even forbidding her to attend church. Ian had already known in his heart that leaving his home and taking his family with him was the right thing to do. The need to protect Bethia and Wren had simply facilitated making that decision quickly and precisely. Now there was no turning back.

"Of course I know Greer is dead," Wren said to her sister, startling Ian back to the conversation. "I only meant that he surely lives on in spirit, and I'd like t' think of him being with us. Perhaps he's looking out for us."

"A pleasant thought," Ian said. Bethia smiled and looked out the window.

The rain continued with unfaltering consistency through the remainder of their journey to Liverpool. The coach wedged its way into the bowels of the dirty city just as the rain decreased to a colorless drizzle. Ian could see the shock of city life on the faces of the three women as they silently took in the noise and chaos reaching through the carriage windows. Wren said nothing, but she squeezed his hand tightly, and he detected a slight tremor in her fingers. Bethia and Shona held to each other as if they were suppressing great fear.

"You mustn't worry," Ian said, sounding more sure of himself than he felt. "I know it's all very strange and different from the Highlands, but that's the very reason we will have adventures we've never had before."

Bethia smiled at him, as if his words immediately soothed her. The other women just continued staring out the windows, having nothing to say.

The first order of business was to find rooms at a decent hotel so the women could rest and be comfortable, especially given the fact that Wren and Bethia were both pregnant. Ian wanted to make certain through every step of the journey that their needs were met first and foremost. Now that he'd actually gotten past the painful severing of himself from Brierley, he was prepared to take as much time as necessary to achieve their destination. The health and safety of those in his care were far more important than his keen desire to get to America and to find people who shared his beliefs—people like the two missionaries he'd encountered in London not yet a year and a half ago. The things he'd heard them preaching, and the book they had put into his hands, had changed his life irrevocably. Wren too had read the book and knew of its truth, and God had made it clear to both of them that their destiny was to find these people and become a part of the religion they lived.

Ian often wondered how it would be when they *did* find them. He imagined a golden city, full of peace and light radiating from the goodness of the people gathered there together. But he knew that he had a tendency toward a vivid imagination, and the imaginings of his youth in believing that a better world existed away from his own home had left him sorely disappointed. This was different, however. Still, he had no idea what to expect and very little to go on in knowing where and how to find these people. The book had been printed in New York, and that's where they would begin. But they had a long journey to simply get *there,* and they needed to take it slowly.

With the kind help of the coach driver who was very familiar with Liverpool, Ian was able to efficiently find adequate rooms for his family at a moderately priced hotel with enough amenities for comfort without being too lavish. While the inheritance he'd brought with him was more than adequate to meet their needs for many years to come, he was determined to be frugal and not waste it away. The one thing that was certain was that the future could be unpredictable.

Ian gave a little extra money to the driver in appreciation for his help, and it was accepted with gracious gratitude and a mention of the man's large family. Ian felt a small pang at the mention of family, imagining his own lost in some measure of grief over his departure. It occurred to him that there would not be such grief if he were not so well loved. He had been blessed to come from a good family, and he was grateful for that privilege. Even in this separation, the memory of his life at Brierley and the lessons of love and living, and right and wrong, would always be with him. In that instant, Ian shifted his pain of parting from his family to thoughts of gratitude and pressed forward with getting his family settled into their temporary lodgings; they would remain here until they could get passage to New York. Since Ian had never traveled beyond his native island at the east edge of the Atlantic, he had absolutely no idea what he was doing. He was glad to have the night to ponder the next step when it was far too late to do anything about it.

By the time they were settled into their rooms, it was past the time when they should have eaten supper, and they were all very hungry. There was a little restaurant on the main floor of the hotel, and they were glad to be able to conveniently acquire a good meal. Bethia took well to the hotel and decided that she would like to eat in the restaurant. She seemed to enjoy taking in the newness of the experience, and she kept very quiet—which was good considering how prone she was to erupting into strange outbursts as a result of the imaginary people talking in her head.

When they'd finished eating, they went upstairs to their rented rooms: two bedrooms that adjoined through a little parlor that was comfortable for visiting and eating meals. Wren made certain that Bethia was settled in, and she left her sister and Shona sitting on their bed, taking turns reading aloud to each other from *The Pickwick Papers*. Wren returned to the room they shared and closed the door, leaning against it a long moment in a way that was typical for her, as if she were breathing in the relief of knowing that her sister was calm and she could now relax. Wren's life had been considerably wrapped up in caring for Bethia ever since her strange mental condition had manifested itself. Ian was only glad that he was also a significant part of Wren's life, and that he could help her carry these burdens. Their eyes met across the room, and he too felt the relief of being alone with her, and being safe and secure in this place, with this first portion of the journey—however brief—behind them. He kissed her in greeting, as if they'd not seen each other for hours—or days—then he held her close and took advantage of such precious time with his beloved wife, renewing the love they shared and finding a peace and serenity that he could find nowhere else.

While they held each other in peaceful silence, neither speaking but not prone to sleep, Ian prayed silently that he would be guided in the unknown journey that lay before them, that he could keep those in his care safe and well, and that they would be led to be joined with God's people in a faraway land. He prayed for his family back at Brierley, and imagined them happy and laughing together around the dinner table. Then he thanked God for all he had been blessed with before he tightened his hold on Wren and kissed her good night.

* * *

The following morning, the rain had stopped, but the city had a grayness that was only enhanced by an overcast sky. Ian went out early to take inventory of their surroundings and make some inquiries. He returned to find the three women sitting on the bed in the other bedroom, giggling like little girls. But their laughter made him smile.

It was typical for them, and he loved hearing it. He hoped they kept giggling through the months ahead. They'd had breakfast brought up to the room and had already eaten. Ian ate the portion they'd saved for him while he read a local newspaper and listened to the laughter of the women occasionally wafting from the other room.

Ian went out again, leaving the women still engaged in that seemingly endless stream of female conversation. He felt firm in his mind on purchasing passage to New York, and returned to the hotel with the arrangements made for his family to depart in six days time. He concluded that in the time between now and then, he would research traveling tips from the people who inhabited this shipping community, and they would do everything they could to be as prepared as possible for a smooth crossing.

Upon his return, the women informed him that they would all be having lunch in a tea shop down the street that had come highly recommended by one of the hotel maids, and then they would like to wander about the city on foot and do a little shopping. They teased Ian about coming along to protect them and carry their packages. He graciously accepted the challenge, and they walked down the street away from the hotel. Wren had her hand over his arm, and he exchanged a smile with her. He loved to see her taking in these new experiences with more joy than fear. Bethia and Shona walked ahead of them, with Shona on the lookout for the recommended tea shop.

"Oh, there it is!" she declared excitedly, and Bethia let out a delighted laugh that was contagious among the others.

The tea shop was somewhat crowded, but it had a jovial atmosphere and it was filled with pleasant aromas. They were guided to a table by the window that was actually set up to seat six, but it was the only available table that would seat more than two people. The view of the busy city street wasn't necessarily pleasant, but it was undoubtedly interesting—especially for these three women who had never traveled beyond the valley of their birth. Being in Liverpool reminded Ian far too much of his time in London, which held no pleasant memories for him at all. The cities had a different feel to them, as if they each had their own character and personality, but the essence of busy city life did not suit his taste. He focused instead on the women chattering as they took in all that was new and different around them.

While they were enjoying a simple lunch and tea in pretty china cups, the shop quickly filled up, and every seat was taken except for the two extra chairs at their own table. A moment after Ian had glanced around and become aware of this fact, he noticed a man and woman coming through the shop's door together. A serving maid approached them to explain that they would have to wait for a table. Ian saw their disappointment and the obvious fatigue in the expression of the woman, who was near the age of Ian's mother. The man with her appeared to be her son; they had similar features, although the man's hair color was darker than his mother's light brown, graying hair. The man was thin with very dark hair, not unlike Ian's—although his own was curly, and this man's hair was decidedly straight, but was cut long enough over his ears and neck to show it to its best advantage. Ian figured they were close to the same age, but this man was nearly a head shorter, which made him more of an average height.

Before Ian even realized what he was doing, he stood and approached these strangers, saying to the maid while he motioned toward the table, "They are welcome to sit with us if they would like."

The maid looked startled by this uncustomary solution to the problem. Ian looked directly at the man and woman and said, "We are new to the city and would enjoy your company. Please join us."

Only then did Ian realize the man was blind. His eyes didn't look at all disfigured or strange, except for the way they gazed off toward nothing.

"That's very kind of you, sir," the woman said. "We're always open to making new friends."

"I'll bring more dishes straightaway," the maid said and went to the kitchen. Ian motioned the newcomers toward the table. He noticed that the man held casually to the woman's arm in a manner that would not bring attention to his blindness, but she was clearly adept at guiding him when they moved about.

"My name is Ian MacBrier," Ian said as the woman guided the man's hand to the back of a chair. He found the edge of the table with his other hand, and managed with little difficulty to sit down. Ian helped the woman with her chair and motioned toward his own family. "This is my wife Wren, her sister Bethia, and our friend Shona."

"How very pleasant to meet you all," the woman said, beaming with pleasure and displaying not the slightest hint of awkwardness at joining strangers for lunch. Ian took his seat again, and she returned the introductions. "My name is Millicent Mickellini. The first name doesn't match the last, I know. I'm British, born and bred, but I married a fine Italian man. His life was brief, may he rest in peace, but he left me a fine son who is very much like him." She put a gentle hand over her son's arm. "This is my son, Howard, although he prefers to go by Ward. He was never fond of the name Howard, but we named him after my father, may he rest in peace."

"I never knew my grandfather," Ward said, "but I choose to assume that he'd not mind my shortening his name for my own use."

"It's a pleasure t' meet ye, Mrs. Mickellini," Wren said, "and you as well—"

"Please, call me Millie," she interrupted firmly. "It was never in our nature to stand on formality. My dear husband, may he rest in peace, came from one of the best-known families in Italy when it comes to wine making. Anyone in the country who knows fine wine knows the name, that's for certain. He left us plenty well off when he died . . . may he rest in peace. But I was raised a simple woman, myself, and we certainly don't stand on formality, now, do we, Ward?"

"No, Mother," Ward said with a kind smile in the direction of his mother's voice, as if he were humoring her eccentricity; but he did it respectfully. "We certainly don't stand on formality." He turned more toward where Ian was sitting and added, "Please call me Ward, and understand that . . . as new friends, we will gladly respect your wish to be called whatever you choose."

"The use of given names is definitely our preference," Ian said. "By all means."

"That's a lovely accent you have," Millie said. "Ian, is it?"

"Yes," he said.

"I assume you're from Scotland with a name like MacBrier," Millie added. "The name certainly declares its heritage right off, doesn't it; the same with ours. You can't say *Mickellini* without people immediately knowing that it's Italian. So you're from Scotland?"

"We are," Ian said.

"From a different area than your wife?" Millie asked. "I detect a difference in the accents."

Ian caught a subtle smile from his wife and was glad to know she would never take offense from such a comment. The difference in their speech was the difference between his being raised as the son of an earl, and her being raised the daughter of a tailor. Those differences had never mattered to them. They'd been friends long before they were married, and they had always been equals in every respect. But Millie was obviously very sharp, and curious—and bold—to pick up on the difference in the few words they had exchanged—and to comment on it.

"No, we grew up in the same valley," Ian said and changed the subject. "What brings you to Liverpool?"

"You can't get to America without finding a ship to take you there," Ward said.

His mother quickly backed up the comment with a zealous, "We're going to become Americans!"

Ian felt as if time stopped for a long moment, while seconds stretched out to allow him to take in a powerful feeling and a great deal of information in the amount of time it would take to sneeze. He could likely never put the experience to words, but he knew the feeling. It was the same way he'd felt when his prayers had finally been answered and he'd known beyond any doubt that he needed to take his family to America. And now, he looked across the table at Ward Mickellini and felt as if they'd known each other far longer than a few minutes. He knew this was no coincidental meeting. He knew their lives had been destined to cross. He knew their being together through this journey was necessary and meant to be. Ian took a deep breath in an attempt to take it all in, and to convince himself that he was not crazy for acknowledging such feelings. Then he felt his wife's hand take hold of his beneath the table with an extra-tight squeeze that alerted his attention to the expression on her face, one that surely mirrored his own. Without a word spoken, he knew that she'd felt it too. They'd always been like that, sensing each other's thoughts. Only recently had he come to understand that it was God who had connected them that way. They kept each other from doubting the things they both knew that were true and right. He smiled at her, and she smiled back before she said to their new friends, "How very marvelous! That is the very reason that we've come t' Liverpool, as well."

"Truly?" Millie asked in a histrionic tone that made Ian chuckle. "What port are you sailing to? We just purchased passage yesterday to New York City; the ship sails in six days."

Ian shared another smile with his wife, then nodded toward Millie. "The very same," Ian said, and everyone at the table laughed at the remarkable coincidence, or perhaps more so from the warm chill of destiny that seemed to rush over the group of six gathered in the tea shop.

The newcomers told the serving maid what they would like, and it was brought to the table promptly. Light conversation and more laughter continued while they shared their meal.

The laughter stopped when Bethia spoke with direct soberness to Ward. "You're blind, aren't you?"

Ian was stunned but not surprised by Bethia's blunt approach. He was hoping Ward—or his mother—wouldn't take offense when Wren said, "Bethia dear, it's not polite t'—"

"I don't consider it impolite," Ward said, his face turned toward the sound of Bethia's voice. "In fact, I prefer having the matter addressed, as opposed to people pretending it's not true or trying to avoid it. Yes, Bethia," he said as he leaned slightly more toward her even though he couldn't see her, "I *am* blind. I wasn't born this way, so I do have memories of what the world looks like. The blindness came on slowly when I was a child. By the time I was ten, I could see nothing except that I have a vague sense of daylight, as opposed to darkness."

"It seems as though ye're looking at me," Bethia said to him.

"I'm looking at the sound of your voice," he said, and Bethia smiled.

"How do ye know I'm not very homely and repulsive?" she asked.

Ward chuckled comfortably, and his mother said, "Ward can teach us all a thing or two about seeing a person's heart."

"Can ye see my heart?" Bethia asked as if she were a child. If she *were* a child, the situation might not have been so awkward.

"I can only say that I hope to get to know you well enough to do so," Ward said, apparently unaware of any awkwardness.

"How do ye know what a person looks like?" Bethia asked him.

"You *sound* very beautiful," he said, and Bethia laughed softly. "But I must rely on my hands to see what my eyes cannot."

Bethia immediately took Ward's hand from where it rested on the table and put it to her face. Ian heard Wren gasp over her sister's boldness, but again Ward didn't seem put off or discomfited by it at all. Ward gently explored Bethia's face with his fingers while Millie just watched the exchange with a pleasant smile.

"You *are* beautiful," Ward said to Bethia, and again she laughed softly.

Ian realized what neither Ward nor his mother could know while they were all seated around a table. As Bethia's only protector in this world, he felt the need to point out the situation before any more flirting took place. Bringing it up couldn't possibly make the situation any more strange or awkward than it already was. Ward's hand was back on the table, but he seemed to be staring at Bethia as if he were thoroughly smitten. Bethia was looking back at him the same way. Millie looked utterly pleased, and Ian wanted to blurt out that these people had no idea of the dark secrets carried by this woman they were admiring.

"Bethia's husband passed away recently," Ian said, "and she's going to have a baby." He didn't add that she was also very mentally unstable, and possibly even dangerous when the personalities in her mind took over.

Ward's expression hardly changed. Millie said, "Oh, you poor darling. Of course we'll do anything we can to help. You can't have too many friends when life deals you a difficult hand. I too lost my husband when I was young, may he rest in peace. Perhaps we can give each other solace."

"Perhaps we can," Bethia said, smiling at Millie.

"Perhaps we can," Ward repeated, still gazing blankly toward the sound of Bethia's voice.

Ian wasn't sure what to make of the situation, but he reminded himself that only minutes ago he'd been overwhelmed with strong feelings of affinity toward this man. Surely the matter was in God's hands, and there was no need for concern. For the moment, he was content to lean back in his chair and enjoy the conversation as it bounced around the table and involved everyone. He became distracted by watching his wife. He thought of how beautiful she was, and how glad he was that he could see her. She turned to smile at him, and he was *very* glad to be able to see her!

Chapter Two
Seeing Bethia

Wren quickly developed a fascination for the city that left her continually eager to take in the sights and sounds, the smells and tastes of a world so completely different from the only world she'd ever known prior to embarking upon this journey. Ian had many times expressed his concerns on her behalf with how their travels might affect her. She understood the source of his worry. His own time away from home had not been positive for him, and of course, there was great uncertainty in leaving the security of home. But this was entirely different from the time that Ian had spent wandering London in an effort to hide from the difficulties of his life. Now they were together, and they were a family. They had already made new friends, and Wren was finding the energy of the city exciting and exhilarating.

Each day they embarked on some new discovery or adventure, wanting to take advantage of their day in the city. Wren loved going to the pier and seeing the ocean. Its magnificence and power was impossible for her to comprehend. To think of sailing such a huge expanse of endless water in order to reach their destination left her breathless. She loved the sound of the waves and the call of the seabirds. And she loved the beauty of the sailing vessels docked there in Liverpool after having visited vast and exotic ports only to make preparations to sail again to a new destination. She wondered what the ship might be like that would take them to America. When she shared her enthusiasm with Ian, he warned her that the reality of sailing for approximately six weeks, with only a tiny cabin below deck in which to live, might not fulfill her romantic expectations. She assured him that she was a reasonable and practical woman, and she would surely be able to handle whatever came along.

"I have no doubt of that," Ian told her with his typical loving smile. She would never get tired of—nor take for granted—that look in his eyes that left her absolutely certain every day of her life that Ian MacBrier loved her.

Wren also loved wandering the crowded streets of the city, watching the people as they passed by, peering into shop windows and sometimes going inside to further investigate the wares for sale. She'd never imagined such finery! She'd never even thought that such a variety of merchandise existed anywhere! Having been raised by a well-reputed tailor, and having learned his trade—even though she'd never been nearly as good at it as her sister—Wren was especially fascinated with the clothes available in such a thriving city. Ian tried to talk her into purchasing a fine traveling suit that he was convinced would look stunning on her. But she insisted that it was altogether impractical for the journey ahead, and it would simply be extra baggage.

Exploring the city quickly proved to be an interest that Wren's sister did *not* share with her. Bethia preferred to remain in the security of her hotel room for the most part and have meals brought to her. She became even more immersed in her voracious habit of reading, and she always had a sewing project close by that she could pick up in order to keep her hands busy. She was actively working on a few different objects of tiny clothing for her own baby, and for Wren's. Recently, she was sewing more and reading less since she had found such comfortable company in Ward Mickellini and his mother. Shona entirely shared Bethia's preference for staying in. After that first day out, she declared that she'd seen enough of the city and was abundantly pleased to stay with Bethia and watch out for her while Ian and Wren spent their days in exploration. Since they'd never had a honeymoon, never gone away together, just the two of them, anywhere, it was nice to have this time while Bethia was in Shona's capable care, and they could just do whatever they pleased with their hours.

Wren quickly became aware that there were parts of the city— perhaps even the *majority* of the city—that were unsavory and wretched. A person didn't have to look very far or very hard to see evidence of poverty and crime and depravity. Wren felt haunted by the glimpses she'd gotten into that world, and she was glad for Ian's generosity in sharing the coins in his pocket with some poor children they encountered. Beyond that, she had to accept that there was nothing that either of them could do to change such appalling conditions, but still, it haunted her.

Each day when Wren and Ian returned to their cozy room at the hotel, they found Ward and Millie there, visiting with Bethia and Shona. They were all usually talking and laughing as if they were longtime acquaintances, and had not just met here in Liverpool. When it became evident that this was becoming a habit, Ian said privately to Wren, "Should we not be concerned about Bethia's condition and how it might affect these people?"

"We probably should be," Wren said, "but I'm not certain what t' do about it. I can't tell Bethia t' refuse their company, especially when it makes her so happy."

"No, of course not," Ian said. He'd already shared with her the inexplicably warm feeling he'd gotten in regard to Ward. Since she had felt something strikingly similar, she heartily agreed that they needed to encourage this friendship. With their traveling on the same ship to the same destination, they both heartily concurred that their coming together was surely not a coincidence. And yet, Ian had brought up a very good point.

"I admit that it's concerned me," Wren said, "even if I've not wanted t' talk about it. But I'm not sure what's t' be done short of just telling Ward and Millie that Bethia is not mentally stable."

"I'm thinking that's *exactly* what needs to be done," Ian said.

Even though Wren wasn't surprised, she couldn't deny that the idea was upsetting. "And what if it pushes them away? What if they don't want anything t' do with her—or us—once they know the truth?"

"And what if Bethia goes into one of her fits and takes them completely off guard and scares the life out of them?"

Wren sighed. "You're right, of course."

"They've already spent many hours with her. I wonder if they haven't already noticed that something is amiss."

"Perhaps I should speak to Shona and find out what she's observed."

"I think that's an excellent idea," Ian said. "In the meantime, I'm going to try to figure out how to tell our new friends the truth."

"Perhaps *I* should be the one t' do it," Wren said. "She's *my* sister."

"She's *my* responsibility," Ian said firmly, and Wren wished he could know how loved she felt when he shared her burdens with such zeal. She'd told him many times, but she often felt that words were inadequate to describe the full depth of her feelings. "I think this conversation should be man-to-man, but I do think it would be well for you to speak with Shona first, and find out if anything out of the ordinary has occurred in our absence."

Wren *did* speak with Shona the very next morning while Bethia was soaking in a hot bath and Ian was out buying a newspaper before breakfast.

"She's quite taken with the young man's company," Shona said. "In fact, I've never seen her so lively. Truth be told, she's seemed more normal with him than I've ever seen her."

"That is quite remarkable," Wren said, taking a moment to absorb the implications. Bethia had been more *normal* with Greer than she'd ever been with anyone else. No, Wren thought, Greer had simply had a way of connecting in spirit to Bethia that could never be explained. He'd understood her even when she'd had trouble understanding herself. But that's not what Shona had said, and Wren felt the need to clarify. "You say she's been more *normal?*"

"I don't mean offense, Mrs. MacBrier," Shona said.

"Of course ye don't. I know that. And now that we're away from Brierley, I must insist that ye call me by my given name. I insist!"

"It's quite a habit," Shona said and bit her lip as if to keep herself from once again saying *Mrs. MacBrier.*

Wren went on purposefully. "Do ye suppose, then, that Ward and his mother have a way of simply bringing out the best in Bethia?"

"I would say that's true."

"But that does not mean that Bethia has been cured of her ailment. It's only been a few days. Ian is right when he says that she could suddenly go int' one of her fits and frighten them t' death. I think he's right when he says that he needs t' tell Ward about the problem, and if it frightens them off, so be it. We certainly can't have a comfortable friendship with *anyone* if they don't know the truth."

"I would agree with that," Shona said. "Truth be told, I'm feeling some relief t' have ye bring it up. I've been wondering what I'd do if she *did* have one of her fits with them around. And might I say that I know well enough she's certainly *not* cured, and I don't imagine she ever will be."

"What d' ye mean, Shona?" Wren insisted.

"I'm meaning I think Jinty and Selma are still in her head when we have company, but I think she's just become better at learning t' ignore what they're saying t' her, just as ye've taught her t' do when she's in public or around others. If Ward and his mother were staying longer hours, it might not be so easy for her t' keep it a secret."

The mention of Bethia's imaginary *friends* bristled Wren, especially when she considered all the turmoil they had caused. "We'll be crossing an ocean on the same ship with these people," she said to Shona. "I doubt that it's wise t' try and keep it a secret."

Wren spoke with Ian later that morning about her conversation with Shona, and he decided firmly that he would arrange a time when he and Ward could talk privately.

"How will ye tell him?" Wren asked, wishing for the millionth time in her life that her sister *could* have a normal life.

"I'm going to pray very hard and hope the right words come to me when I need them."

Wren admired her husband's faith, but she still felt nervous about the whole thing. She'd seen the way Bethia looked at Ward. And even though Ward couldn't *see* Bethia, he still had the very same expression on his face when they were together. He was smitten with her, and had quickly become very comfortable in her company. And Millie seemed utterly pleased, as if she were expecting matrimony to be the inevitable outcome. Wren knew there was no one in this world that could handle and understand Bethia the way that Greer had, and for all of Ward's fine qualities, he could hardly take on such difficult circumstances with Bethia when he had his own severe limitations.

Wren hoped the conversation between Ian and Ward would go well, and that the revelation of the truth would not damage the friendships that had been so quickly formed among the little group that had met in the tea shop. She didn't want Bethia to lose the friendship of these people; their time spent with Bethia was very good for her—for all of them. She just didn't want something horrible to happen and catch them unaware. Wren recalled some of the *dreadful* things that Bethia had done while she was out of her mind, and she prayed very hard that no such horror would ever recur. She also prayed very hard that this would all work out and they could all remain friends. It just seemed meant to be.

* * *

Later that morning when Ward and Minnie came to call, as expected, Ian eased Ward aside and said quietly, "I wonder if you and I might speak privately. Perhaps we should go for a little stroll."

"I would enjoy that very much," replied Ward.

Ian took Ward's hand and guided it to the back of his shoulder, so that Ward could walk where Ian walked without encountering obstacles. Ian announced to the ladies that they would be out for a while, and they all teasingly declared that it was about time for the men to be divided from the women for the sake of more stimulating conversation. Ward chuckled heartily and followed Ian out of the room, but Ian did not feel so jovial; this conversation was weighing heavily on him, and he wanted to have it over.

They shared some friendly small talk while exiting the hotel and going down the street a ways, but Ian soon realized he could not have a serious conversation with a blind man while on the move this way. He now wished he'd encouraged the women to go out together and do some shopping while he and Ward remained in the little parlor where they could have a quiet, private conversation. Settling on the next best thing, he said, "How about if we go to that tea shop where we met? It shouldn't be too crowded this time of day."

"Sounds delightful," Ward said with enthusiasm. Ian had realized that he was a very positive person, in spite of his blindness. He hoped that Ward's positive attitude would serve him well in dealing with this challenge in regard to Bethia.

Ian was pleased with the lack of crowds as they entered and were shown to a table for two across the room from the only other customers present. After they had ordered the standard tea and biscuits, Ward took Ian off guard when he said, "I may be blind but it's easy to see that you want to talk to me about something specific. There's no need to gracefully ease into what it might be. Just tell me what's on your mind."

"Very well," Ian said, amazed at Ward's perception when he couldn't see facial expressions or any gestures that might imply what he'd clearly sensed.

While Ian was trying to gather his words, Ward said, "Are you concerned about my intentions toward Bethia?"

"I do wish to speak to you about Bethia, but it's not really your intentions that concern me."

"I *am* in a position to provide well for a woman," Ward said, "and I am very fond of Bethia. But I'm also well aware that becoming attached to a woman would present certain difficulties. I can't expect my mother to take care of me indefinitely. And actually, I would never want a woman in my life simply to *take care* of me. I can hire someone to do *that*. I just want you to know that I very much enjoy Bethia's company, but we have known each other far too short a time for my mind to even be drawn to considering any steps that might cause you concern. I *cannot,* however, vouch for my mother on that account. She's rather straightforward about finding me a wife." Ward laughed at this, then became more serious. "I do hope she hasn't said or done anything to cause you any concern."

"Not at all," Ian said. "I mean . . . I've not been around much of the time that you've been visiting with Bethia and Shona, but Shona hasn't given us that impression. We all enjoy your mother's company very much—*and* yours, of course."

"Well then," Ward said, "what *can* this be about? It's in regard to Bethia, but not any concern about my intentions." He took a sip of tea. "You must spill the beans, Ian. The suspense is dreadful." Again Ian tried to find the words, and again Ward spoke. "Is it to do with her being pregnant? Or the fact that her husband hasn't been dead very long? Or perhaps I should stop guessing and just let you speak. Sometimes I think I'm far too much like my mother."

"I'm glad for your straightforward manner, Ward. I can start by saying that the situation surrounding Greer's death—Greer being Bethia's husband . . ."

24

"Yes, I know."

"The situation was highly unusual. I fear we had a great deal of drama over it."

"And yet Bethia seems to be handling it so well," Ward said. "She seems very at peace over losing her husband."

"That entirely depends on her mood, you see. I fear you've not been around her enough to know that there are times when the grief overtakes her with a great deal of confusion, and it can be quite . . . dramatic." Ian saw Ward's brow tighten and sensed his concern. "I feel responsible for Bethia," Ian said. "In fact, when I married Wren it was simply expected that if I were to take on the care of Wren, I would need to also take on Bethia's care, as well. And I'm fine with that; I truly am."

"You love both of them very much," Ward observed and took a small bite from a biscuit. "Bethia is like a sister to you, as much as she is to Wren."

"In many ways, yes," Ian said. "We all became well acquainted in our youth."

"And so you've known each other many years."

"Yes, we have. The thing is . . . I don't want this conversation to be in any way disrespectful of Bethia, but Wren and I both agree that you need to be aware of the situation with her."

"I don't understand," Ward said, ignoring his tea *and* the biscuits.

"Bethia has always been somewhat . . . unusual; different. Greer was my best friend, and he always had a way of understanding Bethia in a way that no one else could. They got married and were very happy. Then Greer died under very dramatic circumstances. Or rather, we *believed* that Greer was dead. He'd gotten into some serious gambling debts, which precipitated a rather terrible brawl at the pub, which ended in a fire. Apparently Greer had escaped and gone into the woods to hide from the men who were after him. Then when he realized that people believed he was dead, he stayed in hiding, believing it was safer for him *and* for Bethia."

"That's extraordinary!" Ward said.

"Yes, but it gets more so. I had trouble dealing with Greer's death. It's complicated at best. But I left my home for nearly two years. When I came back, Bethia had . . ." Ian struggled for the words and uttered a quick prayer that they would come and be well received. "Bethia had . . . descended into a place that . . . utterly shocked me, to be truthful."

"A place?" Ward asked.

"In her mind, Ward." Ian blew out a stilted breath and forged ahead. "She is not well, Ward. Her mind is very unstable." He could see Ward's confusion in his expression and hurried to try to explain and get the worst of it over with. "There are people who exist only in her head; two in particular." Ward's eyes widened, and Ian pressed on. "They have names and they have a great deal of power over her. One of these imaginary people is very aggressive and angry. This . . . part of Bethia's self . . . when it overtakes her . . . she is . . . well, she's a completely different person. And she's actually been . . . violent." Ward made no comment; he seemed lost in studied concentration as if he were trying to take in and process what he'd just been told. Ian could certainly understand that, but he took advantage of the silence to explain further. "I know it's difficult to believe when she sits there with her sewing, and she's very amiable and sweet. I realize you can't see her, but she *is* very beautiful."

"I *know* that she's very beautiful," Ward said. "And she *is* very sweet."

"A *part* of her is very sweet, Ward. And thus far you've only seen that part of her. Or perhaps I should say that you've only *been aware* of that part of her. Trust me when I tell you that she's hearing voices in her head, and she's trying very hard to ignore them when she's in your company, but eventually they will overtake her, and I don't want you or your mother to be caught off guard when that happens. As long as Wren or Shona are with her, they know what to do; they can guide her through these episodes and usually keep her calm. She's never left alone for more than a few minutes here and there. Even when she's bathing, one of the women stay close by in the next room to monitor her behavior. It's the best way we know how to keep the problem under control."

"But you *can* keep it under control?" Ward asked.

"In a manner of speaking," Ian said, then he felt the need to reiterate. "My intention in sharing these things with you is not to speak disrespectfully of Bethia. Only heaven knows why a perfectly sweet and innocent woman would come to this world with such a bizarre ailment.

All I know for certain is that she is my sister, and unlike Wren, I *chose* to take on her responsibility. Wren was born to it, but she cares for her sister with an open and compassionate heart. We love her dearly, and Shona has grown to love her, as well. We work together to care for her, and to guide her through her . . . episodes . . . so that she can be safe, and hopefully happy. But we never know when something strange might occur, and none of us can deny the fear that she may worsen. Wren's worst fear has been that people would misunderstand Bethia's condition and have her put away in some ghastly asylum."

"Is that why you left your home?" Ward asked.

"That was part of the reason," Ian said. "There was some harsh judgment in the community toward Bethia, but it had more to do with her being pregnant. Since no one knew that Greer had actually been alive and in hiding, no one knew that there was a valid reason for Bethia to be having a baby."

"But Greer is truly dead now?" Ward asked. "Do I understand you correctly?"

"That's right," Ian said.

Ward leaned back in his chair and let out an astonished sigh. "You certainly *have* had some drama in your lives. May I ask how he died . . . when he really died?"

Ian closed his eyes and shook his head, glad that Ward couldn't see his reaction to the question. He wondered for a moment if there was a way to gracefully skirt around the facts. But so far Ward seemed to be taking in all of this information with an open mind, and he didn't seem upset by it. If Ian's feelings had been correct, and Ward was to be involved in their futures, he needed to know the whole truth. But it wasn't easy to talk about.

"I've asked a difficult question," Ward said. "Your silence makes it evident you either don't want to tell me, or it's not easy to talk about."

"Both," Ian said. "As I told you, Greer was a friend to me; a true friend. Losing him once was difficult; losing him twice was . . ."

"You can't think of a word," Ward said with an air of perfect compassion.

"No, I can't," Ian said, increasingly amazed at Ward's perception. It was as if his absence of sight had given him an uncanny ability to sense things going on around him.

"Are you going to tell me how he died? Or would you prefer to just leave that part unspoken between us?"

Ian pondered the question and had trouble weighing the choice, but he already knew the answer. "I think you need to know how he died, Ward." Ian took in a deep breath and let out the answer on his exhale. "Bethia stabbed him in the shoulder with a kitchen knife." He took a tiny breath, only enough to finish the explanation. "Because he was in hiding, and Bethia didn't tell anyone, the wound became gangrenous." Another little breath. "By the time Bethia finally came to us for help, it was too late. He died from the infection." Ian inhaled, then let his breath out slowly. He could see that Ward was thinking deeply, and he allowed silence to stand between them in order to let all this new information settle.

Ward finally said, "Then Bethia knew he was alive all that time, when no one else did."

"That's right. She spoke of him openly, but we believed she was just *imagining* him to be alive, the same way she imagined that Jinty and Selma are actually real people."

"Jinty and Selma?"

"Her imaginary friends. Although one is more like an enemy. The two argue with each other, and Bethia gets caught in the middle, trying to make them both happy. Jinty is generally angry and cynical; Selma is more quiet and passive, and can usually talk sense into Jinty enough to keep Bethia behaving herself when others are around."

"*You* are talking about them as if they're real people."

"It happens after so many conversations with Bethia when Jinty and Selma are involved." Ian paused, then observed, "You're taking this much better than I feared you would. Either that, or you're very good at disguising your true feelings."

"I've sensed something not quite right with Bethia," Ward said. "And I know you well enough to know that you're a true and honest man, so I have no reason to believe that your intentions in this conversation are any different than what you've said. I'm glad you told me. If I'm going to spend a great deal of time with Bethia—and I intend to—then I certainly should be aware of the problem. So, now that I'm aware, I'll just . . . be prepared should anything unusual take place."

Ian took in Ward's words, realizing he'd expected this conversation to be more dramatic and difficult. He wasn't sure if he'd believed Ward would declare that he wanted nothing to do with any of them, or perhaps that he might express disbelief that a woman could behave in such outlandish ways. But Ward seemed to just be thinking deeply on the matter, and more than willing to remain a friend to Bethia.

"Of course your mother should know," Ian said.

"Yes, of course. I'll speak with her this evening."

"How do you think she'll take it?"

"My mother is very loving woman. I think she fell in love with Bethia at first sight. I believe she's eager to have an opportunity to apply her nurturing skills, and I suspect she might just see Bethia's challenges as a chance to be all the more motherly to her. She often speaks of her wish that I had a sister, and she's certainly full of hope that I'll find a woman who will become a daughter to her. For all of my mother's talkative nature and her complete inability to hold back any thought or emotion, she has much to give and no one to give it to. Perhaps she and Bethia are a good match."

"Perhaps," Ian said, warmed by a more subtle repetition of the feeling he'd experienced when he'd first met Ward and his mother. He knew now more than ever that these people would play a significant role in his life and that of his family members, and that their meeting had not been a coincidence.

"Do you have any advice for me?" Ward asked. "Given your experience in dealing with Bethia, I would like to know more of what to expect."

Ian thought about that for a minute. He knew it was impossible to summarize how it could actually be with Bethia; but he did know one sound piece of advice worth sharing. "It's best just to go along with her. If you behave as if you believe Jinty and Selma are real, as opposed to trying to talk her out of it, the episodes go much more smoothly."

Ward chuckled. "It seems I should make some effort to get to know Jinty and Selma."

Ian chuckled as well. "Perhaps you should."

"I'm glad you told me, Ian," Ward said. "I want you to know that I will always try to keep Bethia's best interests foremost in my associations with her."

"I appreciate that," Ian said, his instincts as well as his logic telling him that Ward was a good man. He then made an impulsive decision to just confront what he'd been wondering since that first day in the tea shop. "You're in love with her." It wasn't a question.

Ward let out a warm, comfortable laugh that let Ian know he was not at all offended by the comment, which was a relief. "You're very forthright, Ian. I like that about you."

"I'm glad you feel that way. I fear I would be forthright whether you liked it about me or not."

"As you should be," Ward said. "And I'm glad for an opportunity to tell you how I feel. I will do my best to be forthright in return."

"I would appreciate that."

"I don't know Bethia well enough to know whether I could love her in the way that you're implying. I will say that I am entranced with her. I'm drawn to her for reasons I can't explain. And yes, for all that I can't actually see her physical self, I am quite attracted to her. But I'm a cautious man by nature, and I will enjoy her friendship and see what evolves—no pun intended."

Ian chuckled. He liked Ward more by the minute, especially his forthright manner and gentlemanly attitudes, as well as his ability to discuss his own impairment with good humor and no shame.

"I'm glad to hear that," Ian said, "because we both know that love can be blind, and . . ." Ian heard what he'd said, and laughter swallowed the rest of the sentence. Ward too was laughing before Ian said, "Forgive me. That was a terrible metaphor to use in this situation, and—"

"No need to apologize, my friend. Now, I wonder if I might tell you something rather personal."

"Of course," Ian said.

"That day we first met—not so many days ago—I was overcome with the strangest feeling that you and I would be very good friends. I felt it as soon as I heard your voice. Does that sound crazy?"

Ian felt a warmth in his chest and a burning in his eyes that he blinked back. "Not at all," Ian admitted, finding it easy to do so. "How could I think it's crazy when I felt exactly the same way?"

Ward chuckled. "You did, truly?"

"Truly."

"How amazing is that!"

"Amazing," Ian said. "Which compels me to admit that I do not believe that our meeting was coincidental. I will confess that I'm a man who believes that God's hand is in our lives more than we could imagine. I know that our going to America is what He wants for us, and I know that He's brought good friends into our lives to share the journey. Does that sound crazy?"

Ward smiled. "Not at all. I don't know that I can say the same for myself, but I *can* say that my mother and I have both felt *very* strongly about this move to America. Perhaps it *is* God guiding us. I would very much like to hear your reasons for feeling the way you do . . . another time, maybe, when we have more privacy." He glanced around, and Ian became aware that the tea shop had become much more crowded while they'd been visiting. He'd not noticed with his eyes what Ward had picked up on with his ears.

"I'll look forward to it," Ian said. "For now, perhaps we should get back and see how the ladies are doing."

"An excellent plan," Ward said. He insisted on paying the bill at the tea shop, then with his hand on Ian's shoulder, they made their way back through the crowded streets to the hotel. They chatted comfortably, as much as was possible while walking through the noisy city.

"You don't have to answer this if you don't to," Ward said, "but you said that Bethia could be violent. Is there any other particular incident that's happened to bring you to that conclusion?"

"Only one," Ian said with a hint of humor in his voice; now that the incident was long in the past, he could see it that way. "She hit me over the head with a frying pan; knocked me out cold."

"Is that so?" Ward said in the same humorous tone. "Well, I should keep a lookout for any frying pans." He laughed at the ridiculousness of the statement in regard to his being unable to see, and Ian laughed with him.

As they continued to walk and share conversation, Ian already felt evidence coming to pass of his initial reaction to meeting Ward. He felt comfortable with him in a way he'd never experienced with any man except for Greer and his own brothers. His oldest brother had died tragically, as had Greer. And Ian had left Donnan behind when he'd made the decision to leave Brierley permanently. An idea occurred to him as they were entering the hotel, and the contrasting quiet to the streets was a relief. In knowing beyond any doubt that God had wanted them to make this journey, He had surely known that for Ian, the greatest sacrifice was leaving behind the close relationships of his family members. After the successful results of his sensitive conversation with Ward, it felt to Ian as if God had sent a friend into Ian's life who might be able to fill the void created by the absence of his brother and his father. He hoped that he was not being too optimistic or unrealistic to think so.

The women were all in good spirits and enjoying their visit. In fact, the men entered to hear them all laughing boisterously, but they refused to share whatever it was they had found to be so humorous. Any mention of it set them off again, and Ian and Ward couldn't help laughing too as they sat down among the women. Ian didn't care what the joke might have been; he simply enjoyed the laughter as he took hold of his wife's hand and exchanged a private glance with her that let her know his time with Ward had gone well. She smiled in a way that implied their sharing of some great secret. Since no one could fully understand the love they felt for each other, nor the joy and peace they shared in being husband and wife, they certainly *did* share a secret, and it was truly great.

With the recent conversation at the tea shop uppermost in his mind, Ian discreetly observed the interaction between Ward and Bethia. He was behaving no differently beyond seeming perhaps more keenly aware of her. Bethia was also keenly aware of Ward, often not taking her eyes off him for minutes at a time. Ian considered that most women who had so recently lost a husband would not be as apt to feel attracted toward another man, but it seemed that she had locked her grief over losing Greer into one of those places in her mind where she hardly ever thought about it. And it was likely better that way. When she *did* go into bouts of grief over Greer, it was crippling for her; those were times when she also remembered that she was responsible for his death, and the reality of that was unbearable for her. Ian far preferred—and Wren had told him that she did too— seeing Bethia with a smile on her face, oblivious to the horrors she'd experienced in her life.

Ward kept his face turned toward Bethia, as if he could clearly see her and couldn't take his eyes away. It was one of those moments when he didn't seem blind. Ian thought of how Ward had said that he could tell the difference between light and darkness with his eyes. It was almost as if Bethia radiated some kind of light that drew him to her. And now that Ward knew the truth and Ian knew him to be a sensible man, he didn't feel nearly so concerned about encouraging their attraction to each other. Perhaps Ward could be very good for Bethia, and perhaps Bethia—for all her strangeness—could fill a need in Ward's life. Greer had been skilled and sensitive in handling Bethia's challenges. Ian had believed that no other man would be able to do the same thing, but maybe he'd been wrong. Ward could not see Bethia with his mortal eyes, but he could see her nevertheless. Perhaps he could see her better than anyone else in some ways. And perhaps Bethia's comfort level with this man had something to do with the fact that he couldn't see her in a conventional way. It was impossible to know what was going on inside Bethia's mind, but it took no effort to see that she and Ward were immensely—and inexplicably—drawn to each other.

Ward and Millie stayed longer than usual, and they all ended up sharing supper together there at the hotel. Ian offered to walk them back to their own hotel, a short distance away, since it was dark and he wanted to see that they arrived safely. Millie was especially grateful for Ian's offer, and it occurred to him that her son's impairment was surely a great challenge for Millie in some respects. The idea of a man being a protector and defender on behalf of the women he cared for was simply not the case for Ward and his mother. Ian felt sure that Ward was a wonderful companion to his mother, but there were just things he could not do *for* her, and there were likely a great many things she had to do for him that most people would take for granted.

Ian gave his wife a quick kiss and told her, "Now you can tell more private jokes and laugh to your heart's content until I return."

"We just might do that," Wren said.

"Indeed we will!" Shona added with enthusiasm, and the women all giggled.

Chapter Three
Embarking

Ian walked through the less crowded but dark streets with Ward's hand on his shoulder and Millie holding to his other arm. He felt comfortable and at ease, and glad to be able to do this simple service for them. At their hotel, Ward said, "Thank you for your assistance, Ian. I wonder if I might impose on you and have you come in for a few minutes for some conversation." Ward discreetly tightened his hand over Ian's shoulder, and Ian understood the implication. Ward wanted Ian's support in the conversation with his mother.

"I'd be happy to," he said, and they were soon seated comfortably in the little parlor attached to their rooms in a fashion similar to that in the hotel where Ian was staying with his family. Ian lit the fire that had been left prepared in the grate while Millie lit the lamps.

"Ward has no need for the lamps," Millie said lightly, "but I certainly do."

The idea was one more point that illustrated what life might be like for Ward, and Ian felt grateful for the gift of sight, something that he'd never given any thought to before meeting Ward.

Once the three of them were seated close to the fire, Ward said, "Mother, Ian has shared something with me in regard to Bethia that we must be aware of. I wanted him to be here while I share the same with you, so that he might answer any questions you might have."

Ward then did an excellent job of accurately repeating the situation with Bethia, and he did so respectfully and with kindness. Millie took it in with more astonishment than her son had, but her only emotional response to it was compassion and—as Ward had predicted—a keen desire to help Bethia and perhaps be a source of support that might ease the burden for the family. Ian observed the conversation in humble awe and growing gratitude, occasionally answering a question. Millie was more interested in the details of Bethia's behavior than Ward had been, but this gave Ian an opportunity to comfortably share more about what they had observed and experienced. The situation surrounding Greer dying—both times—was also discussed in more detail. But Ian didn't feel as uncomfortable talking about it as he might have thought. In fact, it felt good to talk about it, and to be completely open with these people. Ian was astonished to realize how much he had healed since losing Greer. While it was still a sensitive topic for him, and he would always feel some sadness in recalling the difficult memories, he had achieved a degree of peace with it—a peace that he credited wholly to God's miraculous healing of his heart. He longed to share *those* experiences with Ward and Millie as well, but there would be plenty of time for that.

Back at the hotel, Ian found Wren sitting up in their bed reading from that precious book that had changed their lives, the book that was leading them to America—the book that he wanted to share with their new friends. She reported that Bethia and Shona had gone to bed, and he was eager to recount his conversations with Ward and Millie. She was pleased with the outcome and relieved that they had been made aware of the situation.

"Perhaps," she said, "with any kind of luck, Bethia will continue t' do as well in the future as she's been doing since we left home."

"We can hope," Ian said, but deep inside he didn't believe it. He felt certain this was just a temporary reprieve, and he knew if he pressed his wife she would likely admit that she felt the same. But he didn't press her. He was fine with enjoying the momentary peace, and he knew that she was too.

The following day they had one final excursion into the city, and then packed their things in a way that would be best for the crossing. They packed the majority of their belongings into trunks that would go into the cargo hold of the ship and not be accessible until they arrived in New York; they packed their daily necessities in smaller bags that could remain with them in their tiny quarters on the ship.

Early the next morning they all left the hotel and rode in a carriage to the pier, where their belongings were taken on board and they were shown to the two tiny cabins that would become home for the coming six weeks give or take—depending, as Ian had been told, on the cooperation of the wind and other factors. Shona and Bethia would share one room that was directly next door to an identical room that Ian would share with Wren. The beds were smaller than those normally made for two people, and the space around them could barely be considered space. But at least it was secure and private. Ian knew that many people, unable to afford these accommodations, would be living in the steerage of the ship where it was even more crowded and afforded little to no privacy. He felt a new awakening of gratitude for having been born to privilege, and for his father graciously allowing him to have the whole of his inheritance in advance so that he would have ample means with which to travel and live on for the rest of his life if he were careful. Ian had prayerfully considered the best way to travel with a large amount of money, and he had invested some of it in precious metals that would have value in any country. He knew that the currency of his own country could be exchanged for the American equivalent upon their arrival in New York, but he wanted something to fall back on in case something went wrong. With that in mind, he divided up his money and tucked it carefully away in hidden places in all the different pieces of luggage. Should something happen to a trunk or a bag, they would still have something hidden elsewhere and not be left destitute. Given that he'd done all he could to protect his means to provide for his family, he put the matter in God's hands and prayed that all of their belongings would be protected throughout this endeavor. Even more importantly, he prayed that he and those he loved would be protected as well. It seemed a constant prayer in his heart that they would all remain healthy and safe. Any other alternative was unthinkable!

Once settled onto the ship, they quickly discovered that Millie and Ward had cabins a short walking distance from their own. Another unlikely coincidence. If they'd not met these people at the tea shop last week, they would have met them now. Ian felt sweetly comforted to consider that God likely had a back-up plan in the important events of His children's lives.

Ian helped see that Ward and Millie had everything organized and in order before the entire group left the ship to walk a short distance down the pier to enjoy lunch together. It would be their last meal on dry land for many weeks. The captain of the ship required that all passengers be on board some hours before the high tide of evening allowed them to leave port, which gave them just enough time to eat and then to explore a book shop and make some purchases that they all felt certain would serve them well in the coming weeks that promised an abundance of boredom. The women all conspired over the books they chose, knowing they would either share books back and forth or might read aloud to each other. They came away with a few books each, but Bethia was most excited about her discovery of the latest Dickens novel.

That evening they ate aboard the ship, all with a degree of chagrin in realizing that the food that would be provided on the journey didn't promise to be necessarily appealing. But the purpose of the journey far outweighed any discomforts they would endure, and they all encouraged each other in this regard. They were all settled into bed before the ship began to move, but Ian and Wren were wide awake when they felt the movement of the vessel beneath them and knew that they were underway. They said very little, but held tightly to each other in the darkness, quietly pondering the dread of uncertainty and the thrill of adventure that battled in the atmosphere around them.

Nearly four weeks into the crossing, Ian wondered hourly if he would die of the tedium of the experience. They had all initially experienced some sickness and nausea caused by the motion of sailing, but it had settled quickly and they had kept each other company from day to day, encouraging each other and putting some effort into offering assistance to new acquaintances who were enduring different degrees of discomfort that far outweighed their own.

Ian had stopped shaving when it had proven to be far too much trouble under the circumstances. Ward continued to have a clean-shaven face every day, but only because it was one of his mother's favorite tasks. She loved the conversation she shared with her son while she did something for him that he could not do for himself without risking nicks and cuts. "Or worse," he'd said to Ian, "I'd miss a spot and look like a fool. As if being blind doesn't already make me look plenty fool enough."

Ian had laughed in good nature at the comment and replied, "I simply look like a fool because my beard grows unevenly, and when my curly hair gets too long it looks like a mop."

"You have curly hair?" Ward asked, and they both chuckled.

The books had proven to be priceless in easing their boredom, and Wren had begun a daily habit of sitting down in the steerage and reading a novel aloud to fellow passengers. It was a time of day that many people looked forward to, and it created a grand diversion as people discussed what they thought might happen next, and wondered how the story would end. Sometimes when Wren's voice grew tired, Bethia would read aloud, since she was usually by her sister's side during the reading sessions. Ian felt proud of his wife for her gentle compassion with others, for the easy way that she made friends, and for her seemingly effortless gift of making others feel comfortable.

When they were not reading, the women kept busy sewing clothes for the babies. Little by little, items were completed and tucked away in anticipation of the new arrivals. It was agreed that both babies could likely wear the same clothes, since Bethia's child would always be just a little larger than Wren's would be—at least in the beginning. While Wren and Bethia were both skilled at sewing and had brought plenty of materials along, Shona too enjoyed working on the stitching of little gowns and blankets while she listened to Wren or Bethia read from the current novel of interest.

Despite all the tedium of the journey, Ian thanked God every day that they had all remained healthy and safe. He prayed that the pattern would hold out until they arrived in New York, and that all would continue to go as smoothly as possible.

The relationship between Bethia and Ward grew stronger, and it had become natural for them to hold hands and stroll around the deck of the ship, or to sit in quiet conversation. Everyone on the ship that they'd become acquainted with was well aware that Bethia was a recent widow, but there didn't seem to be any speculation over her apparent courting so soon after her husband's death or while expecting a baby. In most cases, people assumed an attitude of sympathy, bordering on pity, in regard to the oddly matched couple, and Ian felt sure it had mostly to do with Ward being blind.

As of yet, Bethia had not manifested any strange behavior that had been observed by anyone but family since they'd been on board. Ian hoped it would remain that way, and that Bethia might continue to enjoy Ward's company without her mental condition inhibiting the relationship. While the others helped keep an eye on Bethia from a distance, no one was privy to the things they talked about, and it was impossible to know—without prying—the actual status of their relationship. Wren had carefully asked Bethia about her feelings for Ward, but Bethia would just gracefully skirt around the question— usually while a warm blush rose in her face. Ian had occasionally commented to Ward that things appeared to be going well with Bethia, or that Bethia had certainly become comfortable with him. Ward would agree but not expound, and Ian didn't feel he could say more without being blatantly nosy.

With Bethia's pregnancy blossoming, Ian couldn't imagine how Ward would fit into her life once she gave birth and had a baby to contend with. Since no one knew for certain when Bethia had started showing signs of pregnancy—due to her keeping it a secret for a good, long while—no one knew for certain when the baby would come. But she was looking about ready to burst if she didn't give birth soon. Ian had hoped they would arrive in New York before the baby arrived, but it was beginning to look like that wouldn't be the case. The ship's doctor had seen Bethia more than once to make certain all was well. Thankfully, he seemed to be a kind and decent man, and he assured them that whenever labor *did* begin, he would be on hand to do everything he could to make certain that Bethia gave birth safely. Of course, he warned them that there were always risks associated with childbirth. The very idea distressed Ian, not only in regard to Bethia, but also in regard to his pregnant wife; however, she was not as far along as Bethia—which meant that at least Wren would be able to give birth on dry land. He wasn't certain what difference it would make, given that they had a good doctor on board, but he just felt better thinking of his own child coming into the world with the uncomfortable and tedious reality of this part of their journey behind them.

Exactly a month from the date of their departure from Liverpool, Bethia started having pains just after breakfast. Ward was deeply concerned by evidence of her discomfort that merged into severe pain, and Ian had never seen him so ruffled. Ward sat next to Bethia's bedside in the tiny cabin, holding her hand and encouraging her. The doctor was summoned but assured them it would be a long while before he was needed. He told the women the signs to watch for that might indicate there was a problem, or that she was getting close to delivering, and told them he would then come straightaway. Ward wanted to remain with Bethia, but as the ordeal worsened it wasn't appropriate for him to stay. The women crowded into the tiny cabin and rallied around Bethia, while Ian took Ward to the deck of the ship where they could walk to relieve his nerves and get some fresh air. They walked and walked, occasionally being found by one of the women who came to give a report, but the day dragged into evening with what seemed like little progress, and Ward could barely bring himself to eat.

"You really love her," Ian observed while sitting across a table from Ward, who helplessly stirred his food around but hardly put a morsel into his mouth.

"You sound surprised," Ward said.

"Not surprised," Ian said. "Not at all surprised. Just . . . concerned, perhaps. I fear you've not yet seen the extent of how challenging she can be. By *seen* I mean metaphorically, of course."

"I know that," Ward said, more testy than Ian had ever seen him. In fact he'd never seen him even a *little* bit testy. "There's no need for you to clarify your metaphors with me. Perhaps I've not *seen* how bad the situation can be, but I've had *many* conversations with Jinty and Selma during the time I've spent with Bethia."

"You have?"

"I have," Ward said. "In all humility, Ian, I think I'm well suited to understanding Bethia and helping her keep the other parts of herself more calm and under control."

"Apparently you are," Ian heartily agreed. "I didn't know. Obviously I couldn't know because you hadn't told me. I'm *glad* to know that. You *are* very good for her."

"And she for me," he insisted. "And yes, I love her. I would hope that in spite of my limitations, when we get to America and find a place to settle down, I might be in a position to care for her, and she for me. I think that we can compensate for each other's challenges, Ian. I really do. Forgive me if I'm being naive, but that's how I feel." He paused as if for effect and added, "And don't tell me that love can be blind."

"I'll not say a word," Ian said. "With as much as I love my dear Wren, I would never presume to tell you what to feel—or not feel. We're as good as family, and we will all work together to take care of each other."

"I'm glad you feel that way, Ian," Ward said. "It means a great deal to me. I do believe you're like the brother I never had."

"And you are like the brother I left behind," Ian said. "If we . . ." He stopped when he saw Wren enter the galley, looking distressed. He rose to his feet and said to Ward, "Wren is here."

Ward turned toward the direction of approaching footsteps, expectant and concerned. "Is everything all right?" he demanded kindly in the general direction of where he assumed Wren to be.

"She's in a great deal of pain, but apparently that's normal." She wrapped her arms around Ian and held to him tightly as she added, "I feel so helpless. I don't know what t' do for her. We just take turns holding her hand and trying t' encourage her. The doctor says that everything is fine so far, but . . . it's so . . ." She couldn't finish. Instead she just held tighter to Ian, and he returned her embrace, attempting to give her the strength he knew she was seeking, the same kind of strength he sought from her when *he* was struggling.

"Is there something else wrong?" Ian asked after a long minute of silence when he sensed that his wife was holding something back.

Wren sat down at the table and put a hand over Ward's. Ian wondered if that meant she had something to say that would be especially difficult for Ward to hear. Given the look on Ward's face, he was surely wondering the same thing. Ian sat beside her, and she said, more to Ward, "The pain is playing with her mind."

Tears spilled down her face, and she wiped them away with her free hand. Ward couldn't see this, but she sniffled, and he said, "You're crying."

Wren said, "It's hard t' see her this way. Labor under any circumstances is an ordeal more horrible than I'd imagined, but . . . I've rarely seen Bethia this way. Perhaps not ever *quite* this way. She keeps going back and forth between her real self and those parts of her we can't begin t' understand. But now she's . . ."

"She's what?" Ian encouraged, putting his arm around her.

She put her head to his shoulder but kept her hand over Ward's. "She's asking for Greer." Wren sniffled again. "She keeps saying that this is Greer's baby and he should be there."

"What have you said to her?" Ward asked.

"Telling her the truth and arguing with her would only make her more upset. I told her that it was not customary for the baby's father t' be with the mother during labor. She insisted that he had been there with her earlier. I don't know if she's imagining Greer, or if she thinks that ye are Greer." She squeezed Ward's hand when she said it.

"If she were imagining him, she wouldn't be wondering why he's not there," Ward said. "Perhaps I *should* be with her. It's not as if I can see anything I shouldn't see."

"He makes a good point," Ian said.

"Perhaps," Wren said, "but I think for now we women should just keep doing what we're doing. If she gets worse I'll come for ye, Ward. I just wanted t' warn ye that . . . when this is over . . . she might think ye're someone different than ye are."

"I have been sufficiently warned," Ward said. "It doesn't matter. I'll do or say whatever I can to help her through this."

"Ye're a good man, Ward," Wren said and kissed his cheek before she turned to share another embrace with Ian. "Ye're both good men, ye know."

"We have much to be inspired by," Ian said, "being surrounded by such good women."

"Such a sweet man," Wren said and stood, keeping a hand on Ian's shoulder to encourage him to stay sitting. She kissed his brow. "I'll let ye know if something changes. I'm hoping it'll be over soon."

"Amen," Ian and Ward said simultaneously.

When it became clear that Ward was not going to eat anything more than the few tiny bites he'd eaten—which was only a little less than Ian had eaten—the two men returned to the deck to keep walking off their nervousness. The dark chill of night overtook the ship completely, and the deck became quiet except for the subtle noises made by the night watchmen. But still they kept walking, with Ward occasionally saying, "What on earth could be taking so long?"

Ian finally ventured to pose a response to the question, rhetorical as it was. "Perhaps we should go to your cabin and wait there." He sensed Ward debating the possibility, and Ian felt sure if he were not blind and incapable of finding his way back on his own, he would have insisted that Ian go back without him. As it was, Ian just kept walking and said, "Or we can stay here."

"Thank you, my friend," Ward said and switched to Ian's other shoulder in order to use a different hand.

Only a few minutes later Shona found them and breathlessly reported, "It's over. She's had a girl. Doctor says everything is going t' be all right."

"Oh, praise heaven!" Ward said and leaned against the hand on Ian's shoulder. Ian's own relief was immense, but he could find no words that would be any better than those Ward had spoken.

Shona then said, "Wren said that ye should come, Ward. But ye should know that . . . Bethia keeps asking for Greer."

"It doesn't matter," Ward said, and Ian guided him to the cabin where Bethia had just given birth. There was a smell of sweat and blood in the tiny, confined cabin that was almost nauseating to Ian when he entered. He caught sight of his wife while he was guiding Ward to the edge of the bed. Her exhaustion was as blatant as the sweat glistening on her face and the blood on her apron. She squeezed past Ward and his mother, who was attempting to tidy the tiny room, and pressed herself into Ian's embrace. He eased her into the narrow passageway and held her tightly.

"It's over," he murmured, "although I fear for you when our own child is born."

"I fear the same," she said and looked up at him with a sparkle of moisture in her eyes, "but when I saw the baby . . . when Bethia saw the baby . . . it didn't seem so bad, Ian. It's such a miracle . . . in spite of the suffering." Ian smiled at her faith and perspective. "She's a beautiful little girl, Ian. And I can see a look of Greer about her, tiny as she is."

"It's a good thing we know now he wasn't dead all that time, or the resemblance would certainly have left us baffled."

"It would indeed," Wren said. "Ye must see her," she added and guided him back to the open doorway of the cabin.

They peered inside just in time to see Bethia reach for Ward's hand and smile at him. "We have a daughter," she said. "I want t' name her Greer . . . after yer name."

Millie cast a concerned and compassionate glance toward Wren, who eased onto the narrow bed to sit beside her sister, on the opposite side of where Ward was kneeling by the bed.

"Greer is a fine name," Wren said, and Bethia turned toward her. "I'm sure yer husband would be pleased to have his daughter named after him, although it is a man's name, Bethia. Are ye certain yer daughter would want t' go by such a name for the whole of her life?"

"I want t' name her Greer," Bethia said.

"Then Greer it shall be," Ward said. Bethia turned toward him and smiled, then she looked down at her baby, nestled in the crook of her arm.

"She looks like ye, my darling," Bethia said, as if she'd become as blind as Ward in her inability to see that the man kneeling by her bedside had no physical resemblance to her dead husband *or* to the baby she was holding. But no one argued with her. They were all just simply glad to have the ordeal behind them, and to know that both mother and baby were going to be all right.

Bethia wanted Ward to hold the baby, although she was clearly convinced that the man she held the baby toward was not blind, that he was Greer. Wren gracefully helped ease the baby into Ward's arms, saying gently, "It's all right. Don't be nervous. She's tiny but she's strong."

Ward held the baby close and pretended to look down at her while he said, "She's beautiful, Bethia."

Bethia became completely and suddenly exhausted only a minute later and quickly drifted off to sleep. Everyone had a turn holding the baby for a few minutes. Ian was glad he'd had a little bit of experience with his brothers' babies. And he had to admit, for all that he'd been aware of Bethia's suffering and his own worry, he greatly anticipated the day when he and Wren would have their own child to cuddle and love.

Bethia and the baby were left in Shona's capable care. Ian made certain Ward had everything he needed before he went to his own cabin and crawled into the narrow bed, snuggling up close to his wife. The moment she was in his arms, she cried and cried over the suffering she had seen her sister endure that day—and the miracle of the new little life that had emerged from the difficulty. Wren's tears eased into a gentle lament, and they talked about the irony of Greer not being around to see this child, when he had been alive all that time without anyone but Bethia knowing. They also talked about the seemingly equal irony of Bethia believing that Ward was actually Greer. They doubted that he could keep up the pretense, especially with his blindness, and they prayed together that Bethia's mind would soon come back to its awareness of Ward's place in her life and the realization that the father of her baby was dead and buried in the woods near Brierley.

The following day Bethia *did* recognize Ward and seemed to remember everything that had passed between them, except for the episode the previous evening where she had been speaking to him as if he were Greer. She also remembered clearly that Greer was dead, which brought on a bout of continual crying, and no one was able to console her. Wren, Shona, and Millie all worked together to care for Bethia and the baby, not wanting to leave Bethia by herself *or* alone with the baby, for reasons none of them dared say aloud.

The day after that, Bethia's tears settled into a quiet that was unnerving. She dutifully fed the baby with an emotionless detachment that the other women privately declared was simply not normal. The doctor checked on Bethia and reported that she appeared to be doing fine for having given birth, but he did mention that sometimes women could suffer varying degrees of melancholia following childbirth.

"What does that mean, exactly?" Wren asked him.

The doctor stated, "It can have many variable symptoms, but it is a mental condition that can cause a person to feel very depressed, or even to be very unstable."

Wren said to Ian later, "Perhaps melancholia is what she's suffered from all along."

"Perhaps what she suffers from doesn't have a name. This . . . melancholia sounds very vague to me, at best."

Little Greer thrived and was a healthy and contented baby, in spite of her mother's continuing melancholia. Bethia did little more than stare at the walls. Occasionally they could get her to eat something or use heated water to wash up and clean herself. She continued to be willing to feed the baby, but she showed little to no interest in her at all. Wren put forth many attempts at conversation with her sister, sometimes gently pleading and sometimes firmly insisting that she come out of this stupor and be a mother to her beautiful child. Ward visited Bethia often, but she often just asked him to go away, which was devastating for him. Shona and Millie also tried to reason with her. Ian didn't try at all. He just did his best to buoy up all of the people who were so diligent and devoted in trying to buoy up Bethia.

In counting the weeks they had been at sea, Ian found hope in believing that Bethia might be stirred out of her poor state of mind if she could be exposed to some new scenery. She'd done well in Liverpool. He had hopes that New York City would have a similar effect on her. It would not be that many days until the six-week anniversary of their departure from England, and Ian prayed that they might arrive ahead of schedule and be able to remove Bethia from this frightening place within her own mind where she had disappeared. He'd seen her go through stages of being quiet and turning inward, but never like this before, and never for so long without some kind of evidence that she was really in there somewhere.

* * *

Wren was finding it difficult to sleep while she counted the remaining days until they would arrive in America. She and Ian both agreed that getting Bethia off of this ship would be the best possible thing for her. Even the captain of the vessel was aware of Bethia's situation, and both he and the doctor agreed. If the winds remained constant and they didn't encounter a storm, they might see New York harbor in three or four days. The *if* in the captain's calculation haunted Wren. She couldn't put words to the uneasiness she felt, but there was no denying the urgency inside of her in regard to her sister. She almost felt as if she were going to lose her sister, and for all her praying and talking her feelings through with Ian, she could not decipher whether her feelings were meant to be some kind of preparation for the inevitable, or some kind of warning so that she could do something to prevent this from getting worse. Wren had fought and struggled and grasped for *anything* she might do to help her sister, but she could come up with nothing. She couldn't imagine actually *losing* her to death when her physical health was fine for a woman who had recently given birth. But still, the idea nagged at Wren, making it impossible to relax.

Wren had become accustomed to sharing the less-than-adequate bed with her husband. He was tall with nowhere for his long legs to go, and she was pregnant, increasing in size around the middle. But they were comfortable sleeping very close together, and they'd gotten used to exactly how to do it, almost as if they were one person. Ian's nearness was a strength and a comfort to her, but he didn't have the answers either. They were both equally baffled and concerned.

Wren heard hurried footsteps the same moment she felt Ian lean up on his elbow, alerted to the sound as well. She'd thought he'd been asleep, but obviously he hadn't been. A moment later a light knock at their door made Wren gasp. For all that Bethia had been struggling since the birth of the baby, Shona had not once sought their help in the night. Ian was on his feet first and groped his way to the door. They'd long ago taken up the habit of sleeping in their clothes, anticipating a moment such as this. Wren was beside Ian before he pulled the door open to see not Shona, but Millie, clutching a robe tightly around her middle with one arm and holding a lantern high in the other hand.

"What's happened?" Ian demanded.

"Ward knocked on the wall between our cabins, a signal that means he needs my help. When I went in it was dark, but I heard him say that Bethia had gone to the deck, that she was completely out of her mind."

Ian moved past Millie at the word "deck," and Wren followed him, unable to keep up with the way he ran, aided by the fact that his feet were bare.

"Get Shona," Wren said to Millie. "Bethia must have sneaked out while she was sleeping."

"I'll get her," Millie said, barely able to say it through her frightened tears.

Wren emerged onto the deck, and fear gripped her so suddenly and so tightly that she almost collapsed and had to put great effort into finding her footing. Bethia was standing *on* the side railing of the ship, holding to one of the rigging ropes, her nightgown blowing against her in the wind as if it were one of the sails.

"Come down from there!" Ian shouted.

"Don't come any closer!" Bethia shouted back at him. They were the first words Wren had heard come out of her sister's mouth in nearly a week. "Ye can't stop me! Ye mustn't stop me! I need t' do this!"

"Stop you from what, Bethia?" Ian shouted. "Come down from there and let's *talk* about what you need to do." Bethia looked as if she were thinking about it, and Wren held her breath, praying frantically in her mind. Thoughts and feelings of losing her sister had taken on a whole new meaning in the past thirty seconds.

"No!" Bethia shouted. "Ye're trying t' trick me! I'm not coming down! I have t' do this!"

"Do *what*, Bethia?" Ian pleaded.

"I need t' be in the water," she said as if the idea gave her immeasurable pleasure.

"Ye'll die if ye go in the water, Bethia," Wren said, moving to Ian's side. "Is that what ye want?"

Bethia acknowledged the presence of her sister, then turned to face the darkness enveloping the ocean that surrounded the ship. "Greer is out there. I need t' be with him."

"Is that what Jinty told ye?" Wren demanded. "Because we'll not be doing anything that Jinty tells ye t' do unless we talk about it first."

"Jinty and Selma are already out there," Bethia said in a quiet, dreamy voice, as if she were being lured by the song of sirens that were falsely telling her she would finally find total peace if she jumped. "They're out there with Greer."

"Please come down, sister," Wren pleaded, aware that the crew members on deck were all keenly aware of the problem and were frantically trying to lower the sails and slow the ship down. For a moment she wondered how they could ever stop the momentum of the huge vessel enough to be able to save Bethia if she *did* jump. Her attention went back to Bethia, and she was once again mindful that Ian was at her side, as helpless over what to do as she was. Wren feared that if Ian tried to grab Bethia, it would only spur her to jump. She prayed for the right words to say to her sister, and all that came out of her mouth was, "I love ye, Bethia. Ye need t' know that."

Bethia turned and met Wren's eyes, and Wren felt momentarily convinced that she could talk her into getting down from there and going back to bed. Through the span of a deep sigh, Bethia's countenance showed a momentary glimpse of sanity. Her eyes delved into Wren's as she said with conviction, "I love ye as well, sister. Ye've been so good t' me. But it's time we were both set free."

Wren didn't even have time to take in her meaning before Bethia let go of the rope and disappeared into the darkness like a bird taking flight.

"No!" Wren screamed, and less than a second later Ian dove into the ocean. "No!" Wren screamed again, assaulted with images of never finding either of them.

A sailor shouted, "Two overboard!"

Ring-shaped life preservers on ropes were thrown into the water. The ship had slowed immensely but was still moving forward, and Wren felt as if the world would fall out from beneath her. She was surprised to find Millie and Shona at her shoulders, and she gratefully leaned into their support, gasping for air as if she herself were drowning. While her panic over never seeing Bethia or Ian alive again was threatening to smother her, a thought grabbed hold of her mind and tore her instantly from the extreme cold of one fear and threw her harshly into the flames of another.

"Where's the baby?" she demanded of Shona.

Shona's momentary hesitance threatened to snatch away the tiny inkling of stability that Wren had been clinging to. "How could I tell where it is when . . ." She didn't finish the sentence, but instead bit her trembling lip.

"Where is the baby?" Wren shouted.

"She's not in the cabin," Shona said on the crest of a sob. "I was hoping t' find her here with one of ye, but . . ."

Wren took a moment to be assured that the crew of the ship were doing all they could to bring Ian and Bethia back to the ship. A couple of sailors had even gone into the water with ropes tied around their waists, attempting to search for them. Knowing she could do nothing here, she dashed back below deck, grabbing the lantern that Millie was still holding. Trusting that Shona had thoroughly searched her own cabin in order to know for certain the baby wasn't there, Wren could only find one possible reason to hope that Bethia in her insanity had not done the unthinkable and done away with her child before she herself had gone into the waves.

Wren burst into Ward's cabin without bothering to knock or offer any forewarning. The sound of the baby's crying struck her ears the same moment her eyes focused in the dim lamp light to see Ward holding the infant against his chest.

"I think she's hungry," Ward said, and Wren sank to her knees, heaving a sob of relief that forced the entire quantity of air from her lungs. She sobbed again, trying to take air back in that wouldn't come as her mind went back to the horror she had just witnessed on deck.

"Is Bethia all right?" Ward asked, and Wren saw black spots swimming before her eyes just before she saw the cabin floor coming hastily toward her face.

Chapter Four
Crossing Over

Wren rushed back into consciousness to find Shona gently slapping her face. She heard the baby crying, as if from very far away. Then the sound came closer, and the memories all came back at once. As if Shona had read her mind in knowing that they needed to get back to the deck, she helped Wren up, and they both hurried out.

"Stay with Ward and the baby," Wren heard Shona say to Millie, and again felt certain they were thinking the same thoughts.

They came on deck to see a very wet—but very alive—Ian helping a group of sailors pull on a rope that was dangling over the railing of the ship. Wren's relief at seeing her husband tempted her to faint again, but she found Shona at her side, helping to keep her steady on her feet. Knowing that the baby and Ian were safe, Wren breathed a silent prayer of gratitude, then breathed a desperate plea for God to spare her sister as well. Seconds stretched out beyond their normal span as she watched a very wet sailor come over the rail, soon followed by Bethia, who was dangling limply in the center of a life preserver being hoisted up by the rope that Ian and the other men were pulling. Another wet sailor came over the rail seconds afterward, pushing Bethia up from behind. Wren heard a loud voice yell indiscernible syllables that seemed to indicate everyone was out of the water and accounted for, then orders followed, and the sailors, except for those who were either wet or gathered around Bethia trying to help her, set to work raising the sails once again. Wren's eyes were fixed with horror upon her sister. Bethia's skin was a ghastly bluish-white color. The doctor was there on his knees, doing something that was apparently meant to coax the water out of Bethia's lungs. But it took only a long moment for him to declare its uselessness.

"She's gone," he stated breathlessly with his fingers pressed to the side of her throat, searching in vain for evidence of a beating pulse.

Wren could hardly breathe and felt certain if not for Shona holding her steady, she *would* have fainted again. Shona's stifled sobs rang in Wren's ears, but she felt too much in shock herself to even comprehend the ability to weep. Wren's eyes drifted from the dreadful sight of her dead sister to her husband, who was kneeling beside Bethia, his head bowed over her, trying to catch his breath. He was clearly freezing and exhausted. He'd clearly given everything he had to save Bethia's life. He turned to meet her eyes, as if he'd sensed her looking at him. Apology and regret consumed his countenance. Neither her mind nor her spirit could begin to accept the shock and horror that Bethia was dead. The evidence was starkly before her, but she pushed it all away and chose instead to center her attention on her husband. He was alive! But suffering. She could do something for *him*, and his unspoken need for her comfort drew her gratefully away from having to face the loss that hovered at the edge of her consciousness. Refusing to let it press beyond certain boundaries, she rushed to Ian's side and knelt beside him, pressing herself into his embrace, taking the water from his clothes into hers, as if she could take his sorrow and regret into herself and dissolve it.

"I'm so sorry," he muttered close to her ear. "I tried, Wren. I tried."

"I know ye did," she said, strengthened by a source that could only be divine. For a long moment it was as if she could see herself from a detached point of view, kneeling beside her sister's body, wondering why she was not crumbling and falling apart, but was instead finding strength to comfort and encourage her husband. "Ye did everything ye could," she added. Ian nodded, then hung his head as a harsh sob escaped through his lips. The sound encouraged Wren's shock to start to give way. She turned to look at Bethia's body but couldn't bear the sight. It didn't look like Bethia. It looked like a nightmarish apparition, its eyes frozen half open, its skin an unnatural color. The blanketing numbness crumbled a little more, and a tight burning gathered in Wren's chest as if to give her fair warning that a full-blown eruption was about to occur.

With severe haste Wren stood and took hold of Ian's arm, urging him to a standing position as well. She was wondering how to gracefully depart and leave her sister's body here on the deck when the captain himself appeared behind them and put a blanket around Ian's shoulders. "You should get yourself into some dry clothes, young man," he said. Wren glanced again toward Bethia's body, just as a blanket was put over her ghastly face. The captain noticed and said, "We've dealt with death at sea before, Mrs. MacBrier. We'll take care of everything. In the morning we'll discuss burial arrangements."

"Thank you, Captain," Wren said, and the burning in her chest became more hot, prompting her to urge Ian toward their cabin, certain her composure and strength were short-lived, their life quickly running out. The distance to the cabin suddenly became much, much farther than it had ever been. Wren could feel the numbness crumbling around her, as if she were made of porcelain and the fragile shell of herself had been broken and the pieces were falling away. *Bethia's dead,* her mind told her. *No, it can't be true,* another part of her protested. Wren wondered if this was how it had felt to live in Bethia's head, with different parts of herself asserting opinions and getting into arguments. The very fact that she was empathizing with Bethia's insanity brought her closer to the point of losing all reason with what she had just witnessed.

"Bethia's dead." She said it aloud this time, and the echo of it provoked a whimper, a foreshadowing of many tears to come.

"I know," Ian said and held more tightly to her as they traversed the final steps to the cabin door.

Millie appeared at that very moment and declared that a miracle had occurred, that a member of the crew had been aware of a woman traveling in the steerage who had been in the process of trying to wean her own baby who was older, and she was only too happy to feed the new little orphan. The baby was currently being fed, and Shona would see to all of the arrangements, making certain the baby's care was complete.

"Thank you," Wren said in a calm voice that was barely steady. Anticipating the inevitable grief that she knew was prowling at the edge of her consciousness, she was glad to know that the baby was being cared for, and grateful beyond measure for the help of Millie and Shona. She wondered how Ward was doing but couldn't bring herself to think of *his* grief, when she could barely acknowledge her own.

"Thank you," Ian echoed to Millie in a voice that indicated he was shivering, and Wren opened the cabin door.

Once inside the safety of their private space, Ian frantically worked at getting out of his wet clothes and into dry ones. Wren sank to the edge of the bed and gripped it so tightly that her hands began to hurt in seconds. "Bethia's dead," she said again, as if one part of herself were trying to convince the other. "Bethia's dead."

"I know she is, my dear," Ian said, still shivering while he buttoned his shirt. "I know she is and I'm so sorry."

Wren gazed at the wall, recounting the incident in detail. Another whimper escaped her, then another and another. Her head fell onto the pillow and her feet lifted off the floor onto the bed. Her knees gravitated toward her rounded belly and the whimpering was overtaken by harsh, painful sobs.

"Bethia's dead," she howled, oblivious to the possibility of being overheard by the people in neighboring cabins. Of course, one of those was Shona, who was likely responding much the same way.

"I'm so sorry," Ian murmured through his own tears as he eased Wren into his arms and wrapped a blanket tightly around the both of them.

Wren cried harder than she ever had in her life, and she'd certainly done a fair amount of crying. Her father's death came to mind. But never had she cried like this! She had been so deeply and intricately connected to her sister that it felt as if pieces of her had literally been torn away. She cried until she slept, and she woke up with tears overtaking her as soon as she'd had a brief moment to orient herself to the fact that her sister was gone.

For days Wren became utterly lost in her grief, the same way that Bethia had often become completely lost inside of her own mind. She pulled together as much composure as she could manage to go on deck for the brief ceremony that took place there before Bethia's tightly wrapped body was buried at sea. No grave to visit, Wren thought; no tangible evidence that this was real except for the horrible memory of seeing Bethia dead on the deck of the ship.

Wren felt selfish for her obliviousness to the grief of their friends. A part of her longed to be able to reach out to them and offer the comfort they were in need of, but a more powerful, consuming part of her had only the strength to face her own grief. Seeing the faces of Shona, Millie, and Ward when they were gathered for the burial made it clear to her that they were all suffering deeply. But Wren could only feel her own suffering, and she indulged in it with little thought for anyone but herself. At Ian's insistence, she forced herself to eat. She couldn't argue with his plea that she needed to remain healthy for the sake of the baby inside her. But she hardly saw Bethia's baby at all. Having been assured that the baby was being well cared for, Wren could only concentrate on her own unfathomable adjustment to Bethia's absence.

Four days beyond the tragic event, Wren found that she could be tolerably composed, and her first thoughts in moving past this loss was an aching to be with Bethia's baby. Ian spoke to Shona, who brought the wet nurse *and* the baby to meet Wren and Ian in the galley at a time between meals when the room would be mostly vacant. Shona declared that they should all become acquainted with one another. Shirley was a kind, robust woman with five children of her own and a husband named Ronald who was brawny and jolly. The entire family came, wanting to meet the aunt and uncle of the sweet baby they'd been caring for. They had all taken to little Greer with great fondness, and Wren expressed her deep appreciation to these people for taking such good care of her tiny niece while she'd needed to adjust to her sister's death.

"We is glad t' do it, Miss," Shirley said, holding the sleeping infant comfortably in her arms. "She's as sweet a baby girl as I has ever seen. Sleeps and eats and doesn't give much fuss. Miss Shona tells me you'll be goin' t' New York, but you don't know quite where you'll set off t' go after that."

Wren looked at her husband, who looked back at her. They'd not shared with anyone their true purpose for choosing New York as a destination. And she knew this was not the time to share that purpose with virtual strangers. They'd told Shona and Bethia that they had a desire to seek out a religious group that they believed to be based in New York somewhere, but they had offered no explanation beyond that. Wren and Ian had both agreed that once they got to America, they could more accurately assess the proper steps to take from there.

"We haven't made specific plans," Ian said. "Of course our biggest concern is for the baby."

"My point exactly," Shirley said. "Ronald's got family in New York. They got a house big enough t' take in the lot of us without too much of a crunch, and we'll be stayin' on there for a bit. I'm saying that I'd be happy t' keep feeding the little miss until you can figure out another way. Goat's milk can suffice if it comes t' that, but for some weeks at least, I'm happy t' keep doing this for you until we go our separate ways."

"That's so very generous of ye," Wren said. "Perhaps it would be wise for us t' find a hotel t' stay that's near the house where ye'll be living."

"That's exactly my thinkin'!" Ronald volunteered heartily.

"Thank you," Ian said. "We're very grateful to accept your help for the time being."

"That's all settled then," Shirley said and handed the sleeping infant over to Wren.

The moment the baby settled into her arms, Wren absorbed a deep peace and comfort from the warmth of Greer's little body, or perhaps it was more the warmth of her spirit. Wren felt better after holding the baby for a long while, then she returned her to Shirley's care when she needed to be fed.

Walking slowly back to the cabin, taking a detour around the deck of the ship, Wren's mind tried to catch up with thoughts it had skipped over throughout these days of grieving.

"I've been thinking that we should raise little Greer as our own," she said to her husband, "but I should not just assume that ye feel the same. If ye—"

Ian stopped walking and forced her to face him. "I cannot believe that you would even have to ask—or wonder. Of *course* we will raise her as our own. We're the only family she's got. There is absolutely *no* question about that." He began walking again, and she settled her hand on his arm to walk beside him.

"Ye're a good man, Ian MacBrier."

"It's no sacrifice, if that's what you're implying. Greer was my dearest friend, and Bethia is family to both of us. I must assert one thing about the situation that I'm struggling with, however."

"What is that?" Wren asked, nervous with concern.

"I would prefer not to call her Greer. It's a strange name for a girl, but that's not the problem really; I could get used to that. I simply don't want this child's name to remind me of how hard it was for us to . . . lose him . . . the way we did. I submit that we use Greer as a middle name, and since you and I will be her parents, we should decide on an appropriate first name."

"I think that's a marvelous idea. I'm certain we would have managed with calling her Greer, but I was never that comfortable with it myself." As an afterthought she added, "Do ye think it's dishonoring Bethia t' call her daughter something different?"

"I would like to think that Bethia is now in a place where the illness of her mind no longer distorts her thinking, and that her spirit completely understands our best wishes on behalf of her daughter."

"What a lovely thought," Wren said, and they ambled slowly in silence until another idea came to her that she'd wanted to share with her husband. She talked about the conflicting thoughts and emotions she had been feeling through the process of grieving over her sister. She spoke openly of the shock, the numbness, the horror, and the blinding grief. And she talked about the times when she had felt different parts of herself seeming to need to convince other parts of herself of what had happened. She related it to other times in her life when she'd endured different levels of inner conflict. In conclusion, she said, "It makes me think that perhaps the human mind *is* divided int' different parts and places that are sometimes conflicting, and for Bethia those parts simply became more dominant."

"I'm certain we all have inner conflicts, my dear. But most of us don't attach names to them."

"I promise ye that I'm not doing that. I've no intention of taking on my sister's illness."

"I am not at all worried about that," Ian said and smiled. "Let's just come up with a name for our daughter, shall we?"

"I have a few ideas; perhaps ye do as well. Do ye think it's best to have her keep her legal surname, or should we call her by our name so that she'll grow up feeling more a part of the family?"

"I'm not certain. What do you think?"

Wren thought about that for a long minute, maybe two. "I think we should teach her—when she'd old enough—who she came from, and she should know her parents' names. But I think she should have the name MacBrier, so that she'll know she belongs to us, and so that she'll not feel different from her brothers and sisters."

"Brothers and sisters?" Ian chuckled. "How many children do you intend to have, my dear?"

"One at a time," Wren said firmly.

Ian declared that he felt the need to check on Ward. The bond of their friendship had deepened immensely through the grief they had shared over losing Bethia. Ian had been dividing his time between Wren and Ward, attempting to console them both and offer support and empathy. Ian had told Wren that Ward was taking Bethia's death *very* hard, and he had been very open with Ian about his feelings. But with anyone besides Ian and his mother, he was very good at putting on a brave face and giving the appearance of doing well.

With Ian gone to check on his friend, Wren felt compelled to stand in the place where Bethia's body had been lifted over the ship railing and laid on the deck. She had to exert some courage to bring herself so close to the memories of that horrible experience, but then she leaned against the rail and closed her eyes, allowing the mist off the sea to kiss her skin and cool her grief. Wren preferred to recall the moment that Bethia had let go of the rope and disappeared into the darkness. She liked to imagine her sister's spirit taking flight and going directly to heaven, with the omission of her actually drowning and being buried at sea. Wren knew that the scriptures taught of a resurrection and redemption, and even though she didn't understand the principles in any way beyond their most simplistic implications, she found peace in thinking of such principles being applied to Bethia.

Wren had recalled over and over the final words that Bethia had spoken, but now they had a soothing effect on the grief that hovered so close to Wren's heart. *I love ye as well, sister. Ye've been so good t' me. But it's time we were both set free.* Wren had felt some anger over the implication. She had never *wanted* to be set free from caring for Bethia, even though she could easily acknowledge that it was more often a burden than a pleasure. Still, she had gained much joy and fulfillment from her association with her sister. They *were* sisters, after all. On the other hand, Wren had worried continually about Bethia, and far worse, she had ached for Bethia's struggle to find peace in her own mind. Bethia had certainly known some stretches of happiness in her life—times with Greer, and her more recent association with

Ward. But for the most part, Bethia's life had been tainted with fear and unhappiness. Wren was not so narrow-minded that she couldn't see Bethia's death as a release from all that she had suffered, and she could not deny some relief in knowing that she would never have to worry about Bethia again. She would always feel some sadness over the separation, and she would always miss her. But she could find peace enough to go forward.

As the idea settled more firmly into Wren that all was well with her sister, a sensation of warmth and power crept from her heart outward until it consumed her every nerve. The peace became palpable; the warmth completely overcame her. She knew that she would be with her sister again one day, and in the meantime, she would never be terribly far away. It was easy to imagine Bethia watching over her little daughter as she grew, and this impression in her mind added to her peace.

Wren lifted her face toward the sun and inhaled the fresh sea air. The suffocating pain she'd been feeling over her sister's death was lifted from her. She'd been praying and praying for such a miracle, and now it had happened. Of course she would always miss Bethia; of course the grief over her death would continue. But a warm peace had filled her with hope. Overcome by the miracle, she felt added peace in their decision to go to America. They truly were in God's hands.

"Beggin' yer pardon, Miz MacBrier," a gruff voice said, and Wren turned to see a sailor she recognized as being one of those that had gone into the water to try to help her husband and sister. "I don't mean t' interrupt yer thinkin', but I did so want t' offer my condolences on yer loss."

"I thank ye very much for that," she said.

"And I did so want t' say that yer 'usband's a fine man, Miz MacBrier; a fine man."

"He certainly is."

"There was a good deal o' commotion, I know," the man went on, "but ye should know that yer 'usband found 'er, Miz MacBrier. We found 'im 'oldin' tight to 'er . . . keepin' 'er 'ead above water while 'e was tryin' to keep afloat 'imself. Twas 'im that found 'er. We'd a never found 'er otherwise. But I do believe she was already gone afore 'e pulled her up. I do believe she was."

Wren nodded and forced a weak smile, unable to comment.

"I do 'ope I've not offended ye."

"No, of course not," Wren said.

"I just thought ye should know what a fine man yer 'usband is."

The sailor walked away, and Wren once again turned her face toward the sea, allowing the wind to dry her tears as they fell. The image in her mind of Ian risking his very life to save Bethia was both stirring and unsettling. One thing was certain. Her husband *was* a good man, and she was grateful to have him in more ways than she could count or imagine.

Wren returned to the cabin when she felt especially tired. Ian wasn't there, and she knew he was likely engaged in deep conversation with Ward. She laid down and drifted to sleep, awaking to find Ian sitting beside her on the edge of the bed, reading from the book that they both considered priceless above all their worldly possessions.

"How is Ward?" she asked, alerting him to the fact that she was awake.

"As well as could be expected," Ian said, setting the book aside. "He feels more like he lost her when she went into that depressed state after the baby was born."

"I can understand that."

"This is very hard for him," Ian said. "He'd grown to love her very much in a short time."

"It's such a strange irony."

"What is?"

"These people that we didn't even know two months ago have now become so very involved in this tragedy that has affected us all."

"That is very ironic, indeed."

Wren sat on the bed and held Ian's hand while she told him how she'd found some peace with Bethia's death, and that she could let her go with love and hope on her behalf. Ian bristled at the comment and stood abruptly, turning his back to her.

"Whatever is wrong?" Wren asked gently.

Ian hesitated to answer, but Wren quickly assessed that in her own grieving she had overlooked something very important. Her husband was grieving too. He'd likely been suppressing his own emotion for the sake of being there for her—and for Ward.

"Ye must talk t' me," she said, standing beside him. "This has surely been at least as hard for ye as for me. I've been selfish in not thinking how it is for—"

"You've not been selfish," Ian insisted.

"But ye're upset."

"Yes, I'm upset, Wren. She was your sister; *my* sister. And I couldn't save her." Tears came with his confession, and Wren realized she'd hardly seen him cry at all since Bethia's death. Had he been holding all of this inside? "I should have been able to stop her, Wren. We were trying to reason with her. I thought we could get through to her. I don't think I believed she would really jump. I should have grabbed her and pulled her back instead of stewing over it, and . . ." He sobbed and sniffled and wiped his face with his shirtsleeve. "If I'd just *grabbed* her, she'd still be alive, and . . . we wouldn't be talking about . . . raising her child for her, and . . ."

"We would be raising the child anyway, Ian. Ye know that we would. She never could have been left alone with the care of a child."

"I know that," he said, a little more calmly. "I know you're right, but . . ."

"Ian, Bethia's free of her suffering now. Maybe . . . just maybe . . . her insanity lured her int' the sea because it was time for her t' go."

Ian turned to look at her sharply. "What are you saying? That she's better off dead?"

Wren said nothing, but she tightened her gaze on Ian's until she saw the words come back to him, and he squeezed his eyes closed. "There was not a day," Wren said, "in these last years that she did not live with feelings of fear and confusion. If we believe there is a peaceful place beyond this earth life—and we do—then we must know she is free from the illness of her mind."

"How is it that you can have such peace over this in so few days?" he demanded as if it made him angry.

Tears trickled down Wren's face as if to declare that her peace had not erased her sorrow. "Perhaps because I've done nothing but grieve for days; perhaps I got it all out of me. Ye've been so strong for those around ye that I wonder if ye've taken time to feel it properly and come t' terms. I miss her, Ian; I'll always miss her for as long as we're apart. But I *do* feel peace over it. I *do!*"

"How?" he asked, slightly less demanding.

"The same way that I knew we were t' leave Brierley and come t' America—and ye knew it as well, Ian. Neither of us could put it t' words if our very lives depended on it. But we both know the truth. And that's how I know that Bethia is all right now. I can so easily imagine . . ." her tears increased, "her as an angel in heaven, watching over her little daughter, watching over us in our journey. My heart tells me that she'll forever be my sister, and I will be with her again. I don't know how it's possible, but I feel that it is."

Ian slumped onto the edge of the bed and hung his head in his hands. Wren sat beside him and put an arm over his back. "Do ye know what it means t' me t' know that ye love me—and my sister— enough t' jump in the water t' go after her without a moment's hesitation?" Her voice cracked. "I feared that I'd lost the both of ye, and I thank God every hour that ye came back t' me." Ian turned his head to look at her. "But ye must know, Ian, that ye're a hero t' me. Ye did everything ye could." She pushed his dark curls back off his face with tender fingers. "Ye did more than most men would have, I'm certain. And I will never forget how ye tried t' save Bethia, and how much ye've sacrificed t' help care for her."

"It was never a sacrifice," he said firmly.

"T' me it is," she said and kissed his face. "Ye must let go of these feelings of guilt, Ian."

"That's easier said than done."

"Perhaps, but let me remind ye that ye once tortured yerself with feeling responsible for Greer's death. And then ye did the same when James was killed." Ian grew defensive at the mention of his brother's death, but Wren pressed on. "Ye blamed yerself when there was nothing ye could have done, and now that time has passed ye know it as well as I. Ye've found peace over their deaths, have ye not?"

Ian thought about it. "I have, yes."

"And ye've told me how that was possible," she said and knew he was remembering the remarkable experience he'd had that had cleansed him of his pain. It had been deeply integrated into the experience that had let him know that God wanted him to take his family to America. Wren could still remember the glow that had seemed to envelop him and the unfaltering conviction he'd felt regarding this decision.

He leaned against her and sighed. "What would I do without you to remind me of what I know is true? You're right, Wren. I know I couldn't have saved Greer *or* James, and I know that God took that burden from me. It might take me some time to make peace with what's happened to Bethia. But if *you* feel that peace, then I believe it's possible." He sighed again. "It's funny how I miss her more than I think about how worried I felt for her almost every waking minute."

"I feel exactly the same. Perhaps we're both in such a habit of worrying, that getting out of the habit might be one of our biggest adjustments."

"Perhaps you're right," Ian said and dropped his head into the portion of her lap that was not occupied by her pregnant belly. Wren toyed with the curls in his hair while they talked about Bethia for a long while, both the good memories and the difficult ones. They shared tears and laughter, and together came a little closer to being able to move forward without her.

* * *

The next morning the captain announced that the New York harbor was on the horizon and they would be coming into port with the evening tide. An air of excitement was kindled among the passengers, prompting Ian to the realization that he needed to have a specific conversation with Ward before they all left the ship and embarked upon the next stage of this journey. Ian knew that Ward and Millie had no particular plans once they arrived. Their goal had been to become Americans, and they had openly discussed their desire to simply spend some time in New York City and then decide if they wanted to remain there or move on to a different location. They all knew from hearsay that America was a huge and vast land with the possibility of many different opportunities that could suit anyone's taste. They had all agreed that once they were actually on American soil and had done some research and gathered information, they would know where to go and what to do. But Ian and Wren had never shared with Ward and Millie the *real* goal in their American journey. Part of their purpose in leaving Brierley had been to protect Bethia. Having her gone made that decision ironic at best. But Ian and Wren both knew that their decision had been rooted in something far deeper and more complex than they believed they could ever explain to anyone else. And yet, Ian had not been able to shake the feeling that he needed to try to explain it to Ward. They'd been through so much together in the less than two months they'd known each other, and their bond was strong. Ward had a right to know what mattered most to Ian, and it felt important to Ian to share it now, before they left the ship.

Ian found Ward on the deck with his mother. He greeted them with the exchange of some customary small talk, then he asked Millie if it would be all right for her to join the other women while he had a little chat with Ward.

"How delightful!" Millie said with a smile that was somewhat unconvincing. It was constantly evident among all who had grown to love Bethia that her death was continually on their minds and that they were trying to adjust and muster the courage to move forward.

Ian guided Ward's hand to his shoulder and they began to stroll around the deck. Ward said right off, "If your intent is to tell me that my mother and I cannot follow you around America, it won't work. The two of us will track you no matter where you go."

Ian chuckled. "You can't *track* me. You can't even go for a walk without me."

"Precisely! My mother's a fair tracker, however. And she *will* find you." They both shared a hearty laugh, likely the first since Bethia's death. "She's a competent woman, my mother. But I can't rely on her for these man-to-man chats, now can I!"

"No need to worry, my friend. My intent in this conversation is quite the opposite. I just want to be assured that wherever we end up, that we end up there together."

"I thought that had already been established," Ward said more seriously. "I confess that with Bethia gone, my plans for the future have become dramatically altered, but you're a fine friend, Ian. I wonder how I ever got by without you. We all enjoy each other's company—unless you've been lying to me."

"I have many shortcomings, Ward, but you never have to question my honesty. If I had an aversion to your company, you would have discovered it by now. The thing is . . . there's something about our reasons for coming to America that I've not shared with you, and it will certainly have an influence on where we end up."

"And where is that?" Ward asked, turning more toward Ian as if he could see him. Even though he couldn't, the gesture implied an increased interest in what Ian was saying.

"I don't know exactly, but . . . somewhere in New York state, I believe."

"You believe?" Ward echoed, confused. "Perhaps you'd better start at the beginning."

"I intend to, but I think we should go to your cabin where we can sit and have some privacy."

"Lead the way, my friend," Ward said.

Once they were inside the cabin, Ward sat on the bed and leaned up against the wall, stretching out his legs. It had become a comfortable position for him, and his mother or Bethia had often sat at the foot of the bed to visit or to read to him. Ian sat in that spot so that he could comfortably face Ward. Even though Ward couldn't see him, he always wanted to converse toward the sound of the voice he was talking to. And now, more than ever before, Ian wanted to see Ward's facial expressions. If Ward believed that what Ian had to share was strange and unfounded, it could dramatically alter their friendship.

"The story begins in London," Ian said. "No, I must go back. The story begins in Scotland. For as long as I could remember, I had this uneasy feeling inside of me that made me want to leave my home. I had no logical reason to leave. It was beautiful there. I had friends and family who loved me. But the feeling persisted terribly; I even turned to drinking far too much, and one of the reasons was to try to block out that feeling."

"What were the other reasons?" Ward asked, proving his sharpness.

"Truthfully, I was in love with Wren but unable to admit it, and she was in love with my brother. That's a different story for another day. We're together and so that has a happy ending."

"Indeed it does."

"When Greer died, or rather when I *believed* he had died, I took it very hard. And that was when the feelings inside of me took over. I left home with no explanation to my loved ones and ended up in London. I wandered aimlessly there for many useless, ridiculous months, drinking myself into oblivion and waking each day, amazed that I'd not been robbed or even murdered. I kept thinking I should return home, *wanting* to return home, but I didn't know how to face the people I loved. I felt like such a fool. Then one morning I overheard two missionaries preaching. They spoke of redemption in a way I'd never heard before, and what they said suddenly put me on the path to home as if I'd been shoved there by some divine hand. These men had a book; a unique book of scripture. I purchased a copy, then put it in my bag and forgot about it. Many months later, during an especially difficult time, my mind suddenly became awakened to a remembrance of the existence of that book. It seemed to call to me. I started reading it and soon found answers to many questions in my life. Over time and through much prayer, I came to know that this book was true, and I realized that the men I'd heard preaching that day were surely missionaries connected to the religion this book represents."

Ian took a deep breath, realizing how zealous he was sounding. He calmed his voice and said, "I don't really know how you feel about religion, Ward. For all of my own feelings on the matter, I confess that I've avoided the subject, not wanting the possibility of opposing views to come between us."

"You should know that any difference of opinion between us would always be treated with respect."

"I *do* know that, Ward. But this is . . . very close to my heart."

"And how does Wren feel about what you believe?"

"She's read the book as well. She knows it's true. We both had profound, unquestionable experiences where impressions came to our minds and feelings to our hearts with such intensity we could not deny their truth. We both knew beyond any doubt that God wanted us to come to America, to find this religion, and to become a part of it. We both believe that this decision will make a better life for our posterity, and we are willing to do whatever we need to do to make that happen."

Ward was silent, expressionless. Ian's heart began to pound, and he tried not to hold his breath. He couldn't believe how important it was to him to have Ward's approval and support. Of course, just as Ward had said, they would always respect each other's differences, and he didn't expect something like this to actually come between them. But if Ian followed the path that led to these people, Ward and his mother might not follow the same path if they had no interest in such a thing as a new religion.

Ward finally spoke. "I've never taken you for the kind of man to get caught up in something impetuous or unfounded."

"I'm not!" Ian said, wishing it hadn't sounded so defensive.

"Exactly. There must be something to what you're telling me if you feel so strongly about it." He chuckled. "I'd ask you if I could borrow the book to read it, but . . ."

"I'll read it *to* you," Ian said. "Perhaps your mother might find it interesting, as well."

"Oh, my mother is always up for a new adventure," Ward said.

Ian breathed in deep relief. He'd quickly come to believe that he and Ward were meant to be on the same path, and Ian knew there was no path more significant or important in his life than this one.

Chapter Five
America

Wren was grateful and relieved to hear that Ian's conversation with Ward had gone well. That evening Millie sought out Ian and Wren and asked questions about this religious book. She wanted to start reading it to Ward right away. It was impossible to know if she had any interest in it herself, or if she was simply acting on Ward's request. Either way, they would both end up reading the book, and Wren didn't know how *anyone* could read it and not feel its truth. It was difficult letting the book out of their hands, when she and Ian were in the habit of reading from it together every day. But they had both agreed that they could not share its message without parting from it for a time. It was their hope that when they found the people they were looking for, they would be able to acquire more copies of the book. Ian had told her more than once that he'd imagined sending copies to his family back in Scotland. He'd not told them anything of his experiences before leaving, but when the time was right, he felt sure he would want to explain himself in a letter, and sending at least one copy of the book with it would be wonderful. He couldn't think of any greater gift he could give to his family; he only hoped that it might be received with open hearts rather than cynicism.

Over supper Ian announced to their friends that he and Wren had finally decided on a name for the baby. "Gillian," he said, "after my sister."

"It's a lovely name!" Shona said.

"I don't believe you've mentioned that you have a sister," Millie said. "Or if you've mentioned it, you've not said much about her."

"We were never close," Ian said. "It wasn't that anything negative was present between us; we simply had little in common and no reason to be close to one another. She moved quite far away when she married, and I saw her very little."

"Were you able to tell her good-bye before you left Scotland?" Ward asked.

"Only in a letter," Ian said. "There simply wasn't time, once our decision was made, for her to travel to Brierley, or for us to visit her."

Silence followed his words, as if he didn't know what more to say, and everyone else sensed his sadness in speaking of the fact that he would likely never see his sister again.

Shona relieved the tension when she said in a light voice, "Naming the baby Gillian is an excellent idea. It's a beautiful name, and a grand way t' honor yer sister."

"I agree," Wren said. "We will use Greer as her middle name."

"That would please her poor, dear mother," Millie interjected. "May she rest in peace."

"Speaking of names," Ward said with an obvious desire to steer the conversation away from any mention of Bethia, "Mother and I have decided that we're changing our surname . . . in order for it to sound more American, you see. Or perhaps more accurately so that it doesn't immediately sound so Italian. Therefore, in honor of embarking upon a new life, we shall start out with a new name and be certain it is on all the records of our family from here onward."

"Wherever did you come up with such an idea?" Wren asked.

Millie said, "I heard some folks on deck talking about it one morning, and I intruded upon their conversation and was quite taken with their friendliness, as well as by the idea. I've got nothing against the name Mickellini, and of course I'll always love my dear Mr. Mickellini, may he rest in peace. But it *does* sound so Italian. I am *not* Italian, as you well know, and even though my dear Ward is half Italian by birth, he was raised in England; therefore, the name doesn't seem entirely suitable—especially with us becoming Americans. Therefore, I shall hereafter simply be Mrs. Mickel. There, that's it. Mrs. Mickel. I do like the sound of it. Short and sweet. Your name does sound very Scottish," she said to Ian. "I wonder if you might not consider doing the same with your name. It's quite a common practice, I understand."

Wren could see that Ian felt irritated by the comment, and it was good when Millie went on to talk about her speculations on what it might be like in New York City.

After supper Wren and Ian checked in with Shirley and spent some time with the baby. Shona had taken to spending a great deal of time with Shirley and her family, initially because she'd wanted to look out for the baby, and then gradually coming to genuinely enjoy the company of a new friend that helped fill the emptiness in her life that had been created by Bethia's absence. The two women joked about believing they *should* have been born as sisters, and this was further evidenced by the fact that their names both began with the same *Sh* sound. Wren considered it a huge blessing that Shona had found such congenial companionship, when her days had previously been so filled with watching out for Bethia. Following Bethia's death Shona had confessed that she felt useless and helpless. Now she was able to help keep Shirley's children entertained, and she'd found purpose in being needed there.

The ship docked very late in the evening. Since it was too late for newcomers to go ashore and find their way, most of the passengers stayed aboard the ship that night, all packed and ready to set foot in America right after breakfast. Lying close beside Ian in the little bed they'd shared for many weeks, Wren found it difficult to relax while her mind tried to make sense of the dramatic changes that had occurred in their lives since they'd left Liverpool and the uncertainty of making themselves part of a new country.

"I know you're not sleeping," Ian said out of the darkness, and she snuggled closer to him.

"There's far too much t' think about," Wren said.

"There is indeed."

"Then tell me what ye're thinking, Ian."

"You go first," he said, and she talked about how difficult it was to believe that Bethia was really gone. She speculated over how it might have felt when they'd embarked on this journey to realize that Bethia would not ever see the shores of America. She cried some as she spoke of her sister, and then she expressed her gratitude for Shona's friendship and devotion, and for the wonderful way that Shirley had taken on the care of the baby. With Shona's help as well, little Gillian was in good hands, and Wren was grateful.

Ian heartily agreed with her on everything she said, but when she had no more to say, he was reluctant to admit to what *he* had been thinking about. She prodded him further, and he finally said, "I keep thinking about Ward and Millie changing their surname. At first the very idea of doing so felt like such a dishonor to my family . . . to my father. I'm proud of my Scottish heritage, and as you and I both know we can hardly open our mouths without being pegged as Scottish—and I'm fine with that."

"As am I," Wren said.

"But a name gets passed down indefinitely. I want to think more about the generations to come than about offending generations past. It feels right to me, Wren, to change our name. What do you think?"

"How would ye do it?"

"Take off the Mac at the beginning; the Scottish prefix."

"Just Brier?" she asked.

"Yes, that's what it would be," he said, but even through the dark she could tell he was still not firm on it, still having trouble with the idea. And yet drawn to it.

Wren had to admit she felt drawn to it herself, but she expressed her feelings on the matter. "Brier seems a little too plain. Millie might like short and sweet, but . . ." An idea came to her mind, so obvious and yet so perfect. "Brierley. It's the name of the house where ye were born and raised, Ian. The name is a great respect to yer home and yer family. Brierley. What do ye think?"

Ian let out a comfortable laugh followed by a contented sigh, and even through the darkness Wren could tell that he liked it very much, even before he said, "I thinks it's perfect . . . Mrs. Brierley."

"It might take some getting used t' saying it, but I like it as well."

They practiced the name back and forth, considering possible names for their unborn baby that would go well with the new American version of their name. Sleepiness came on for both of them at the same time, and they were finally able to rest, anticipating a new life before them.

* * *

Wren was glad for their time in Liverpool, which made their arrival in New York City not quite so shocking. She'd never imagined so many people, and was glad to be able to hold on to Ian and little Gillian, while Shona held on to her. Ward and Millie stayed right beside them as they followed Shirley and Ronald and their children through the streets to where they would meet up with Ronald's cousin who had established his family here some years earlier, and had been writing to Ronald ever since and urging him to bring his family and join them.

Ronald finally found his cousin, and their reunion was sweet. Ernest gave them all a hearty welcome and they all walked a significant distance farther, winding through many streets that manifested the reality that America had its share of poverty and filth, the same as any other place in the world. They finally came to the home of Ernest and his family, and they received an equally hearty welcome from his wife, Maxine. She insisted that they all stay and have some lunch, that there was ample of the stew she'd made. It was joyful to observe the absolute delight Ernest and Maxine took in having their cousin's family under their roof, and they were almost as delighted to meet these new friends of Ronald and Shirley's. While the adults were crowded tightly around the table to eat and the children sat on the floor nearby with their bowls, Shirley and Ronald worked together to tell the story of Bethia's dramatic death and how everyone on board the ship had known of it and had grieved over the loss of the poor girl. But the story shifted to their pleasure at being able to help care for little Gillian. The baby was passed around and admired while she remained awake and completely content.

"Look at her!" Wren commented, noting how the baby's gaze was so intently fixed on a point where there was nothing to look at. Just as Wren said it, the baby's gaze shifted as if she were clearly watching something move.

"All babies do that," Shirley said with the voice of experience. "It's my thinkin' that when they're new out of the womb they're still seein' the angels what sent them here."

"Do you really think so?" Ian asked, fascinated by the idea.

"Just a theory o' Shirley's," Ronald said. "I thinks that babies is just babies and they do funny things. They all stop doin' it once their eyes gets strong enough to look at those around 'em."

"Or when they gets used t' not bein' in heaven and they can't see the angels no more," Shirley said.

The conversation moved on, but Wren couldn't take her eyes off of little Gillian, who seemed utterly fixated on something unseen. The idea came to Wren's mind that it could be Gillian's mother watching over her. Perhaps it was a silly idea, as Ronald had declared. Or perhaps infants *could* see angels as Shirley had declared. Whether or not it was true, Wren liked the idea and chose to believe in it. When Gillian craned her head for no apparent reason, as if to follow some kind of movement, no one else was paying attention, but Wren was even more convinced that the spirit of her sister was hovering nearby. She hoped that wasn't some indication of the same kind of madness that Bethia had experienced. It certainly didn't *feel* like madness. It felt like truth. It warmed her heart and gave her peace and joy. What was it she'd read in that marvelous book? *Every good gift cometh of Christ.* And she knew she'd read something about angels too. She wanted to see if she could find that part again, but the book was currently in the possession of Millie and Ward, and she would just have to be patient and wait until they'd finished reading it.

Ian left as soon as he'd eaten, taking Ward with him, so they could find a place to stay that suited their needs and that hopefully would not be too far from this home where Shirley would be keeping the baby with her so that she could feed her. Shona was also somewhat anxious about being apart from Shirley, but there was nowhere for her to sleep in this home with so many children underfoot. If they could find a place nearby, then Shona could go back and forth easily and help care for the baby, as well as maintain her blossoming friendship with Shirley. Maxine had taken quickly to Shona as well, and Wren was glad to see them all so comfortable with each other. Shona was a sweet girl, and Wren wanted her to be happy. She'd asked her once if she wanted to go back to Scotland, now that Bethia was gone and no longer needed constant supervision. Shona had expressed a keen desire to live in America, just as she had from the start, but Wren wanted to be certain. Shona in turn expressed her concern in not wanting to be a burden to Wren and Ian, but she was enthusiastically assured that she would always have a place with them, and they would gladly support her needs in return for any help she could give them with whatever might arise. Shona was hardworking and sensitive, and Wren knew she would never take advantage of the support being given her. If anything, she worked *too* hard on their behalf, always seeking out opportunities to be of assistance. Throughout the long ocean journey she had been very helpful to Millie, as well. They all got along much better than most families, especially in such close quarters, and Wren hoped that wherever this journey led them, Shona would be able to find fulfillment in her life.

The day dragged on while Wren and Millie waited for the men to come back with good news of a place to stay where they could be comfortable. Shona was content being with Shirley and Maxine, and seemed not to mind the noise of the children in a home that was adequate for one family, but not for two. Wren began to feel very fatigued and longed for a place to rest. Millie became mildly agitated over the lengthy absence of the men. All of the women remained polite and gracious, but the strain was evident. Wren was about to ask if there was a place she *could* lie down for just a short while, when a carriage pulled up and a knock at the door followed only moments later. Wren was visibly relieved to see Ian and to know that he was all right. He quickly reported, "I apologize for the delay, but we did have trouble finding a place that was suitable. However, it's all taken care of now." Turning more to Millie he said, "Ward is there now. I've got a carriage to take you ladies back to our rooms, where supper will be waiting."

"Oh, delightful!" Millie said, clapping her hands together.

"Thank you so much for your hospitality," Ian said to Maxine.

"You've been so very kind," Wren said to her.

"'Twas a pleasure to have you in our home," Maxine said. "We'll be seein' you again soon, I suspect."

Wren glanced toward Shirley, who was holding the sleeping Gillian in her arms. "I'm certain we'll be seeing each other a great deal," Wren said.

Shona promised to see Shirley the next day, and kind farewells were exchanged before Ian got all three ladies out the door and into the carriage. Once inside and underway, Ian said, "It's not as close to here as we would have liked, but hiring a cab is not difficult, and we can go back and forth as much as we like."

Shona nodded gratefully, as if the separation from Shirley and the baby felt painful. Wren wanted to see the baby as much as she possibly could, but at the moment she just felt so dreadfully tired she only wanted to crawl into bed and stay there for a week.

Ian also said, "I've arranged for the remainder of our luggage to be delivered here first thing in the morning, and then we'll have all of our things that we've not had access to since we left England."

"Oh, that will be nice!" Millie said. Wren agreed with her but didn't comment.

The carriage ride was quite brief, but Wren could imagine that walking the distance would take significantly longer. Their rooms proved to be more of an apartment than a hotel, which Ian and Ward had agreed would conserve financial resources more frugally but still meet their needs. There were small bedrooms adequate for everyone, and they all adjoined the living area they would share. The rooms were not spacious, but compared to ship cabins they felt that way. There were many shops nearby where they could purchase anything they needed or wanted, and there were even laundry services as well as restaurants and cafes that would deliver food if the need arose. Shona took warmly to the little kitchen area, as if she would very much like to have tasks with which to keep herself occupied. There was a quaint parlor where a fire burning in the grate took off the autumn chill in the air. Ward was sitting close to it, but stood up when they all entered the room. His mother greeted him with a kiss on the cheek, and then he announced that their meal had just been delivered and was waiting to be eaten. Wren felt more tired than hungry and barely assuaged her hunger before she made herself at home in the lovely bedroom she would share with Ian. She washed up, changed into a nightgown, and crawled into the bed that seemed huge and luxurious in contrast to that on the ship.

Ian tucked her into bed and kissed her brow, saying that he was going to unwind by the fire for a while before he turned in.

"Thank ye, Ian Brierley," she said.

"For what?"

"For taking such good care of us."

"I love you, Wren Brierley," he said, and she smiled at the name before she closed her eyes and fell almost immediately to sleep.

* * *

Soon after Ian returned to sit by the fire, Millie and Shona went off to bed themselves. Ian and Ward talked for a long while, with part of the conversation focused on the book that Ian had loaned him. Ward wanted to know more about the spiritual feelings Ian had experienced that he'd interpreted as answers to prayers. Ian did his best to explain something that was very difficult to explain, but Ward seemed to take it in with an open mind. Ward admitted that religion had never held much interest for him. His mother had taken him to church now and then, but only when it was convenient or she had been in the mood to go. He did admit, however, that he certainly believed in a supreme being, and the things Ian had told him had induced a desire in him to find out more for himself. Ian felt warmed by his hope that Ward would come to know the truth of these things for himself, and that the bond between them would be strengthened even more. In a way, having Ward come to such knowledge this way seemed far too easy. But then, he concluded, truth was truth, and if a person were earnestly seeking for the truth, surely God would open it up to him.

Ian helped Ward to his bedroom and made certain he had all that he needed within easy reach so that he could be on his own through the night. Then Ian went to his own room and found Wren sleeping soundly. He quietly washed up and dressed for bed, basking in the luxury of having ample water and ample space. The bed felt especially luxurious, and he relaxed into it, gravitating toward Wren in a way that made him realize how much he'd grown accustomed to sharing a smaller space with her for sleeping, and he was fine with that.

Ian fell asleep quickly, but he woke up in the night and couldn't go back to sleep. His mind recounted his conversations with Ward, and he recognized the impatience he felt for Ward and his mother to read the book and take in its wonders. He longed to talk to him about the magnificent stories of great prophets and vile oppressors and the ongoing battles between good and evil. He craved conversation concerning the eternal principles contained in the book, and the great witness of the saving power of Jesus Christ. Future discussions went round and round in his head, making him increasingly restless. Then a thought rushed into his mind so suddenly that it took his breath away. He was in America! The missionaries he'd met were Americans. The book had been printed in America! New York, to be precise. He was in New York! Wren was weary of traveling and needed to rest. Her health and that of the baby were most important. Little Gillian needed to stay with Shirley for the time being. Other arrangements could surely be made; goat's milk could be used if necessary, but surely it was best for Gillian to be in the care of a good mother, especially when Wren was moving toward the final stages of her own pregnancy. They were stuck here for the time being, but that didn't mean Ian couldn't leave on his own to find the place where the book had been printed, to find these people who worshiped according to his own beliefs. He couldn't remember the name of the city where he needed to go, but it was printed in the front of that book. Once morning came, he only had to look in the book and then he could proceed to make his own travel arrangements. The state of New York wasn't so terribly big compared to the whole of America. He wouldn't be gone very many days. And then they would know where to settle once they were up to moving on. Oh, the thought of it filled him with such great joy that sleeping became even more difficult!

Ian finally slept and dreamt of standing at the rail of a large sailing vessel, but instead of ocean before him, it was a wide beautiful river, and he could see the shore that was parallel to the course the boat was moving. In the distance he saw a beautiful city nestled against the shore. It shone brilliantly, as if it were a heavenly city, all aglow. Ian woke to sunlight streaming into the room, and the recollection of his dream very clear in his mind. Pondering its possible meaning, he recalled something Wren had once told him that seemed to relate to the dream he'd just had, but he couldn't remember what it was. He wanted to ask her but she was still sleeping, and he left her to do so, knowing how exhausted she had been last night.

* * *

Wren slept well but woke up still feeling excessively tired. Ian suggested she just spend the day resting, and since he assured her that everything was taken care of and there was nothing she needed to do, she was easily convinced and went back to sleep. She woke in the middle of the morning and didn't bother getting dressed. Instead she just put a robe on over her nightgown to go to the kitchen, where she enjoyed tea and biscuits and some fresh fruit that Shona had gone out to get earlier. Shona had just put some bread in the oven, and Wren looked forward to eating some when it came out, but she wasn't up long before she felt sleepy again and decided to lie down while she waited. She was surprised to wake up and realize she'd actually fallen asleep again. She rolled over to see Ian sitting in a chair, his expression concerned.

"Are you all right?" he asked.

"I'm simply tired," she said. "I feel fine otherwise."

"Nevertheless, I've sent for a doctor," he said, "just to make certain nothing is wrong."

Wren didn't protest, wanting to do everything she could to protect the health of her baby—and she knew that meant protecting her own health. The doctor arrived just after Wren had enjoyed a few slices of Shona's bread with fresh butter and some apricot preserves that she'd purchased that morning. The doctor reported that Wren appeared to be in good health, and that he guessed her to be about six to eight weeks away from delivery, according to her size—but he cautioned that it was impossible to know exactly, because women varied a great deal in the way they carried their babies. He was a kind man and seemed competent. After he left, Wren thought about the doctor on the ship, and how kind he had been in helping Bethia through her pregnancy and delivery. Her mind wandered to thoughts of Bethia, wondering what it might be like now if she had lived. She pushed the thoughts away, knowing there would be possible joys and possible challenges if she were here with them. She chose instead to concentrate on the present, and spent the rest of the day reading until she ate some supper that Millie and Shona prepared. Then she went to bed early.

She had just gotten into bed when Ian came and sat beside her, taking her hand. "I'd like to talk to you about something before you go to sleep," he said, "if that's all right."

"Of course," she said, squeezing his hand.

"I had a dream last night," he said, and her eyes widened with interest. He told her about the city on the river, then asked, "Didn't you once tell me something about a city on a river? Something about—"

"Yes!" she said and sat up. "It was that dream I had . . . when I knew that we should come t' America." Ian felt a chill as he now recalled what she had told him, and its connection to his own dream. Unable to remember details, he was glad when she reiterated it. "I saw us together . . . with our children. We were far from Scotland, in a beautiful city next t' a river wider than I've imagined a river could be. We were happy there. God was with us. And when I awoke, I knew that it was our destiny t' be there . . . even though I don't know where it is."

"I remember now your telling me," he said with enthusiasm. "Do you think it's possible that God has shown us both the same place in our dreams?"

"I believe that anything is possible, Ian. Anything!"

"I'm glad you feel that way, Wren, because . . . I believe I need to leave for a few days and see if I can find these people." Her eyes went from wide to narrow, and her brow tightened. "I purchased a map of New York today. Palmyra is the place where the book was printed. Surely they must be there, or nearby at least. If I can go to Palmyra and find them, then we can go there ourselves before winter sets in, and we'll be settled before the baby comes. What do you think?"

Wren was quiet for a long moment that became longer, and Ian's heart quickened with dread. When she still didn't speak, he continued with his reasoning. "If I go alone on horseback, the journey shouldn't be so terribly long or difficult. I can find out what I need to know and be back straightaway. You'll not be alone, and if there's a problem while I'm away, Shona or Millie can hire a cab to go and get help from Ronald or Ernest."

Wren thought for another long moment. "Of course ye must go. I hate t' be apart from ye even for a day, but it's the obvious thing t' do, really. I'm certain we'll all be fine."

"Then I should go tomorrow," he said. "The sooner I leave, the sooner I can return, and the sooner we can be settled with these people . . . where we both know we belong."

"Ye're right, of course," she said with a little more enthusiasm, and they discussed more specific details of their plans for his travel, and her being without him. Ian left Wren to sleep, but she found it difficult to do so now that she'd slept so much during the day;

in addition, her mind was struggling with her reluctance to let Ian go. She wondered for a long while why it was bothering her so much, then she connected it in her memory to the time before their marriage when he'd left home unexpectedly with no explanation and he'd been gone for nearly two years, wandering aimlessly and leaving her to worry and face the challenges of her life without him. She reminded herself that he was a different person now, and this was a completely different situation. She didn't want to be without him, even for a short time, but she completely agreed with his reasoning and knew that it simply had to be.

* * *

Ian spoke to the others about his plans. Shona seemed to have no opinion about this quest to find some strange religious group. But Ward and Millie were enthusiastic and supportive of his decision to take some action in finding them. They told him they'd been reading the book and they were both intrigued by it. Ian was thrilled by their interest, and hoped that this would all turn out the way that he'd been hoping. He hoped too that Shona might eventually find some interest in the things that were being discussed, and perhaps she might want to read the book when the others were done with it. All in good time, he reminded himself, wishing for the hundredth time that he had multiple copies of the book. He also wished he could go back in time to that day he'd met those missionaries in London. He would have asked them their names, where they lived, and inquired about their families. And he would have purchased many more copies of the book—as many as he could have carried if they'd had them available. He recalled that he'd been traveling on foot and he'd barely had enough money to get home—and he'd arrived home hungry. Still, he could see now the importance of that moment in his life and wished, at the very least, that he'd gotten more information from the men. But now that he'd taken another glorious step, being with people like them felt so close he could almost embrace it.

The following morning, Ian went out early to arrange to use a horse from a local livery and to get more information that would help him in his travels. He purchased some saddlebags and a flask for water, as well as some food that could be carried with him. He knew there were places along the way where he could stay and get a good meal, but he didn't want to be slowed down any more than necessary.

Back at their apartment, he had an especially difficult time saying good-bye to Wren. For all of his assurances that it wouldn't be so many days, she seemed terribly worried and hesitant to let him go. But at the same time, she heartily agreed that he needed to do this and she believed it was right. He finally just had to kiss her one last time and hurry away, praying that all would be well for both of them until he returned.

* * *

Wren went back to bed and cried into her pillow after Ian left. Shona found her there and offered comforting words, reminding her of how a woman's emotions are more sensitive during pregnancy and she mustn't be concerned.

"Whatever would I do without ye?" Wren asked and hugged her friend.

"Maybe we should go out," Shona said. "We could walk t' the market, which is not far from here, and after lunch maybe we could take a cab t' visit Shirley and little Gillian."

"Oh, that's a wonderful idea!" Wren said, very much wanting to take her mind off of Ian's absence. "Let's see if Millie and Ward want t' come along."

"Of course they'll want t' come along," Shona said. "They never want t' be left out of an adventure."

Wren thoroughly enjoyed the day, except for Ian's absence. She felt much less tired than she had the day before, and was glad to be out and about. Signs of autumn were showing themselves throughout the city, and the weather was lovely. Over the next couple of days the weather remained mild, which eased Wren's concerns about her husband riding a long distance on horseback. She missed Ian dreadfully, but she forced herself to keep busy. She continued to have regular outings with the others, and they all spent time here and there at Shirley's home, enjoying the baby as well as the company of the rest of the family. They went to the market and bought food that they worked together to prepare, and they enjoyed some fine meals. Ward proved to be fairly competent in the kitchen, as long as the right tools were put within his reach and someone kept an eye on him.

On the third evening following Ian's departure, Wren went to bed early, feeling especially tired and unable to get warm. She fell asleep quickly but woke up in the night shaking from head to toe. She missed Ian more than ever when she realized that she was ill, then she thought it perhaps better that he was away so that he wouldn't be exposed to the contagiousness of whatever she had. Wren managed to build up the fire in spite of her shaking, and she piled on extra blankets with the hope of warming up. But she felt cold from the inside out and knew that she was feverish. She didn't want to have to wake anyone up to help her and, in spite of her misery, didn't feel so sick that she couldn't care for herself. After a few hours, however, a horrible ache settled into every muscle in her body, and she could hardly move. The chills and shaking came and went while the ache only persisted and deepened.

Shona came to the room to check on Wren when she didn't appear at the usual time for breakfast; Wren warned her to stay back and suggested that she go for a doctor. Shona remained calm in spite of her obvious fear, but she did all she could to make Wren comfortable without getting too close. Then she left Millie with some firm instructions to keep an eye on Wren while she went for the doctor. Once she was alone, Wren wanted to cry, but she didn't have the strength, and even if she did it would have been too painful. Not knowing what the illness was or where she'd gotten it, she had no idea if her life was in danger—and equally frightening was the thought that this could affect the well-being of her baby. Wren had only been this sick once in her life, when she was a child, and her memories of it were dreadful. She prayed that it would not be as miserable as that had been, that she and her baby would come through all right, that no one else around her would become ill, and that Ian would return safely to her and bring good news.

The following days blurred together for Wren. She lost her ability to distinguish night from day, and she was only vaguely aware of those around her speaking in hushed voices and trying to get her fever to come down. She did know that the doctor had declared it to be some kind of influenza. While he'd said it could have been something far worse, he clarified that it could still have dreadful results, and they could only wait and hope that the fever would break. When Wren had asked him if it would harm the baby, he'd only said that she needed to rest and hope for the best.

Chapter Six
The Winter Wind

Ian was overcome with gratitude to finally return to the streets of New York City. He'd felt an inexplicable and urgent desperation to get back to Wren. While he'd convinced himself that it was simply difficult to be away from her, and he knew that she was missing him, he wouldn't feel completely comfortable until he saw evidence for himself that she was all right. As anxious as he felt to see her, he dreaded the news he had to give her. Just recalling the moment the truth had settled into his own heart made him ill. The disbelief and shock had been physically painful, and he only had to ponder the memory for a few seconds for that sensation to overtake him again.

Ian left the borrowed horse at the livery and settled with the man there before he walked the short distance to the apartment. Knowing he was minutes away from holding Wren in his arms again, he quickened his pace and tried not to feel impatient with the crowds on the streets. He entered the outside door with a quickening of his heart and bounded up the stairs, where he opened the door to their apartment. Shona, Millie, and Ward all looked toward him at the same time. It was Ward who said, "Ian?" But then, he knew no one else would be coming through the door without knocking.

"Hello," he said, and before he could ask about Wren's whereabouts, he caught the grim expressions of concern on all of their faces. "What's happened?" he demanded and closed the door.

"She's been ill," Shona said, coming to her feet. Ian dropped his saddlebags and pressed his hands to the door behind him, needing to steady himself. "She's past the worst of it now," Shona added, and Ian was able to draw a breath. But the pounding of his heart didn't cease.

"The doctor's come a few times," Millie said, coming to her feet as well. "He's done very well with her. He tells us she'll be fine with time; influenza, he said. The fever finally broke last night. Poor dear. She's been so miserable. But she'll be fine."

Ian hung his head and blew out a long, steadying breath. "And the baby?" he asked without looking up.

"The doctor said it should be fine," Shona reported.

Ian drew in a breath and blew it out before he looked up again. "And the rest of you?"

"We've all been fine," Ward said. "We've done our best to care for her and not get it ourselves, although who can tell with such things? She said many times she was glad you weren't here so you wouldn't get ill."

"I *should* have been here," Ian said and started across the room to see his wife.

"Wait," Shona said. "The fever's broke like I said, but the doctor said she could still be contagious and we should be careful." She nodded. "Just . . . take care."

"Of course," Ian said, putting away his fantasies about the tight embrace and warm kiss he'd been imagining for days.

Ian slowly pushed open the door that had not been latched. He felt sick himself to see her. She was as white as the sheet tucked up to her chin. He'd never seen her look so wretched. There were dark circles under her eyes, and her face looked gaunt. Her hair was utterly disheveled, and even with only her face visible he could see that she'd lost weight. He gathered his courage and stepped into the room as quietly as he could manage, not wanting to wake her and intrude on much-needed rest. He sat on the chair close to the bed and just watched her, silently thanking God that she was going to be all right, and asking forgiveness for having left her alone to face this without him. He sat there for a long while, just watching her sleep while he recounted the fruitless disappointment of this journey. Knowing now how his wife had suffered in his absence only stung his spirit more deeply. His being here couldn't have kept her from getting ill, but he should have been here for her.

When she began to stir, his heart quickened painfully. He waited a moment, then said her name. She opened her eyes with difficulty and turned her head toward him. Her expression implied that she doubted what she was seeing. "Ian?" she asked as if she feared he might be an hallucination.

"It's me," he said, scooting the chair a little closer. He wanted to be close to her, to hold her hand, but he understood the need for caution. He couldn't care for her if he became ill himself.

"Ye're back," she said, her voice rough and faint. "Ye're safe."

"I am," he said, "but I'm told you've had a terrible ordeal, my love. I'm so sorry. I'm so . . . very, very sorry. I should have been here with you."

"Ye're here now," she said. "It doesn't matter. I'm so glad t' have ye back."

"I'm so glad to be back, my darling. I don't ever want to be apart from you again!"

She smiled weakly. "I would agree with that."

Ian hoped that she would be too weak and tired to think about asking him how his journey had gone. When he feared that she *would* bring it up, he asked, "Are you hungry? Thirsty? Can I help you?"

She nodded toward a glass of water on the bedside table and he helped her drink some. "Shona gave me some broth earlier," she said. "I *am* feeling a bit hungry. Could ye see if—"

"I'll get it straightaway," he said and went to the kitchen to find the very broth kept warm on the stove in anticipation of Wren needing some. Shona put some in a bowl while he found a spoon and a napkin, then he returned to the bedroom to help Wren sit up. He was stunned by her weakness and felt keenly afraid at the thought of her being strong enough to give birth in not so many weeks. Refusing to think of that now, he fed her the broth, glad for the absence of conversation when he knew what the most likely topic would be, and he preferred to avoid it.

When the broth was gone and she declared that she was satisfied for now, he helped her get comfortable again, and she asked that he stay and sit with her.

"Of course, my darling," he said.

"Ye haven't told me." She looked right at him with a piercing gaze that had not been affected by her illness. "It must be bad news, or ye would have been eager t' tell me. Instead ye're avoiding it."

Ian sighed and resigned himself to just say it and get it over with. "I found Palmyra easily enough, and it's a lovely city. But . . . I was told that . . . the people . . . they called them *Mormons* because they believed in the Book of Mormon and followed the prophet who claimed to have translated the book. The Mormons . . . I was told . . . left New York years ago." He hung his head and suppressed that sick feeling. He fought back the sting in his eyes, but it was impossible to resist both the tears *and* the nausea. "I spoke to different people . . . asked a lot of questions. Some felt badly about the way the Mormons had been treated, but . . . most people spoke of them harshly; said they were glad the Mormons were gone, and no one—*no one*—had any idea where I might find them. No one, Wren. I . . . ." He sniffled and wiped a sleeve over his face. "I . . . don't know what to do now, Wren. I don't know where to begin to . . . look for them."

"God will show us the way, Ian," she said weakly. "He would not have let us know so clearly t' come here only t' leave us t' never find these people. He would not have brought us this far only t' abandon us."

"Are you sure, Wren? Are you sure we got the right message? Perhaps we were caught up in worry over Bethia, and our need to get her away affected our judgment. Perhaps we should have—"

"I cannot believe what I'm hearing, Ian Brierley. Ye know very well what God told ye t' do, and ye know why. And I know it too. Ye must remember it. Ye must!"

"Of course," he said and nodded. "Forgive me. I'm just . . ."

"Disappointed, I know," she said.

"And worried about you," he said. "I should have been here."

"There's nothing ye could have done that wasn't taken care of. Ye mustn't worry, Ian. It will all work out."

"You seem so sure," he said as if he resented it.

"Whether or not I'm sure, it's likely wise t' hope for the best."

"I'm sure it is," Ian said, but mostly because he didn't want to upset her or have her expending any more energy on the conversation. "You rest, my love. I'll stay close by. Perhaps later you'll feel up to eating a bit more."

"Perhaps," she said and closed her eyes, quickly becoming lost in sleep.

* * *

The following day, Ian walked to the market with a little list from Shona for the ingredients she would need to prepare meals for the day. He felt inclined to buy Wren some kind of gift and stopped in a book shop before he started weighing down his arms with grocery purchases. He felt disappointed but not surprised over being unable to find another copy of the Book of Mormon, but he did decide to buy a beautiful Bible. He'd studied from it a great deal throughout his life, and he knew that Wren had too. They'd had many discussions about stories they'd read or heard about in church. But Wren's family had never actually owned a Bible, and Ian's family Bible had, of course, remained in Scotland. He felt sure that reading from it now would help compensate for having loaned their precious book to their friends, and it would give them something to do together and to talk about. He was intrigued by the idea of comparing it to what he'd now learned from a new volume of scripture. After he'd acquired everything on Shona's list, he also bought some hothouse flowers for his wife; they would brighten up her room, and hopefully brighten her pallid countenance as well.

Autumn's pleasant breezes were swept away by the wind of winter while Wren slowly regained her strength, and fortunately no one else in their household became ill. Ian read stories from the Bible to Wren, while he knew that Millie was reading to Ward from the Book of Mormon. Sometimes they all sat together and shared what they were learning from both books. Ward and Millie maintained their intrigue with this new book of scripture, which gave Ian and Wren a growing hope that their friendships would in time have greater meaning and purpose. Shona sat in on their reading when she was there, but she never commented, and she was more and more prone to be gone, spending long hours at Shirley's home. Now that Wren was doing better and Ian was home, they assured her that they could manage without her and she was welcome to spend her time where she chose. She always more than earned her keep by the work she did with cooking and laundry in between her visits with Shirley.

Wren said more than once that she was glad not to have the responsibility of caring for little Gillian, as weak as she felt and as ill as she'd been. But they all missed the baby and looked forward to the day when she no longer needed a wet nurse and they could take on her care. As soon as they were certain that Wren was no longer contagious, they resumed regular visits to Shirley's home so that they could spend time with Gillian, but it simply wasn't practical for them to spend too much time there with it being as crowded as it was. Shirley had brought the baby to their home a few times, but she was very busy caring for her own family, so that wasn't very practical either.

Shona brought word on a very cold day that Ronald had been hired at the same factory where Ernest had been working for some years. Apparently it was a place reputed for treating its employees well, and the wages were sufficient to care for a family. Ronald and Shirley would now be able to afford their own rent, and would soon be moving out of Ernest and Maxine's home, although they'd all gotten along so marvelously well that everyone knew the families would remain inseparable.

Once the family found a place and got settled in, they invited everyone over for dinner to celebrate. Millie and Ward stayed at home since Millie was feeling a little under the weather, and Ian wished he could have used that excuse. Wren was almost back to normal except for becoming easily fatigued, but the doctor had said that could have as much to do with being very pregnant as it could with having been very ill. She was looking forward to their dinner engagement at Ronald and Shirley's new home, but Ian found he was dreading the event. It wasn't that he didn't feel pleased that they'd been able to rent a home of their own, just as he felt pleased that Ronald's work was going well and he was bringing in enough income to provide an adequate living for his family without relying on his cousin's hospitality. Ian simply wished that he and his own family were no longer here in this city. And he wished that he had any idea where to take them. His discomfort over being in New York had become so much like the wanderlust he'd endured throughout the majority of his life that it had begun to feel like a disease that would eat him alive and destroy him from the inside out.

During the course of a fine meal with the typically boisterous family, Ian noted—not for the first time—that Gillian was doing well. She looked healthy and happy. But she was also very attached to Shirley as a mother figure in her life. Ian could see how Wren longed to fill that role for Gillian, but she was so consumed with the discomfort of her own pregnancy that it would be nigh to impossible. Even if they weren't reliant on Shirley to feed the baby, they would have to rely on Shona to see to most of the baby's care. Of course, he would help as much as he could, and if he *had* to take care of a baby he would manage. But under the circumstances, blessed as they were to have Shirley available and so willing and eager to care for Gillian, it was better this way. Still, Ian knew that Wren felt distressed over the situation, and he knew that in spite of the fact that she was very pregnant and miserable and that traveling right now would be foolhardy, and even dangerous, he also knew Wren felt the same restlessness in wanting to leave this city and move on. But neither of them had any idea where they would go, and he wondered how they might ever find out.

Recognizing that his thoughts were not new, and therefore very depressing, Ian did his best to focus on the conversation around the dinner table and to put on a cheerful face. The children finished eating and went off to play. Shona went with them, having taken a strong liking to interacting with the children at every opportunity. Shirley loved the way Shona kept the children occupied, and Shona simply loved children. She'd confessed more than once that she'd never had the opportunity to work with children in her employment, but if she had her way she'd be a governess to a large family. Since Ian and Wren *wanted* a large family, it wasn't difficult to imagine Shona being with them always and blessing their lives with her unique talent in that regard. However, Wren had told Ian that she hoped Shona might find a good man who could love her so that she could have a family of her own. Ian felt some reluctance over the thought of losing Shona for any reason—even to a good man. But he had to agree that ultimately he wished this for Shona. With the joy and fulfillment he'd found in his own marriage, he would certainly want the same for anyone, especially those he loved most. It had crossed his mind more than once that Shona and Ward might be a good match. They certainly enjoyed each other's company and had spent a good deal of time together, but it was readily evident they had little in common. Ward did well at keeping his feelings concealed most of the time, but they all knew his heart was still grieving over the loss of Bethia, and Ian wondered if he would ever find another woman who could fill the place that Bethia had come to hold in his heart, even though their time together had been so brief. Whatever Ward or Shona chose to do with their lives—and whomever they might end up with—Ian just hoped that they could all stay together through the course ahead, even if he had no idea what exactly that course entailed or where it might lead them.

Ian mostly just listened to the conversation swirling around him, making only a comment here and there to indicate polite interest. He was barely aware of their observations regarding the expansion of America as explorers continued to venture farther west and create communities and new opportunities. He only had a thing or two to say about the weather in New York City in comparison to that of their homeland. And he didn't comment at all on a rather long debate over the ongoing slave trade. He personally felt revolted by slavery of any kind, but felt too weary with his own thoughts to express his viewpoint. He was surprised, however, to hear Ernest talking about the vast diversity of religions available here in America. Ian knew that to be true. But his search to find one in particular had proven fruitless. Ernest and Maxine both agreed that attending the church geographically closest to their home was the most practical option, and that it really didn't matter so long as they were attending church on the Sabbath. Ronald and Shirley passively agreed, although they didn't have as much conviction about whether they went to church at all. Shona quietly seemed to agree with them, and Ian wondered what she truly thought about the reasons he and Wren had come to America to begin with. Of course, she knew all about Bethia's challenges, and the need to get away in that regard. But she was also aware of their desire to find a new religion.

Ian paid more attention to the conversation on religion than he had any topic thus far, but he still didn't comment. Ernest emphasized his preference for convenience in regard to religion and went on to tell the story of a coworker who had up and taken his family to some "godforsaken place out in the middle of nowhere" in order to meet up with some "religious fanatics who actually believed that God spoke to their leader like he was some kind o' Moses or something."

Ian had to acknowledge that his heart was pounding before he could accept that something had been said that connected with his spirit for no logical reason. Wren put a hand on his thigh beneath the table and squeezed tightly as if to say that she was feeling something too. He took her hand and returned the squeeze of her fingers before he gently cleared his throat and asked in a tone that was entirely neutral, "And what is the name of this fanatical religious group?"

"Call themselves Mormons, they do," Ernest said, and it took all of Ian's willpower not to gasp for breath and slide under the table as his every cell seemed to melt. Wren tightened her grip on his fingers until they hurt, but he returned his grip with equal firmness.

Ian wanted desperately to ask if Ernest knew where these people were, but he didn't want to draw attention to his interest, given the negative tone of the conversation. A mutual desire for Gillian's well-being created a strong bond between their families, and it needed to stay that way. But Ian had to know! He was inexplicably relieved when Wren asked in a perfectly normal voice, "Out in the middle of nowhere, ye say? I wonder where that would be, exactly."

"Somewhere on the Mississippi, I hear," Ernest said. "The fool's sister is still workin' at the factory and she talks about him all the time."

"I wonder if ye might ask her where her brother lives," Wren suggested.

Everyone but Ian looked astonished. "Why in the world would you want to know such a thing?" Shirley asked.

Wren didn't answer; she turned to Ian as if he might rescue her. For a moment he felt completely stumped and a little scared over how this would turn out. Then an explanation came abruptly into his mind and he was able to say, "I met some missionaries in London years ago. They were very kind to me, and I do believe they were . . . Mormons, as you say. I've always wanted to find them and thank them for their kindness. If these people are gathered together somewhere, perhaps I could write a letter or something and get it to one of these men."

Ian knew the very idea was ridiculous when he had no inkling at all of the names of either of the missionaries, but the story was mostly true and somewhat plausible. Apparently it worked when Ernest said, "I suppose I could do that. I'll ask her t'morrow, then."

"Thank you," Ian said, and the conversation thankfully shifted to another topic.

Late that evening when Ian and Wren were finally alone in their bedroom, they both expressed their amazement at the subject having come up that way, and their excitement at the possibility that they might actually have access to information of where and how to find these people.

"What do you think," Ian asked, "about the negative things he said?"

"It's just like we talked about before, Ian. There will always be people with different opinions, and some of them will be opposed t' good things . . . or things they don't understand. We have t' remember what we know t' be true and trust in God."

"Yes, you're right, of course," he said.

"And did ye hear what he said . . . about the Mississippi?"

"I did," Ian said, recalling the thrill he'd felt at the time.

"Is it not said to be a tremendously large river?"

"That's what I've heard."

"It can't just be chance, Ian. It can't!"

"I hope you're right, Wren. I do hope you're right."

* * *

The following day the city was assaulted with a tremendous snowstorm. The wind blew horribly, and the snow flying outside the windows had a blinding effect. They were all glad for plenty of firewood and enough food in the house that they could get by and not have to go out at all. Ian felt disappointed because he'd wanted to get the information from Ernest after he returned from work in the evening. But the storm was still intense, and it would be ridiculous for him to go out in this kind of weather so that he could stop by casually and bring up this topic without sounding too eager or ridiculous. So, he stayed close to the fire and did his best to take care of Wren, both anticipating and dreading the day when their baby would finally arrive. He didn't want his sweet Wren to go through the suffering of childbirth, but he *did* want to have the ordeal over with, and they were both looking greatly forward to having this child become a part of their family.

While Ian was gently rubbing Wren's swollen feet, he glanced toward the snow pelting against the windows and realized that even if he had the information in his hands this very minute about where to find the Mormons, he wouldn't be doing anything about going to look for them until spring. It would be completely unwise to set out anywhere toward the frontier of America with the potential for such harsh weather at any given moment. And his wife was pregnant! She needed time here in the comfortable security they'd found for her to give birth safely, and for the baby to get old enough to be able to travel without difficulty. Gillian also needed to be at a stage where she was not dependent on Shirley for sustenance. They had talked about the possibility of Wren being able to feed Gillian once she had a baby of her own, but Shirley had cautioned her to wait and see how much milk she produced and if she was able to sustain both children; she might have to work into it slowly. While Ian knew next to nothing of such things, it made sense to him in theory. All things considered, he had to accept that they would be staying here at least until spring, and he needed to learn to be patient and enjoy this time.

That night, soon after going to bed, Wren whispered to Ian that she felt uncomfortable in her lower back and across her belly. Within an hour the discomfort had evolved into pain, and they knew that the time had come. Even though Wren had been doing fairly well, Ian knew she had not fully recovered from the harsh effects of the influenza, and he felt more afraid than he could begin to express. Recalling the intense difficulties that Bethia had experienced while giving birth, his fears were only heightened. All he could do was pray and stay close by.

It was morning before Shona told him that he should go for the doctor; once the doctor was there, he insisted that Ian stay out of the room. In some ways Ian felt sure that was likely best. He wasn't certain he could have endured watching Wren suffer any longer. But he longed to be with her, to help her through this in any way he could. Ward insisted they go for a walk so that Ian couldn't hear the signs of Wren's anguish from the other room. Ian finally gave in, but he couldn't bring himself to stay away long. They returned to the joyful news that a girl had been born only a few minutes earlier. It was over! And Wren was fine by all accounts.

Ian was overjoyed and overcome with relief. A few minutes later he was allowed into the room where he found his beautiful wife, looking almost as bad as she had when he'd come home to find her barely past the fever of influenza. But her countenance was beaming with happiness and pride, and in her arms was their daughter, wrapped in a little white blanket. Ian crept closer and peered down at the baby, and his joy was magnified. She was tiny and precious and beautiful! Wren encouraged him to hold her, and he was glad for his practice with Gillian and with his brothers' babies before he left Scotland. He sat nearby and held the baby for as many minutes as it took them to decide firmly on naming her Bethia Joy, although they would call her Joy; it seemed so fitting. Ian gave the baby back to Wren while the doctor was preparing to be on his way. He was about to put on his coat when Ian noticed that Wren's expression had taken on a look of panic.

"Something's wrong with her!" Wren shrieked in a voice too weak to be very loud.

The doctor grabbed the baby from Wren, and Ian got only enough of a glance to see that her skin had turned blue. The panic and fear he'd felt during Wren's labor came back to him, now intensified. He sat on the bed and put his arms around Wren as the doctor whisked the baby into the other room. Ian wanted to follow but knew he could do nothing, and he was better off staying here with Wren, giving her comfort and allowing her to give it to him. She held to him tightly and cried against his shoulder. He prayed with all the energy of his soul that their little girl would come through this, that the doctor would be able to help her. Then something shifted inside of him; something cold took hold of his heart, and he found himself praying that they could endure whatever God's will might be. A strange sense of comfort buffered a pain that he hadn't fully felt yet, but he knew it was coming. Somehow he just knew it was coming.

A moment later the doctor appeared in the doorway, holding the blanketed bundle that was eerily still. The doctor's expression required no words to explain its meaning. "I'm so sorry," was all he said before Wren wailed and grabbed more tightly onto Ian, who managed to hold his own weeping back behind a curtain of shock while he heard only brief phrases of explanation. The doctor didn't know what had gone wrong; things like this just happened sometimes. Even with all of his training, there were things that were simply out of his control.

Ian managed to ask if his wife's influenza might have caused this. "It's not likely," the doctor said, "but it's impossible to know for sure why these things happen." He encouraged them to hold the baby and say good-bye to her. He'd obviously had as much experience with death as he'd had with saving lives. And what doctor wouldn't? Ian became vaguely aware of Shona and Millie crying in the distance, but he wasn't even sure if they were in this room or in the parlor. The doctor offered to make arrangements with the undertaker. Ian thanked him and watched in numb horror while his sweet wife held their cold, dead baby close to her face and wept uncontrollably.

With the doctor gone, Shona, Millie, and Ward all hovered helplessly nearby. Ian just held Wren while she held to the baby as if she would never let it out of her arms. She became so upset, and was so obviously ill and weak from her ordeal, that Ian finally had to firmly insist that she give him the baby. He held it for only a minute, which was all he could bear before he was glad to relinquish it into Shona's capable hands. It was obviously not the first time she'd seen a dead infant, and he wondered when and how that might have happened. It wasn't the first time it had occurred to him that they knew very little about Shona's life before coming to work at Brierley, but she was very private about herself. Right now he was simply grateful for her calm ability to take control of the crisis. She said to him in a gentle voice, "I'll take care of everything. Ye just need t' grieve with yer wife."

Ian nodded, feeling like a child taking direction from his mother, then he returned to the bed to hold Wren close. She cried herself to sleep, and as her weeping subsided, his own took over. He fought to remain quiet so as not to disturb her, but his grief felt utterly overpowering. He simply couldn't imagine how they would ever move beyond this and find any peace or joy again in their lives. *Joy.* The irony was too painful to consider.

A few days later their little Bethia Joy was buried in a cemetery in a place they would likely leave behind. Wren was too ill to attend the burial, but she did see her daughter resting peacefully in the tiny white casket, looking as if she were asleep. The winter wind was bitter while a minister Ian had never met before spoke a few words over his daughter's grave—but his words felt hollow and lacking in truth to Ian. When the brief service was over, Ian looked at this man and asked, "Where *is* my daughter, sir?"

"In heaven, of course, among the angels."

Ian could agree with that, but he asked, "Will I see her again? Be able to hold her again?"

"Such feelings as you have now will have no meaning in the life to come, my friend," the minister said, and Ian wanted to give him a bloody nose. How could it be possible that his love for those who meant most to him would simply dissipate with death? It didn't make sense, and it didn't feel right, but he knew instinctively that he would not find any answers here in this place. The answers had been driven away from this state, along with the people who believed what he believed.

With Ward's hand on his shoulder, and Millie at his side, Ian returned to the apartment to find Shona looking after Wren, who was growing weaker by the day, when it should have been the opposite. The doctor had reported that she had no logical reason to be so ill, but she *was* ill. And Ian felt helpless and frightened and very near to losing his mind.

Ian stayed close to Wren throughout the remainder of the day, praying with all the energy of his soul that his wife would be spared, that they could find a reason to go on, that they could find hope in the future. He thought he had known despair in his past, but what he'd previously defined as such was merely a selfish kind of hopelessness. Losing a child and seeing his wife suffer so deeply was something his wounded bachelor heart never could have comprehended.

Somewhere in the night, Wren woke up experiencing a new kind of pain. Her milk had come in, and having no baby to nurse was creating a dire problem and a great deal of affliction that only accentuated her grief. Ian woke Shona just past dawn, hoping she had some suggestion as to what to do. She thought about it for a minute and said, "We need to go and get Gillian."

The idea entered Ian's heart like a rush of a warm wind that immediately eased a measure of his grief and gave him an abstract kind of hope. While nothing could take the place of their little Joy, the situation suddenly smacked of destiny. But he could see a problem in this plan.

"Won't that cause an equal challenge for Shirley if she's accustomed to feeding the baby?"

"She knows how t' deal with such things," Shona said. "She's told me all about it, talking on and on the way she does. She can work the milk out enough to ease the pressure until it dries up. She would understand and be willing t' do it; I'm sure she would. She's not the one grieving right now, and needing t' have a baby in her arms. She'll miss little Gillian, but she's known all along it was temporary, and she's got a houseful of children t' love. We must go and get Gillian. I'll come with ye."

"You're brilliant, Shona," he said and impulsively pressed a brotherly kiss to her forehead.

They left Millie at Wren's bedside, explaining only that they would return shortly. They arrived at Shirley's door just as she was about to start cooking breakfast for her brood. Shona explained the situation quickly and efficiently. Since she'd already known about the death of little Joy, Shirley admitted that it had occurred to her just the night before that this would happen, and she felt prepared to let Gillian go, knowing it was the right thing to do. Within minutes she had the baby's things gathered, and said she'd bring over whatever might have been missed. Shirley cried a little as they were saying good-bye, and Ian held the sleeping Gillian during the cab ride back to the apartment. Gillian was just coming awake when they arrived, and Ian immediately placed Gillian next to Wren on the bed. Wren looked utterly stunned. Ian simply said, "You must feed her. She's yours to care for now."

"But . . ." Wren only got the one word out before a different kind of tears filled her eyes and she turned her attention to the crying baby. Gillian was much bigger than the tiny infant they'd just buried, but she was well trained at nursing, and it took only a few minutes for her to figure out how to ease Wren's physical pain. And while the baby nursed, Ian could see a discernible softening in Wren's countenance. He knew the grief was not magically gone. He knew this because he still felt it so keenly, and he knew that whatever *he* felt, Wren had to be feeling it more so. But having Gillian as a part of their lives, ready and available to solve this problem, seemed nothing short of a miracle. And with such a miracle, Ian could find reason to hope that perhaps God was looking out for them after all.

Chapter Seven
Waiting for Spring

Ian watched Wren slowly come back to life through her need to care for Gillian. The baby didn't seem at all disoriented by her change of environment, almost as if, in her infancy, she had known this change would come to pass. Ian noticed Gillian often staring at what seemed to be nothing, and then moving her eyes as if she were watching movement. Wren commented to him more than once about noticing the same phenomenon. When Shirley came for a visit, they all noticed Gillian doing this, and Ian said, "I thought you said that babies grew out of doing that."

"Most of 'em do," Shirley said. "I never did see one prone t' doin' that at this age." She chuckled. "Perhaps she's a special one, eh? Perhaps she's blessed t' see the angels longer than most."

"Perhaps she sees her mother," Wren said as if she fully believed it.

"I do think that's a lovely thought," Shirley said.

"Or perhaps she sees her little cousin," Millie said.

"That is also a lovely thought," Ian commented, loving the idea that his little daughter might be an angel in their midst.

"How ironic," Wren said, "that I would be caring for Bethia's baby, and she would be caring for mine."

Ian felt a chill at the thought, but it was accompanied by a strange warmth in his heart, and he couldn't help thinking that the idea was true. Whether or not it was, he felt better thinking it and chose to do so. Watching Gillian as she gazed at things unseen by mortal eyes, it was easier to believe that it *was* true.

* * *

Ian was glad to see Wren becoming herself again, however slowly, even though she cried every day over the loss of their daughter. Ian's grief was less visible, but he felt it nevertheless. He kept thinking of the minister's words, and they haunted him. Ian couldn't believe that a loving and merciful God would make the love felt between family members just disappear at death. He simply couldn't believe it! And when he talked to Wren about it, she heartily agreed with him. Ian admitted that he didn't know if his instinctively believing it necessarily meant that it *was* that way, but he wanted to believe it was, and believing made him feel better. Wren agreed with that as well, and they both agreed to believe, and with any luck when they got to the other side, they would be proven right.

Ian thought of his parents like he hadn't allowed himself to do for months. He couldn't think about them without missing them deeply, and without wondering how they were doing. His father's health had not been good for quite some time, and Ian couldn't help wondering if his father was doing all right, or if he were even still alive. Ian thought of the overt and powerful love shared by his parents, and couldn't imagine how death could possibly be the end of all they'd shared. He thought of his feelings for Wren, and the fear he'd felt in regard to her illness and childbirth. If he lost her, he couldn't imagine going on. But if he had to believe that death was absolutely the end of all they'd shared, his grief would go to a whole new level of unbearable. He just couldn't wrap his mind around such a cold concept!

With his parents on his mind, Ian did something he'd had in mind to do for some weeks now. He started to write them a letter. Given the weeks it would take for a letter to get to Scotland, and then for another to get back to New York, he'd not wanted to write when he'd believed that their address would quickly become obsolete. But now he knew they wouldn't be going anywhere before spring, for the sake of Wren's health if nothing else. Even then, he wasn't sure where they would go, and therefore couldn't be certain if they'd leave here at all. He wasn't necessarily that fond of where they were living, but they were all safe and secure, and anything beyond the present situation felt uncertain and somewhat frightening, especially given the recent reminders of the vulnerability of human life.

Ian felt somewhat hesitant to tell his parents of the tragedies that had occurred in their lives since leaving the highlands of their home, but as he began to recount in writing the course of their journey and their experiences, it all just flowed onto the pages in detail. He could easily imagine sitting in his parents' sitting room, chatting comfortably with them, pouring out his heart as he'd always done. It took a few days and several sittings to finish the very lengthy letter. Intermixed with the tragedies they'd endured, he also told his parents about the wonderful friends they'd made, how priceless Shona had been to them, and how very much they'd been blessed. Ian felt better for having written the letter, as if it had assuaged some of his grief and reminded him of all he had to be grateful for. He just hoped that they would not be faced with any such challenges in the future, and that somehow, by some unfathomable miracle, he would know where and how to find the Mormons.

With the thought came the memory that Ernest had told them he would get information about the Mormons from a woman who worked at the factory—a woman whose brother had become a Mormon and was now living with the Mormons in the middle of nowhere. Ian nearly stopped breathing at the thought. How could he have forgotten such a thing? Then he remembered that the conversation had taken place the day before Wren had gone into labor, and they had been thrown into a whirlpool of grieving and coping. Although Ian couldn't take his family away from here in the middle of winter with Wren's health as fragile as it was, if he had any idea *where* to take them, when the time was right he could have a plan in place.

Ian didn't necessarily know Ernest very well. He'd become more comfortable with Ronald, and Ernest was simply the man's cousin with whom they'd associated due to the fact that Ronald and Shirley had lived temporarily in Ernest's home. He decided it would be most appropriate to send Ernest a message, which he did, but days passed and he got no response. He finally got up the nerve to call on Ernest and Maxine in the evening when they would have just been finishing supper. Ernest was there and invited Ian in, being very friendly and offering a drink. Ian refused the drink—having an aversion to liquor due to times in his past when he'd been prone to losing himself in it—but he did sit and visit with Ernest, engaging in awkward small talk that led into Ernest rambling on about things in which Ian had no interest. After putting a fair effort into humoring Ernest with polite conversation, Ian asked if he'd been able to get that information from the woman with whom he worked.

"Oh, oh!" Ernest seemed to recall the thought from the deepest recesses of his brain.

"Did you get my message?" Ian asked.

"I did. I did," Ernest said. "But I've not thought t' ask 'er. I'll be sure and do it t'morrow and be lettin' ye know."

"I would appreciate that very much," Ian said, now wanting to leave as quickly as possible without being impolite.

"Why was it again that ye wanted t' know?" Ernest asked.

"I met some men in London," Ian said, "and I would very much like to find them."

"Oh, that's right. That's right. I'll be lettin' ye know."

"Thank you," Ian said and visited for a few more minutes before he graciously excused himself, praying that he wouldn't have to endure any more long conversations with Ernest in order to get the information. Of course, he would do just about anything to get the information, so he corrected the thought and simply offered a silent prayer that Ernest would be successful in finding out what felt to Ian like the greatest secret of all time.

The next time Ian spoke to Ernest, he told Ian the Mormons had been somewhere in Ohio, and then they'd all gone somewhere in Missouri, and now he thought they were somewhere in Illinois. Ian resisted yelling at the man and telling him that his information was not helpful at all, except in discouraging Ian with the evidence that the Mormons were apparently some band of gypsies, never settling in one place for very long. With Ernest's promise to get more information, Ian tried not to think too much about what he so desperately wanted to know. Instead he pondered the implications of what he *had* learned. He discussed what he knew with Wren, and his concerns that perhaps they were following a fruitless path—that perhaps associating with these people was not necessarily wise. She reminded him of the obvious: that they knew the book was true, and they had to at least do everything they could to find these people and then press forward from there.

"It's the greatest reason we came t' this land," she said with conviction, "and we can't leave here without knowing we did everything we could t' find these people."

"You're right," he said, and the next day he endured another frustrating conversation with Ernest, just hoping to get the needed information—or at the very least, to be gracious enough to Ernest that he would feel more inclined to help Ian. In an effort to move this along more quickly, Ian asked if he could simply know the name of the woman he worked with so perhaps he could send her a message and get the information himself. But Ernest wouldn't have it, and Ian actually wondered if Ernest was dragging this out for the sake of having a friend to chat with. Ian reminded himself *again* that he would do *anything* to get this information, but he had absolutely nothing in common with Ernest, and these ongoing visits were becoming very tedious.

Winter in New York pressed forward mercilessly. The good things got better, and the difficult things only became more difficult. Ian's friendship with Ward became stronger and deeper for a number of reasons, the first being that Ian was able to open up to him fully about all of the grief and disappointment in his heart. He'd once been able to talk to his brothers and his parents like that, except that even with them he'd never felt entirely comfortable in completely expressing his every secret pain. Perhaps he had grown more mature and therefore able to be more honest with his feelings. Perhaps recent events had forced him to face the monster of grief in ways he never had before. Or perhaps Ward just had a way of making it easier for Ian to be open about his feelings. Perhaps and most likely, it was a combination of all three. Ian could certainly be that open with Wren, but her own grief was hard for her to bear, and he was trying to be strong for her. He did his best to let her know that he was one with her in the loss they'd shared, but he could not take away the ache of her mother's heart. And he found that if he was able to share his deepest feelings with this man who had become such a dear friend, he could talk more easily with Wren and not fear hurting her tender feelings.

While Ian's friendship with Ward grew deeper, he also gained a more keen appreciation for Millie and her sweet maternal ways. She had very little in common with his own mother, beyond having a kind and giving heart, but he began to see her as a mother figure in their lives. She filled the role well, watching over all of them like a little mother hen, always concerned and wanting to do anything she could to ease their burdens. She was clearly happiest when she was doing something for someone else, and she had easily reverted back to skills she'd learned before marrying a wealthy man. She was competent in the kitchen and with menial tasks, and was willing to help Wren with anything she needed as she healed from childbirth and adjusted to caring for Gillian.

Shona too was always kind and helpful, although she often wanted to be sure that everything was in order and that she'd done her fair share so that she could go and spend time with Shirley and her family. Since she was technically employed by Ian, and was reliant upon him for her livelihood, they sat down together and discussed her exact responsibilities now that they'd settled into their little household routine. She was always cheerful and eager to do all that was expected of her, and she always put extra effort into helping Wren and making certain everything was in order. Millie gladly filled in during the times that Shona was absent, and they all developed a comfortable routine and got along fairly well, especially for living in such small quarters. Of course, Ian recalled living in the tiny house behind the tailor's shop with Wren and Bethia and their father. Following his marriage to Wren, it had been the only solution in order for Wren's father and sister to feel secure and comfortable, and Ian had been glad to comply. It had been cramped and more than cozy, but they had managed fine and had been happy there. Now, their circumstances were greatly changed. They were sharing living space with people they'd not even known back then. Bethia was gone, and Gillian was at the center of everything. Ian dearly loved this child they were raising as their daughter. He loved helping with her care, and he grew more attached to her every day, as did Wren.

This sweet little girl that Bethia had left behind was the personification of healing and happiness. Her precious little smiles and cooing noises never failed to make the adults around her smile. She had quickly adjusted to Wren as the mother in her life, and in fact was prone to be more fussy if someone else held her when Wren was in the room.

But Ian was glad for the way it made Wren feel needed and loved by this child who seemed to have an extra sense about filling the hole that had been torn open in Wren's heart. Beyond Wren, Gillian was most tolerant about being held by Ian, and he loved to just hold her and try to make her smile. She had wound her way wholly into his heart; he only wished that their own little Joy were in this world to be a sister to Gillian. They would have grown up much like twins, just as Ian and his brother had, being very close in age.

Ian and Wren were both adjusting to the loss of their baby, and through prayer and the support of friends and each other, they had found strength and comfort enough to press forward. Yet the loss still left them feeling raw and wounded, unable to comprehend such a tragedy. Gillian's presence was a great blessing in many respects, and they thanked God daily to have her in their lives and in their care. But she was not their little Joy, and Ian wondered often if they would ever see their own baby again.

In an effort to find some peace and answers in that regard, he began attending some of the religious "factions" in the area. He could call them nothing less or more than factions when he always came away so disappointed, and sometimes even angry. Ward always went with him, and sometimes Millie came along. Wren refused to go, saying that she knew in her heart the true gospel of Jesus Christ and she would attend services when she found *that* religion. She had no desire to sit in a congregation and listen to hypocrisy. Ian knew Wren had been wounded by the minister in Scotland who had piously refused to let Bethia attend church due to her being pregnant with no explanation. Of course, people had not known that Bethia's husband had still been alive, and it was a secret that couldn't be told. Still, the minister's attitude had been harsh and judgmental, and Wren had no desire to encounter any such supposed clergy again.

On the matter of religion—specifically the fact that Ian knew beyond any doubt that the Book of Mormon was true—he felt a continued longing to know that Ward shared his feelings. He knew that Millie was pressing forward in reading the book to Ward, and they occasionally discussed its stories and principles, but neither of them had expressed any personal feelings beyond an intrigue and a desire to keep reading. Ian didn't want to press the matter too hard, and he simply sought out moments when he could casually express his own feelings without putting either Ward or his mother on the spot. While Ian kept praying for Ward's and Millie's hearts to be softened and opened to the truthfulness of these things, he prayed for Wren to be healthy and strong and for her heart to be comforted. Gradually she was becoming stronger and more color was returning to her face, but the ordeal of her influenza, followed by the ordeal of childbirth, had taken a great toll on her health. Losing a baby to death had certainly not helped the matter any. But Wren was a strong woman in both body and spirit; Ian knew that to be true. And he saw her strength coming through. She had a great deal of faith and courage, and she was continually an inspiration to him. He only wished that he had any idea of how to find the people and the place they were seeking so that he could move his family and friends away from this crowded city and find a permanent home for them.

On a particularly cold evening at the tail end of February, Ian returned home from another fruitless visit with Ernest to the news that Millie had slipped and fallen on the ice on her way out to the market and broken her arm. The doctor was presently in the other room with her, setting the fractured bone. He'd reported that it wasn't a serious break—something that could have required a painful surgery or even amputation. For this they were all *extremely* grateful. Nevertheless, Millie would be wearing a splint and a sling on her right arm for many weeks until the bone healed properly, and the pain was not likely to calm down for some days yet. When Millie's arm was properly set, the doctor left them with a tonic that would help ease the pain for her, and he gave them specific instructions on seeing that she didn't move the arm—at all. The other members of the household all sat down to discuss how they could work together to see that Millie was cared for, and how the household needs and chores could be handled efficiently. Wren was doing much better, and was therefore able to do more around the house, and Shona was glad to stay at home more and help out where she was needed. Ward had proven competent at cleaning dishes and drying them if everything was properly put within his reach, and he could also help with other tasks. His eagerness to do so showed his genuine love and concern for his mother and for his friends.

Two days later, however, Ward became unexpectedly ill. The doctor declared it to be an influenza, similar to that which Wren had suffered. Ian, Wren, and Shona worked together to care for both Millie *and* Ward, taking every precaution to not catch Ward's illness. Wren and the baby were kept far away from Ward, and Ian and Shona were always careful to wash their hands after helping Ward with anything so that the contagion could hopefully be contained. Since no one else in the household had become ill when Wren had been afflicted with influenza, they hoped that the methods they'd used then would be equally effective now.

Ward was dreadfully miserable, and Ian found it difficult to watch him suffer. He thought of Wren experiencing the same symptoms while he had been away, and it tugged at his heart. He told her again that he wished he had been there for her, but of course it was silly to wish such a thing when it was long in the past and could not be undone. He also wished that their baby had not left them, but he kept that wish to himself and tried to focus on things he could actually control. He wanted to go threaten Ernest with life and limb if he did not immediately produce the desired information. But he was too busy caring for his family and friends to have time to worry about Ernest.

Through cold, dreary days with Ward lost in fevered delirium and Millie in pain, Ian found it more difficult not to think about the losses they'd experienced. He reminded himself that they had much to be grateful for. They were warm and safe and dry. They had plenty to eat and good companionship. They had knowledge of God's existence and God's love, if only through the pages of the scriptures in their possession. But Ian longed to be able to attend church with people who shared his beliefs. He longed to be out of the city and breathe country air. He missed his home and his family and found himself aching for the highlands of Scotland. When he mentioned his feelings to Wren, she readily agreed that she felt the same and she was overcome with tears that amplified the evidence that she was struggling just as much as he was over the matter.

"Maybe we should go back," he said. "We could take Ward and Millie with us. We could all be happy there, and—"

"I cannot believe what I'm hearing, Ian Brierley," Wren said in that saucy tone that he'd always loved in spite of how it intimidated him. "We are *not* going t' turn around and go back until we can have peace in knowing we did everything we could t' find God's people. He told us t' come here, and He did not allow any room for either of us t' doubt it. We'll not be turning back until He tells us t' do so and we can feel just as strongly about it."

Ian was strengthened by her conviction, and the reminder of what he knew to be true in his heart. "Of course," was all he said before he left the house to go for a walk, even though it was freezing outside. He returned to find that Ward's condition had worsened and Shona had gone for the doctor.

Ian sat by his friend's bedside and prayed with all his heart and soul for this man's life to be spared. "Please, God," he muttered into his hands. "We cannot bear another loss. We cannot. Please spare him, I beg you."

Ian kept his prayers silent when Millie came in and sat on the other side of the bed, weeping quiet tears and staring at her son as if she were looking into the dark abyss of hell itself. The doctor came and reported that he'd done everything he could. There was nothing to do but to continue with their efforts, and hope that Ward was stronger than the fever afflicting him.

Ian didn't go to bed that night. He stayed at Ward's side, doing his best to help keep the fever down. Millie and Shona took turns resting and being with Ward, but Ian couldn't leave. He'd almost convinced himself that his very presence and his constant prayer might actually be able to save Ward. Whether or not it had anything to do with him, he just kept praying and did everything in his power to keep Ward alive.

Millie remained very brave, except for one particularly difficult moment in the darkest part of the night. She broke down in tears and Ian let her cry against his shoulder.

"Whatever will I do without him?" she muttered over and over.

"We shall keep praying that you *never* have to do without him," Ian said gently. "But I can assure you . . . if the worst happens . . . I will always see that you are cared for. You will always have a place in our family."

She looked up at him in surprise, then a glimmer of comfort showed in her eyes. "You are just the dearest man, my boy. God surely was smiling upon us when he sent us to the same tea shop at the very same time."

"He surely was," Ian agreed, and Millie cried a minute or two longer before she gathered her courage, composed herself firmly, and pressed forward in caring for her son.

* * *

Ian didn't realize he'd slept until he started awake and saw that the room had gone from nighttime to daylight. It only took a moment to see that the scene hadn't changed. Millie was sitting on the edge of the bed, pressing a cool rag to Ward's pallid face. Ward looked almost as if he were dead, and the room still smelled of sweat and fever. Ian knelt beside the bed, on the opposite side of where Millie was sitting.

"Any change?" he asked.

"None," she said and sniffled.

"You should get some rest," Ian suggested. "I'll stay with him."

Millie reluctantly left the room, sniffling more as she did so. He could well imagine her believing that she might return to find Ward dead, but her exhaustion was readily evident in her demeanor. Ian felt Ward's face and thought that it didn't feel nearly as warm as it had, but he couldn't be certain of his judgment, given his own weary state of mind.

Ian knelt there in prayer, trying to keep Ward's face cool, until Shona brought him some breakfast. He left the tray untouched and stayed as he was. He ignored his efforts with the cool water and rag and hung his head, begging God to spare Ward, certain his pleas must be sounding tedious to God after he'd uttered the same words seemingly hundreds of times. He knelt there until his knees hurt and his back ached, then he sat on the edge of the bed and once again dipped the rag into the bowl of cool water near his side, wringing it out as he'd done hundreds of times. Before he could get it to Ward's face, he heard him say in a faint voice, "Is that you, Ian?"

"It is!" Ian muttered breathlessly. "Is that *you*, come back from the dead?"

"I feel more dead than alive, so it must be," Ward said, his voice dry and hoarse.

Ian got a glass of water and carefully lifted Ward's head so that he could drink. "I hope this means you're going to make it," Ian said, trying not to sound as emotional as he felt.

Ward's voice came with little more than a whisper. "It's not time for me to leave this world yet, my friend."

"And how do you know that?" Ian asked with mild facetiousness. The fact that Ward was conscious and speaking gave Ian multitudes of confidence in believing that the worst was behind them, and Ward would indeed stay in this world. But he wasn't quite ready to completely let go of the fear that this might not yet be over.

"I just know," Ward said, his face turned toward Ian even though his eyes were closed, although that would hardly make a difference for Ward. Ian saw Ward reaching for him, and he grasped Ward's hand with his own.

"What is it, my friend?" he asked, sensing there was something important Ward wanted to say. Ian hoped that Ward would indeed pull through, and that this was not some kind of deathbed confession.

"It's true, Ian," Ward said, his voice raspy.

"What? I don't understand."

"This . . . book that came into your hands. These people you are seeking who are affiliated with it. It's all true."

Ian's heart quickened and tears stung his eyes, although he didn't have to worry about Ward seeing him cry. This was what he'd prayed for, ached for. It was a miracle! An answer to prayers! He only prayed now that Ward would live long enough to see this through.

"I know it, Ian," Ward continued. "I know it with my whole heart." He tightened his grip on Ian's hand. "Promise me, my friend, that you will keep me by your side through this search. Your search must be my search. I must find what you find. I must have what you have. I must!"

"I promise," Ian said firmly. "It's what I've wanted all along . . . ever since we met. I believe I knew then that we would follow this path together, but it was not for me to dictate such things. You had to discover the truth for yourself." Ian thought as he said it that Ward's knowledge of the truth had strengthened his own conviction and his own knowledge. His faith had been substantiated through another source; his hope had been fortified.

Millie had apparently heard whisperings from the other room that indicated her son was conscious, and she entered the room in a flurry of tears and excitement, overcome with the evidence that Ward was recovering. Ian wanted to point out that the fact that Ward was conscious didn't necessarily mean he was completely out of the woods, but he didn't want to dampen the mood. He figured it was a good thing he'd kept his mouth shut, when hours later Ward was sitting up in bed, heartily taking in the broth his mother fed him with her good arm. Within a few days he was feeding himself, and color was coming back into his face. Ian's gratitude at having his prayers answered was inexpressible, but coupled with it was an impending sensation of fear. He felt grateful that Ward would live and that Millie would heal and be all right. He felt grateful that they had Gillian and that Wren was recovering as well. But he felt as if something in his spirit had been traumatized by the series of recent events in his life, and the trauma had left him wondering what might happen next—who they might lose, how much they would suffer. It was as if some voice inside of him that he didn't like in spite of its deep familiarity was taunting him to believe that pursuing this course in his life would only bring pain and heartache to his loved ones. And then Millie came down with symptoms of the influenza, and Ian was terrified that Wren would get it again—or little Gillian. He wondered if they would survive if they did. Or what if *he* became ill? Who would take care of his loved ones? He wasn't worried about their financial needs, but Ward was in no position to do most of the things a man needed to do for his family.

Ian was fighting hourly with his inner voices of fear when Shona brought word home with her from Shirley's that one of Maxine and Ernest's children had taken ill. Three days later the child died. Ian felt horrified, as did the others. But he didn't dare speak aloud the full extent of the fears inside of him and the way that this news had made them explode. They didn't go to Ernest's home to offer their condolences, since both households were dealing with the effects of illness and they didn't want to risk any contagion. They did, however, order a fine fruit basket to be delivered to the family, with a sincere note of sympathy on behalf of their loss. Ian felt almost guilty for his impatience with Ernest in the past, and he felt absolutely guilty for thinking that a basket of fruit could begin to ease their grief. He knew it was not intended to; it was simply a gesture of support and concern. But it still felt like far too meager a gesture, and he stewed and fretted over it.

Having lost a child of their own, Ian and Wren both felt as if the news of someone else losing a child brought their own grief closer to the surface. Wren was more prone to tears than she had been in weeks, and Ian's fears mingled with a new level of sorrow until he felt as if he were some kind of shadow of himself, barely existing.

Millie recovered from her illness, and no one else in the household became ill. Ian was truly grateful for that, and he recounted to God every day all that he had to be thankful for. He also prayed that his fears and worries could be soothed and comforted, and that he could find the path that God would have him take. But the battle inside of him only seemed to grow more intense.

* * *

It was a joy to receive a package from Scotland. Everyone gathered around the kitchen table while Ian opened the large box. Inside there was a tin of shortbread, the very kind made in the kitchens of Brierley and served each day at tea. There was a lovely little dress and bonnet for Gillian that was still a bit big but would fit perfectly in a few months' time. There were three beautiful shawls, one each for Wren, Shona, and Millie. And some fine gloves for both Ian and Ward. There were also a couple of novels that Ian's parents had enjoyed, which they were now passing along. And best of all, there was a very thick letter. Wren suggested that Ian read the letter privately, and then perhaps there would be parts that he would want to share with the others later. Ian appreciated the suggestion and found a quiet place to sit down with the letter and savor every word. The letter expressed deep sympathy for their losses, and equivalent joy in knowing they had made such good friends. While most of the letter was written by Ian's mother, there were also personal notes from Ian's father and brother. Ian was glad to hear that his father's health had not declined, even though it had not shown any marked improvement. He was glad to hear details of how his brothers' children were growing, and of their antics, and he was glad to hear of everyday details about life at Brierley. While he was thoroughly engaged in the letter, he was surprised to read a strong plea for Ian to let go of this idea of settling permanently in America and to come home where he was loved and needed. It took Ian so off guard that his initial response was anger. How could these people he loved so dearly not understand his need to do what he was doing? But worse, how could they taunt him with such a plea when he couldn't deny that he was already feeling tempted to do just that? But he couldn't. He just couldn't. He thought of the many times Wren had reminded him that they could not return to Scotland without knowing they had done everything they could to do what they both knew God had asked them to do. And then he thought of Ward's conviction in *his* beliefs, and his plea that they share this quest. He could never let Ward down, nor could he disappoint his sweet wife. If it had been up to him alone, he likely would have buckled under the strain of all that had happened, and he would have given up and headed for home. Thankfully, God had given him a wife *and* a dear friend with convictions stronger than his own who kept him on the right path. If only he knew exactly where that path would lead!

Later Ian *did* read the entire letter aloud to the others, while Gillian sat contentedly on Wren's lap, chewing on a little baby toy that they'd purchased in town. After reading the letter, Ian spoke frankly about his temptation to go back to Scotland. He was glad for the way that Ward and Wren both immediately corrected his thinking and reminded him of his reasons for coming to America. Ian was surprised to hear Millie's conviction about being a part of their quest to find the Mormons. She said nothing specifically about her own beliefs on the matter, and Ward had not told him anything to indicate how Millie felt about what she'd read. But it seemed that knowing Ward's feelings about it were good enough for her, and she would venture into any unknown territory so long as she could be with her son. While Shona didn't share their religious convictions, she expressed her appreciation for being in America and her absolute stand on never going back to Scotland.

"I guess that's that, then," Ian said, closing the letter. "I only wish we knew *where* to find these people. With winter weather and all this illness, we couldn't have traveled before now anyway, but spring is coming, and I would very much like to know how to find these people."

"What exactly is the problem?" Millie asked with a zeal that belied the fact that she was barely up and around following a severe illness.

Ian explained the situation with Ernest, which was the only possible connection he had to knowing *anything* about where the Mormons were. Until now he'd said nothing to anyone except Wren—who had been present when the initial conversation had taken place—about Ernest's possible connection to solving this problem, and Ian's reasons for repeated visits to Ernest's home with the hope of getting the information he needed.

"Perhaps we should just pay him a visit and give him a little encouragement," Millie said as if she might go over there and shake the information out of him if needed.

"They've recently lost a child," Ian said. "Surely we can't be so audacious, although I simply don't know what else to do. My frustration is mounting, I confess."

"I don't think ye need t' involve Ernest at all," Shona piped in.

"What do you mean?" Ian asked, his heart quickening.

"Ronald works at the same factory. If this woman talks about her brother half as much as Ernest says she does, then I'd wager a pretty penny that he knows who the woman is and *he* could get the information. Ronald's not the kind of man to withhold information just t' get someone t' come over and listen t' him ramble on and on, now is he."

"No, he's certainly not," Wren said.

"I'll talk t' Ronald t'morrow, then," Shona said. Then she winked. "And don't ye worry. I'll be discreet about it, and Ernest will never be the wiser."

"You could very well be an answer to our prayers, Shona," Ian said. "Not for the first time, I might add."

"And ye certainly have been t' mine," she said. "I'm glad t' help however I can."

"Good then," Wren said. "With any luck we'll get this problem solved and know where it is we might be going when spring comes."

"With any luck," Ian echoed, and Gillian let out a spontaneous happy noise, as if to agree.

Chapter Eight
Testing Faith

Ian wished that he'd solicited Shona's help many weeks earlier when she reported back three days later with success. There was indeed a woman who worked in the factory whose brother had become a Mormon when he'd met missionaries right here in New York City some years earlier. He'd taken his family to join a Mormon community in Ohio, and had moved to Missouri, then to Illinois, just as Ernest had said. But Ronald's report to Shona had been much more positive. Apparently this woman didn't agree with her brother's beliefs enough to want to follow him into the wilderness, but she respected them, and she had reported to Ronald that her brother was very happy, in spite of many challenges he had faced.

Ian listened to Shona's report with delight, but for all of her talking she avoided the one detail he needed to know. *The name of the city,* he kept thinking. *Tell me the name of the city!* And then she said, "She told Ronald that just the other day she got a letter from her brother, and it came from a place called Nauvoo in Illinois. There ye have it. Nauvoo, Illinois."

Ian laughed and surprised himself as much as Shona when he hugged her tightly and lifted her feet off the ground, much as he would have if she were his sister. She laughed too and said after he'd set her down, "Glad I could help."

That evening Ian discussed with his wife and friends what step they should take next; however, Shona excused herself, saying she had some things she needed to attend to. They heard her fussing in the kitchen some, then she went into her room and closed the door.

"I wonder if she's not feeling well," Wren said.

"Or perhaps she's not so keen on the possibility of leaving here," Millie suggested. "We should just give her some time."

Ian felt concerned but could only focus now on what exactly to do with their newfound information.

"Given that spring is not yet here, and the weather is still so unpredictable," Ward said, "I wouldn't think it prudent to just up and head to Illinois. Perhaps we should write to someone there and gather more information."

"That's an excellent idea," Wren said. "But who exactly would read such a letter when we don't actually know a person there? We could find out the name of this woman's brother, I suppose, but—"

"I know!" Millie said and hurried into her room. She came back a moment later and handed the Book of Mormon to Ian. "There in the front," she said with an enthusiasm that made Ian believe her convictions over the matter were more than she'd verbalized. Ian opened the book to the first page, and Millie pointed to a particular place. "It says here that Joseph Smith, Junior, is the author and proprietor. Although it's evident he's more the translator than the author. I'm certain he couldn't have written it himself, whoever he might be."

"You're certain?" Ian questioned.

"Absolutely!" she countered, seeming appalled that he would wonder. "Aren't you?"

"I am," Ian said, but Millie quickly went back to her point, oblivious to what she'd just admitted, and what it meant to Ian. He saw Wren wink at him, however, and knew that she understood his quiet thrill at the evidence that Millie *did* have her own convictions about the book.

"This Joseph Smith is obviously a very important man in regard to this religion. If we write to him in this city of Nauvoo, surely we'll get some kind of response, and then we might know more what to do and how to get to this place."

"I think that's an excellent idea," Ian said and immediately got out paper and pen. They all gathered round to help dictate the letter, and Ian did a great deal of changing and crossing out. Once they were all pleased and in agreement with the letter's contents, he copied it onto a clean piece of paper, included some money with which he hoped to purchase some copies of the Book of Mormon, and sealed it up tight. On the front he simply wrote: *Mr. Joseph Smith, Junior, Nauvoo, Illinois.* They all sighed at the sight of the finished letter waiting to be mailed the next day. Ian declared that he would go out early in the morning to get it to the post office, and he would buy a map of Illinois while he was out to see exactly where Nauvoo was located.

"You'd best buy a map of everything between here and there," Ward suggested. "We're going to need it."

* * *

Ian kissed his wife and daughter and left them both looking beautiful and sleepy, comfortably close together in the bed. He left the apartment early, dismayed when it started to rain only a minute into his trek toward where he knew that he could post the letter. With the rain came a heavy mist that made it difficult to see very far ahead. It reminded him very much of London, but since his memories of London were mostly unpleasant, he pushed that thought away. Just across the street from the post office, he looked both ways before stepping out onto the road, but he was not halfway across the street when a coach and four horses thundered out of the mist. He barely saw it coming before he was thrown a good distance, landing on his back in the mud. He heard the air burst out of his lungs at the impact, and turned to see the precious letter he'd written lying just out of reach, splattered with mud.

"Are you all right, good man?" he heard a deep voice say.

"My . . . letter," Ian muttered, reaching for it.

"Here's your letter, sir," another male voice said, less deep, and Ian felt it being pressed into his hand just before everything went black.

* * *

Wren began to feel nervous when Ian had been gone an hour.

"He said he'd be right back," she said to Millie and Shona while they prepared breakfast. "It doesn't take so very long t' walk t' the post office and back."

An hour after that she was pacing frantically, and no one had anything to say that would assuage her fears. After another half hour of wondering, she had to consider the possibility that something had happened, and the most logical way to get any information seemed to be to go to the police station. She knew where it was. She'd seen it on many outings. Shona agreed to go with her, and of course they would need to take the baby. They hired a cab and were soon on their way, while Wren felt so afraid she could hardly breathe. What would she do here in a strange land without Ian to care for her and Gillian? Not to mention the others who were in their care. Beyond that, what would she do without Ian under *any* circumstances? The thought was unbearable! He was everything to her! As difficult as it had been to lose a child, the very idea of losing Ian felt worse. So much worse! Shona kept assuring her that there was probably just some silly little problem, that surely he was fine, that everything would be all right. But Wren had difficulty believing her.

The cab left them at the door of the police station. The driver took his fee and drove away. Wren and Shona went inside, Wren holding tightly to the baby as if doing so might give her strength in facing whatever information they received. She wondered what she would do if they had no information to give her. Would it be worse to hear that Ian had been robbed and beaten, or to hear nothing at all and be left to wonder? Unable to know the answer to that question, Wren bravely approached an officer behind a high desk and stated the nature of the problem.

"I think something's happened t' my husband, sir. He's not come home when he should have. Could ye help me, please?"

The officer looked bored by the request, but said he'd check and see if anyone knew anything. Wren fidgeted nervously with the ribbons on Gillian's bonnet while she waited for the officer to go into the other room and inquire. He came back after what seemed an eternal stretch of minutes to announce, "A man fitting that description was in an accident not far from where you say you live, ma'am."

"What kind of accident?" Wren demanded, praying her worst fears had not come to pass.

"Hit by a carriage, they say. He's in the hospital, but since he was unconscious when he was taken there, we couldn't ask him his name and where he came from."

"In the hospital?" Wren said, more in relief than alarm. She had no idea of the extent of his injuries, but she was utterly relieved that she'd not been told her husband had been taken to the morgue and they were waiting for someone to identify the body.

"Yes, ma'am," the officer said, and Wren felt Shona take hold of her arm. Whether it was out of concern for Wren or due to her own shock was difficult to tell. Either way, Wren was glad to have Shona at her side, and for the reminder that she was not alone. "I can have an officer take you there, if you like."

"Oh, that would be much appreciated, sir," Wren said.

It took time for the arrangements to be made for the officer to escort them, and what seemed a ridiculous amount of time for them to get to the hospital. It took more time for someone to figure out exactly which patient "these ladies" were there to see, and more time for them to be guided to the proper room. Wren didn't like this place at all, and while she was grateful that Ian had been brought to a place that could give him the proper medical attention, she wanted very much for him to be able to come home where she could take care of him herself. She pushed away that thought as she was led down a crowded hallway, hoping that she was not being presumptuous in believing that he would be well enough to come home at all. What if her thinking had been premature? What if his injuries were so severe that he *would* die, even though he wasn't already dead? She couldn't think of that! *Refused* to think of that!

Wren nearly fainted when she entered a room with many beds in it to see her husband lying in one of them, not looking well at all. But he was conscious! And he was alive! He gasped with relief when he saw her, and Wren practically shoved the baby into Shona's arms so that she could bend over the bed and hold Ian close to her. He groaned, and she realized that her embrace had caused him pain.

"Ye're hurting!" she declared, looking him up and down as if that alone would assess the damages. "Where?"

"Everywhere!" he said and groaned again. "A doctor looked me over when I first came in," Ian said. "He didn't believe anything was broken, but I'm bruised pretty badly. He said that he wanted to talk with me again before I go home, but I have no idea where he is, and . . . oh!" He sighed and looked at Wren as if she'd sprouted angelic wings. "I'm so glad you found me. I had no idea how I would *get* home in this condition. I was going to ask how I could send word to you, but everyone here is so dreadfully busy, and . . . I'm so glad you found me."

Wren told him her version of how she'd done so, and he told her his version of what had happened. Shona hovered close by and listened to both sides of the story, declaring boldly that it was a miracle he'd not been hurt much worse—or killed. They all agreed, and Wren couldn't hold back tears thinking how grateful she was on both accounts.

It was another hour before the doctor came to speak with Ian again. Wren had to find a place to discreetly nurse the baby while they waited, then Gillian slept peacefully in Wren's arms while they waited. The doctor was pleased that Ian had someone to care for him, and cautioned them that given the nasty bump on Ian's head, it was important that he stay down and do nothing for at least a few days. He also told them that with the excessive bruising all over his body, he was going to be very sore for many days, possibly weeks, until he healed.

It was dark before they arrived at home. Ward and Millie were frantic with worry, even though Wren had sent a message to them earlier to let them know that she'd found Ian and that he was injured but would be all right. Shona carried the baby into the house, while Wren helped keep Ian steady as they ascended the stairs.

"Reminds me of when ye used t' get blind drunk and show up at my house," Wren said with just a trace of humor.

"What a pleasant memory," Ian replied with sarcasm.

"How could it be that," she added with exaggerated irony, "when ye could never remember a thing?"

"Oh, very funny," Ian said with no humor. "Besides, there were no stairs at your house."

"No, but it wasn't always easy keeping ye steady."

Wren was glad to know that his drinking days were long in the past, but she felt horrible to realize how much pain he was in, and how hard he was trying *not* to lean on her.

Once Ian was settled into his bed, Millie insisted that they all needed to eat some supper, which Ward had helped her prepare. Only then did Wren realize that she hadn't eaten a thing all day, and neither had Shona. Ian had been offered a little something at the hospital before Wren had arrived, but he'd had no appetite and had refused it. The stew Millie and Ward had made, along with bread that Shona had made the day before, was especially satisfying when they were so hungry. And now that Wren had Ian beneath the same roof and she knew he was going to be all right, she actually felt like eating. She thanked God that it hadn't been any worse, and prayed that he would heal well and quickly.

The following day Ian was in terrible pain from head to toe. Wren offered to rub some balm on his bruised back, where he said he'd gotten the worst of it. She was astonished when he removed his shirt to see how horribly black and blue the majority of his back had become. He could hardly bear for her to touch him enough to apply the balm, and then he declared that it didn't seem to make any difference; therefore, he refused it when she offered it again later in the day.

Ward was astounded that the doctor at the hospital had not given Ian something he could take to ease the pain. At his suggestion, their usual doctor was called in to offer *his* opinion on Ian's injuries. He concurred with what the other doctor had said, insisting that Ian stay down and take it easy.

"As if I could move even if I wanted to," Ian declared with disdain.

The doctor *did* give him something he could take to ease the pain, and it would also help him sleep. Given that Ian had hardly slept a wink since he'd come home from the hospital the previous day, he was glad for the tonic and made no protest about taking it. Ian slept through the night and into the next day, waking only long enough to have a little to eat and to take more tonic. When he came around in the afternoon, he wanted to stay awake and be with his family for a while, even though he was still in more pain than he'd ever endured before in his life. In the middle of observing little Gillian while she cooed and kicked on the bed beside him, Ian let out a frantic gasp.

"What is it?" Wren asked. "Are ye hurting badly? Is something—"

"The letter!" he said. "I put it in the inside pocket of my coat. It didn't get mailed! We must mail the letter right away and—"

"I already found it when I washed the mud from the coat," she said. "Millie has fixed it good as new, and Shona will mail it when she goes out for groceries."

Ian relaxed again and said, "Tell her to be careful when she's crossing the street."

* * *

Winter finally started to give way to spring while Ian healed slowly, a process that sorely tested his patience. He was entirely unaccustomed to needing to rely on anyone for anything, and the very fact that this accident occurred at all only fed the fears inside of him that he'd been trying so hard to suppress. *What horrible thing might happen next?* he kept asking himself. More illness? Accidents? Death? He couldn't bear the thought! Given the present situation, he far preferred being the victim rather than having anyone else in his household suffer any such mishaps, but he would have far preferred that it hadn't happened at all. He'd rethought the moment a thousand times. If only he'd waited a moment longer, or been a moment quicker about getting across the street. If only he'd eaten breakfast before he'd gone out to mail the letter, or perhaps he should have left the house earlier. *Or* maybe he shouldn't have been trying to mail that letter at all. Perhaps all of these things going wrong were some kind of sign from God that in spite of what they'd believed, this was *not* the right course to take.

Such thoughts ran around in circles in Ian's mind continually, so he was grateful for the welcome distraction when Wren would sit and read to him, and he was grateful for Ward's company, even though he teased him about *not* being able to read to him. Instead Ian read to Ward—as long as it was from the Book of Mormon, Ward insisted. He didn't want to hear anything else right now.

"I'm the invalid here," Ian teased. "Don't I get to choose the text we read from?"

"Do you have a better suggestion?"

"No," Ian had to admit. In spite of his nagging doubts, it *was* his very most favorite book in all the world. "Where would you like me to start?" Ian asked.

"Anywhere," Ward said. "It doesn't matter. It's all good. Just let the book fall open and see where we end up."

Ian did just that and began to read. For the first twenty or thirty minutes, Ian felt distracted by his thoughts of fear and self-pity. But then he gradually began to feel an inner softening. It wasn't the text they were reading that specifically made a difference, he concluded. It was almost as if the book itself held some kind of spiritual power that reminded Ian of what he knew in his heart.

Through the remaining days of his healing, Ian often wished that he were back in Scotland in the comfort and beauty of his family home. He often wondered what it was like in Nauvoo, Illinois. And he wondered if they would all be able to arrive there safe and healthy and alive. When he was able to be up and around more, he found things to distract him from his worrisome thoughts, but they still plagued him. He prayed every day to be able to be freed from such fears, but his inner battle felt constant, and he didn't know how to control it. And perhaps what was even worse, he simply didn't understand it.

* * *

Ian was forced out of sleep by the sound of Gillian crying. That in itself wasn't terribly unusual. But her cries were generally a mild impatience in wanting to be changed and fed, and she was always quickly appeased. This time it was different. It only took Ian a minute to realize that the crying itself had changed. It was the cry of pain!

Ian turned over abruptly to see Wren pacing the floor with the baby. The low-burning lamp left no doubt about the stark worry on Wren's face.

"I don't know what's wrong," she said. "She ate, and her diaper is dry, but . . . something's wrong, Ian; something's terribly wrong." Tears came with the verbalization of her worry, and all of it reached into the center of Ian's chest, grabbed his heart, and twisted it into a painful contortion. He wanted to scream. More specifically, he wanted to scream at God and demand to know why He would allow more suffering and cause for fear into this family. Only Wren's need for him to be a strength for her kept him calm. He would not behave like a child and add to her burdens.

"I'll go for the doctor," he said, needing a task with which to occupy himself as much as he knew they needed a doctor's help. He hurried to get dressed, then paused before putting on his coat to put a hand to Wren's face in an attempt to offer some form of silent reassurance. It was the best he could do when he couldn't find the words in himself to tell her that everything would be all right. How could he, when he felt utterly terrified that it would *not* be all right? He then put a hand to Gillian's head with the same intention. But feeling the heat of her skin sent a fresh shock through his nerves. "She's burning with fever," he said in a raspy whisper.

Wren just nodded, and fresh tears filled her eyes, as if she'd not wanted to tell him, as if she'd wanted to spare him the depth of fear that *she* was experiencing.

"I'll hurry," he said and put on his coat. Going down the stairs and out into the cold, he felt so sick at heart he feared he might lose the contents of his stomach. Wren was the faithful one, the strong one. If *she* was that afraid, where would they find the strength to get through this?

Ian was praying that it wouldn't take too much trouble to awaken the doctor and get him to hurry, but the man's very awake wife answered the door to report that he'd left a short while ago to deliver a baby. She had Ian write a message for the doctor, which she would have their son deliver to him so that he would know to come straight to the Brierley home the moment he was done. She assured him it was their usual practice, that her son was very reliable, and that her husband would come just as soon as humanly possible. Her kindness and compassion were very much appreciated, but did nothing to alleviate Ian's fears, and he hated returning home to hear Gillian still crying as if she were in agony, only to report that he had no idea how long it would be until the doctor could arrive.

"I considered looking for another doctor," Ian told Wren who had stopped pacing the parlor to hear his report. "But it's the middle of the night, and I don't know who we can trust. Surely we can do no better than *this* doctor."

"I agree," Wren said and eased Gillian into his arms the moment he had his coat off. "Please hold her," she said tearfully. "I just need a few minutes." She rushed into the tiny bathing room, and he could easily imagine her sobbing her heart out more than seeing to any personal needs. He was struck anew by the incredible courage of his wife. He knew she had no qualms about pouring her heart out to him, and she was not ashamed of letting him see her tears, but he also knew she was trying to be as strong for him as he was for her. How could he not be inspired by such courage? He loved her so dearly! And for her he could be strong—more so than for himself. He would devote himself entirely to helping her get through this—whatever *this* turned out to be. He couldn't think about the possible reasons for Gillian's suffering, or the possible outcomes. For now he could only hold his little daughter and try to comfort her the best he could, and he could remain by his wife's side to share this difficulty with her and do his best not to let her down.

Wren was gone longer than a few minutes. Ian paced the floor with Gillian and patted her little back. He whispered soothing words to her, even though he had no reason to believe that doing so had any positive effect whatsoever. Perhaps doing so soothed his own nerves. He felt sure the baby's crying was keeping Shona, Millie, and Ward awake—if not the neighbors above and below them. But there was little to be done about it. He wasn't surprised to see Millie appear and ask if he would like her to take a turn. It was evident she'd already been up and had already spoken to Wren. He assured her that he was managing and she should try to rest. A few minutes after Millie reluctantly went back to bed, Shona appeared and made the same offer. He graciously refused, but she set about making a pot of tea.

Wren finally returned to the room, calm and composed. But Ian knew she'd been crying long and hard. He couldn't begrudge her doing so, and he couldn't blame her for wanting to do it in privacy.

"I can take her now," Wren said in an unaffected tone that seemed completely out of place, given how difficult the screaming baby made it to hear any conversation between them.

"Not yet," he said. "I'm managing. Have a cup of tea and sit down. You'll have your turn again soon enough."

He could see her wanting to protest, but she thought about it, nodded, and poured herself a cup of tea. She sat nearby and closed her eyes, inhaling the steam off of the tea as if it could block out the bold indications of the pain their baby was in, and the fear associated with wondering what could be causing her misery. Ian prayed while he paced and tried to comfort the baby. He prayed that his own fears would be calmed, that his sweet wife could be comforted, that Gillian would live through this ordeal—whatever it might be. And he prayed that they could all be strengthened to face whatever had to be faced. Ian knew well enough the principle of accepting God's will in all things. But he wasn't ready to accept that it could be God's will to take this child from them. He reprimanded himself for jumping to the conclusion that this pain and fever was an indication that her life was in jeopardy. But it was difficult not to take that leap when he knew well enough that such a fever was most often an indication of some dreadful, unknown infection that could either burn out of control or gradually dissipate. Illness felt like a game of chance, and he couldn't help pondering the odds. He'd certainly been exposed to illness during his youth, but for the most part he and his family had remained relatively healthy. He'd been more aware of it in people they knew; and once a bout of influenza had gone through the household, mostly among the servants. Ian recalled a death taking place, and it had been very upsetting to his parents. But Ian had not personally known the maid whose life had been lost, and he'd been too young to fully understand the impact. But now he had seen Ward, and Millie, and his own wife suffer the effect of influenza. He'd seen how hard it had been on them, and he'd feared losing them. He didn't know *what* was wrong with Gillian, but her fever and pain were frightening. He kept praying the doctor would hurry and get there, but he knew that doctors were not miracle workers. He might be able to tell them what was wrong, but he had no magic cure for *any* ailment. Ian suspected that the next several days would simply be filled with torturous waiting and wondering and trying to soothe an infant that could not be reasoned with. Poor little Gillian didn't understand the source of her pain, and therefore could only cry helplessly with the hope that the people who loved her would be able to make it go away. Ian was nearly moved to tears to think of the child's suffering, and to feel so helpless in being able to do anything about it.

Wren finished her tea, went again into the bathing room for a few minutes, then insisted on taking a turn with Gillian. Ian watched her for a few minutes, deeply impressed with her warm maternal instincts. For all that he'd tried to comfort and soothe the baby, Wren had a natural tendency with her that was simply beautiful to see. It was as if mother and baby nearly molded together. The fact that Gillian was not Wren's physical child made no difference. Gillian didn't necessarily cry any less in Wren's arms, but she did seem more comfortable there—or perhaps more comforted.

Ian poured himself a cup of tea in an effort to follow his own advice—and Wren's example—and remain calm. He realized the room was getting subtly lighter with the approach of morning, and he wondered when the doctor would arrive. He imagined the doctor being struck by a passing carriage while trying to cross the street, and he wondered if he *would* ever arrive. Ian prayed for the doctor's safety and well-being, and he prayed for the woman whose baby he was delivering. Memories of the doctor delivering their own baby, and then trying to save the baby's life, brought on a mixture of harsh emotions. He felt a deep gratitude to have a skilled and compassionate man available to see to their medical needs, but he had to admit that this man's visits to their home had always been associated with difficulties. Illness and death were the man's business. The only exception to that would be delivering a baby that was healthy; a baby that would live. And Ian prayed that would be the case with the baby coming into the world with the doctor's assistance this night.

Ian extinguished the lamp that was no longer needed, then insisted that he take a turn holding the baby. Wren had tried to feed her more than once but Gillian wasn't interested in doing anything but crying helplessly. While Ian walked with the baby, Wren went into the bathing room to try and express some of the milk that was now causing *her* pain. She returned to report that she hadn't had much luck, and she hoped that Gillian would soon become hungry enough that her need for milk would override her pain.

A short while later the doctor finally arrived. He looked tired, but he brought with him an attitude of assurance and a calm demeanor. He set down his bag, removed his coat, and washed his hands. Then without even touching Gillian he said, "She has an ear infection."

"How do you know *that?*" Ian asked, trying not to sound disrespectful.

"See the way she's pulling at her left ear with her little hand," the doctor said.

Ian and Wren both watched for a minute to be assured that he was right. "So she is," Ian said.

"As with most things," the doctor said, "it's impossible to know what causes these problems, but they happen sometimes with babies. Has she had a cold?"

"A little bit of a sniffle," Wren said. "Nothing that caused us any concern."

"Sometimes the congestion in the head can bring this on." He touched the baby's face to check for fever, then opened his bag and dug into it in search of something. He brought out a bottle filled with some liquid, and poured some of it into a much smaller bottle. He then did the same with a different medicine. One bottle was made of dark brown glass, and the other dark blue. The doctor said it was important to remember which medicine was in which bottle. He then gave them two tiny glass droppers that could be used to administer the medicine. He demonstrated putting drops into Gillian's infected ear, and he put them in the other ear "just in case it too was troubling her." He then put some of the other medicine into her mouth. "Only a tiny drop," he cautioned. "She's very small and shouldn't need much." Gillian protested at the obvious horrible taste, but she did swallow it. "That ought to do it," the doctor said and explained that it should help ease the pain enough for her to eat and to rest. "I would try to feed her right after you give it to her, and then she should hopefully sleep." He told them how often to administer both medicines, and then reported that as with any infection, it was impossible to know how bad it might get, or if it could be stopped. Ian knew it was a diplomatic way of saying that any infection was capable of taking a life, and it was beyond the ability of any medical professional to change that fact. The doctor told them they simply needed to treat the symptoms, and hope that it all cleared up. He assured them that he'd seen many babies with such symptoms that had pulled through just fine. Ian felt sure he deliberately didn't mention the ones he'd seen *not* pull through.

Ian settled with the doctor and gave him a little extra for his efforts in coming at such an early-morning hour. While the doctor was putting on his coat, Ian asked about the baby he'd delivered.

"Mother and baby are doing well," the doctor reported.

"Oh, we're glad t' hear it," Wren said with enthusiasm, and Ian felt proud of her for being able to be so charitable when he knew that she had to be thinking of her own loss in that regard.

As soon as the doctor left, Wren tried again to feed the baby. At first she refused it and kept fussing, but then she took the milk vigorously, as if she were as starving as Wren was desperate to feed her. By the time Gillian had taken all the milk that Wren had to give her, she had drifted to sleep. Ian put his arm around Wren, who was holding the baby, and they heaved a mutual sigh of deep relief at taking in the peace and quiet.

Millie and Shona both appeared at almost the same moment, as if the silence had caused them fear. Ian hated the implication of that fear, but he hurried to say, "The doctor gave her something for the pain and to help her sleep. She just finished nursing." He told them everything the doctor had said, then added, "I think we'll try to get some rest, as you should."

"We'll take care of everything," Millie said. "The two of you just work together to take care of that baby, and we'll take care of everything."

"Everything," Shona echoed.

Ian and Wren went back to bed, with Gillian sleeping between them.

For three days Gillian ate and slept only when aided by the medicine. During the times when it was wearing off but too soon to give her another dose, the evidence of her ongoing misery was still evident. She continued to have a fever, though not terribly high, and the pain was obviously still there—which meant that the problem still existed. But they all worked together to keep their little household running and care for the baby, and they all prayed that Gillian would come through this and be all right.

On the third day, a little bit of a rash began to appear on her skin, and her little hands kept trying to grasp at the affected areas, the same way she would grasp at her ailing ear. They summoned the doctor, and in his agitated state of mind, Ian felt sure that this was an indication that Gillian had contracted some terrible disease that would put the household under quarantine—and that they might *all* die. Waiting for the doctor's verdict, Ian could hardly breathe. He was surprised to hear the doctor say, "The rash is not from the illness; it's from the medicine. I've seen it before. Some patients simply have a bad reaction to the medicine; their body simply cannot tolerate it. I'm afraid you'll have to stop using it."

"But without it she won't sleep," Wren said as if the doctor didn't already know that. "Without it she'll be in pain."

"I'm sorry, Mrs. Brierley," the doctor said gently. "I wish that I had some other option. *With* the medicine, she could develop other complications that I'm certain you don't want to have happen. Along with a rash, I've seen swelling and sometimes difficulty breathing. If her body is rejecting the medicine, it's more dangerous to give it to her than it is for her to experience the pain. Her fever's not ever gotten terribly high; hopefully it will stay that way and this will run its course quickly."

The doctor wished them good day and hurried away to meet with other patients. Ian and Wren heartily agreed that they were grateful to know their daughter didn't have some life-threatening disease, but the thought of her being unable to sleep felt torturous—to Gillian in her suffering, and to her parents in helplessly having to try to comfort and care for her.

"Well," Ian said, resigned but determined to take this on with courage, "it doesn't look like any of us will get much sleep for a while." The next thought that came to his head was an image of Gillian making no sound due to sudden death. He slammed the door of his mind on such a horrible thought and thanked God for Gillian's ability to cry, even if it meant that they would be getting very little sleep.

Chapter Nine
The Letter

For days Gillian's fussing continued. She slept only in spurts, when exhaustion would become stronger than the pain. But then the pain seemed to assert itself through her rest and force her back into consciousness and more crying. She slept better with her head upright, as opposed to lying down. And when she was awake, she would only whimper and fuss if she were being held on one of her parents' laps, or against their shoulder. Her pain was obviously worse with her head down; therefore, Ian and Wren simply took turns holding her, whether she was awake or asleep. The one not holding the baby tried to get some rest or attend to necessities, while the one holding the baby could only fruitlessly attempt to ease pain that could not be eased.

To say that the strain was beginning to take its toll would be a gross understatement. Ian became as worried for Wren as he was for Gillian. And he was worried about himself as well. He feared that he would completely fall apart and make the drama worse by either crying like a baby or screaming like a madman—or both. He insisted that Shona take Wren out of the house here and there, if only for a brief walk, and he did the same, often taking Ward with him so that he had someone with whom he could vent his frustrations and concerns as he walked. But neither of them could stay away very long, and it was becoming increasingly difficult to deal with Gillian's suffering and stay calm.

To make matters worse, the sky seemed to be stuck in a dark heaviness that neither snowed nor rained nor let the sun through. It felt as if winter was stuck against some invisible barrier, unable to move on, unable to allow spring over the threshold. Ian had lost track of the days that they had been in this terrible state, and he found himself wishing one afternoon that Gillian *would* die—if only to ease *her* suffering. He had watched her cry *so* much, had witnessed her pain hour after hour, day after day, helpless to do anything about it. When the part of his mind that was terrified to lose his daughter fully perceived the thought that had been conceived by another part of his mind, he bolted out of his chair and turned to look at Wren, who was futilely trying to comfort the baby. He felt as if he'd betrayed them both in his heart by even entertaining such a wish for a moment. He was glad he'd not verbalized such a horrible thought, but he wished he'd never even allowed it into his mind. Now that it was there, he didn't know how to get rid of it. Feeling as if he might erupt in some inappropriate way, he hurried to say, "I need to get out for a while."

"Of course," Wren said as if she fully understood, as if she were not standing there impossibly trying to do the impossible and take away the baby's pain.

Ian put on his coat while he was on his way down the stairs. He stepped outside to be assaulted by a harsh breeze that made it clear winter had not yet relented. He flipped up the collar on his coat to cover his neck and deflect some of the cold away from his ears. He stuffed his hands into his pockets, glad to find gloves there, which he put on. He walked with a quickened pace that kept quickening, as if walking fast and far could shake off the doom that seemed to be hovering at his shoulders, threatening to devour him. Was God trying to prepare him to lose Gillian? Or were his own fears distorting the strain of the situation into something that it would never be, except in his own warped and damaged imagination?

Ian kept walking while the questions battled back and forth, and his spirit vacillated with his thoughts, certain one moment that he was pointlessly allowing worry to create problems that did not even exist and mostly likely wouldn't, and certain the next that he would lose yet another child and that he and Wren would have to face that horror all over again.

Ian hadn't consciously thought of walking to the cemetery, especially when it was a very long walk from his place of residence. But when he realized where he was, he felt almost angry with himself for coming here—even if it was only a subconscious part of himself that had urged him along. He wondered if it was a sign that he *would* have to face death again. The thought made the wind more biting, but he wrapped his coat more tightly around himself and moved with trepidation into the cemetery and between the array of stones, some recent and new, some old and weathered; some tiny and insignificant, some huge and ostentatious. But all of them represented the passing of a human being, and the reality of someone left behind to see that the dead person would be remembered and honored by some kind of gravestone to commemorate the fact that a person's lifetime had been reduced to the dates of their birth and death. Ian slowed down his pace immensely as he glanced at names and dates and wondered about the stories they told. Then he stood before the grave of his own daughter and saw the story there. *Bethia Joy Brierley.* Her name told the story of an aunt tragically lost, the emotion she'd brought to her parents in her brief appearance, and the heritage of her ancestral home in Scotland. And there was only one date. She had died on the same day she had been born. Her time on this planet had been but a moment, but she'd left a deep impression on her parents and she would never be forgotten. He ached to hold her and see her smile, hear her laugh, and yes, even to hear her cry, just to have evidence of her life.

It was easy to imagine an identical gravestone next to this one. He could see Gillian's name carved into it, and dates that declared a very short life, only a matter of months in this world. The thought was so painful that Ian dropped to his knees, taking only a quick glance in both directions to be assured of his solitude there before he allowed the full force of his anguish to come pouring out of him. The events leading up to this moment marched through his mind. Leaving his home and family had torn at his heart in spite of his knowledge that it had been the right thing to do. Bethia's death and the wretched grief that had followed had felt insurmountable, and his heart still tightened whenever he thought of it. There had been the frightening illnesses that had worn down his loved ones physically, and worn them all down in spirit. And then, worst of all was the death of their little Joy. He still could hardly believe that it had happened, could hardly believe that it was possible for him to keep getting up every day and facing existence in this world when such a loss pressed on his heart every hour of his life, and he knew that his own grief was eclipsed by Wren's. All of it combined had weighed Ian down with worry and fear over what else might go wrong. His greatest fear had become the loss of another of his loved ones, and a close second to that was having something happen to himself that would prevent him from being able to care for his loved ones in the way he would want, the way they *needed* him to.

If Wren knew the secret thoughts of his heart, she would tell him to have more faith, to trust in God, and to know that He would care for them. In his deepest self he believed they *were* in God's hands and that He was aware of their existence and their challenges. But he had also seen harsh evidence that God had placed them in a world full of affliction, and God's presence did not by any means guarantee that hard things would not happen. And Ian just didn't know if he was strong enough to endure anything further. He felt homesick for the highlands of his native land, and for the familiarity of his family there. He knew that being in Scotland would not have necessarily kept his loved ones from becoming ill; illness had no boundaries. And their baby likely would have died regardless of where they had been. But Bethia would probably be alive if she'd not been on that ship, and if they were still living at Brierley they would have been surrounded by the love and security of home. He couldn't think of the advantages of staying in Scotland, however, without conceding that he would not have met Ward and Millie if they'd not ventured out into the world, and he would not trade away the friendship of this good man and his mother.

Ian cried the way he'd felt like crying through the course of each of these events, but he'd fought to remain strong and firm and do what needed to be done. He cried the way he'd wanted to cry ever since he'd first realized Gillian was ill. The tears ran down his face and soaked into his collar. His wet cheeks stung in the cold wind. The sobs heaved out of his chest in painful bursts that he couldn't control. He placed his hands flat on the ground, glad for his gloves but not certain he'd notice the cold ground even if he didn't have them. He hung his head and drained himself of torrents of grief that had been hovering, brewing, and simmering in him for months. His emotion gradually settled into an occasional sharp breath, which eventually subsided into an unearthly quiet. He heard nothing around him, not the chirp of a bird nor the rustle of trees in the wind. In fact, the wind had ceased, and the air was surprisingly calm. Ian didn't look up. He just remained as he was, quietly considering all he'd felt and experienced since he'd left Brierley, and especially since he'd come into the cemetery. Then without thinking about it first, he opened his mouth and began speaking to God. He prayed like he hadn't prayed in weeks. Oh, he'd certainly *prayed.* He'd prayed night and day, hour by hour, minute by minute—especially through the *difficult* hours and minutes. He'd begged God for His help and His mercy to be manifested in miracles. He'd thanked God—over and over—for all with which they had been blessed. But in that moment, Ian prayed from the depths of his spirit. He poured out his darkest fears, those that he'd been afraid to verbalize. And even though he knew that God could read his thoughts, there was something cleansing in actually being able to tell his Maker all the things that he feared, and all the reasons he had to be afraid. As he spoke of things he'd not dared speak of, he found himself better able to understand *why* he was afraid, why the trauma he'd experienced had made it difficult to believe that trauma wouldn't happen again. He felt a strange kind of comfort deep inside that seemed to be telling him God understood such human emotion, and He would not condemn Ian for feeling it, but rather would have mercy and compassion. Then a thought appeared in his mind that could not have been his own, simply because he'd had no conscious reason to think it, and there had been no related thoughts leading up to it. It was simply a thought. He'd not heard a voice either in his ears or in his mind. It was just a thought.

I already suffered these things for you, Ian.

Ian drew in a sharp breath and couldn't let it go. He asked himself if he'd imagined the thought, or if he was imagining what he believed to be its source. Then a warmth gathered in his chest that he recognized very clearly. He had felt it during the unforgettable experience when he'd known beyond any doubt that he needed to take his family to America, and more powerful and important than that, he had known then—as he'd been reminded now—that he had a

Savior who had paid the price for his own mistakes, his shortcomings, his sorrow, and his suffering. He wept tears of a different kind as the pain of all he'd experienced was soothed to a level that felt more tolerable than it had since the occurrence of these cumulative events. He didn't know if Gillian would live, and he didn't know if he and his loved ones would be spared any more heartache and suffering. But he *did* know that God was with him, and that in the end, all would be well. He felt a fresh determination to do whatever it was that God required of him, knowing that the blessings of eternity mattered more than the suffering of the here and now. He felt a renewed conviction to have courage and faith and strength in whatever he had to face, and to be an example and a support to those around him, rather than needing to lean so much on the faith of others.

Ian shifted from his knees to sit on the cold ground, grateful at least that it wasn't wet. While he sat there and pondered all he was feeling, the impression came to his mind that he was not alone. It was so strong that he actually looked around, half expecting to see someone there, and half knowing that he wouldn't *see* anything. While he wondered exactly what the impression meant, he felt a strong desire to read from the Book of Mormon. He and Ward had been taking turns with it, and they had often read together. Since Ward needed someone to read to him anyway, it was most convenient that way. But with Gillian ill, their time for reading had been very minimal. Now Ian felt as if he'd not be able to take another deep breath until he had the book in his hands. It reminded him of how he'd felt when he'd first purchased it. And he'd felt that way again when the book had called to him in his memory from where it had been deposited in a wardrobe and forgotten for many months. Ian held fast to the feeling—and all else he'd felt in the last little while—and jumped to his feet, brushing the dirt and dry grass from his clothes as he walked swiftly out of the cemetery and toward home. He walked every bit as fast as he had on the way there, but this time for different reasons. He couldn't get there fast enough. He needed to read from that book!

Ian was about halfway home when he noticed that the grayness of the sky was starting to clear. Spots of blue were showing through the clouds, and the sun was showing evidence that it indeed still existed.

How appropriate, Ian thought. He didn't know whether or not it was coincidence or was meant to have meaning for him, but he chose to believe in the latter and enjoyed the implication that spring would indeed follow winter, and the earth would be warmed once again.

Ian quickened his pace more when he realized he had no idea how long he'd been gone, and he didn't want Wren to be worrying about him when she had so much else to worry about. Nearing home, he practically ran the final stretch, at least as much as he could while avoiding any possible collisions with passersby. Once inside, he hurried up the stairs, realizing he couldn't hear any crying. His heart thudded painfully as he opened the door, imagining Wren's tears as she told him that Gillian was gone. He held his breath and opened the door to see only Millie in the parlor. She looked up calmly, then she offered a faint little smile and said, "Mother and baby are sleeping. Gillian ate rather well and dozed right off."

Ian breathed deeply and had to lean against the closed door to steady himself.

"Are you all right?" Millie asked.

"I just . . . hurried home and I'm out of breath," he explained, which was certainly true, but it wasn't the biggest reason for his breathlessness. He realized that even with the wonderful feelings he'd experienced only a while ago in the cemetery, it took very little to provoke his fears to the surface again, and he needed to work very hard to combat those fears and put the matter in the Lord's hands.

Ian removed his coat and crept quietly into the bedroom where he found Wren sleeping with little Gillian close beside her. The baby was propped up on a pillow to elevate her head, a sleeping position that seemed to give her relief and comfort. He sat in the chair near the bed without disturbing either of them. While they slept, he silently recounted all that had happened within himself since he'd left here earlier, and he prayed that he would be able to remember the truth of these things in his heart and hold firmly to them no matter what else happened. He'd sat there a long while when he saw that Gillian was beginning to stir. When it became evident she wasn't going back to sleep, and would instead start to cry at any moment, he scooped her up and took her into the parlor, carefully closing the door behind him with the hope that Wren would be able to get more sleep.

Gillian quickly resumed her agitated crying that indicated her ongoing misery. Ian felt weary for more reasons than he could count. Even the remarkable spiritual strength he'd been given earlier was difficult to hold on to when his daughter was suffering so much, and he had to wonder if it would get any better, or if the infection was slowly overtaking her and would end up being her undoing. Millie helped him put drops in her ears and change her diaper, but the fussing didn't cease. Wren appeared, drawn by the ongoing noise, and said she would try to feed her. Usually it took some fighting to get Gillian to eat, but her hunger seemed to be more motivating than her pain, and she was eager to be nursed. Ian sat there for a minute watching his beautiful wife with the baby. In spite of the weariness about her, she was beautiful and precious, and his gratitude for having her in his life was inexpressible. Then Ian remembered the strong desire he'd felt to get home and read from the Book of Mormon. He jumped to his feet and stepped into the kitchen where Millie and Ward were sitting at the table. Ward was eating a piece of pie while Millie read to him from a novel.

"Where is the Book of Mormon?" Ian asked. "I'd like to read from it."

"On my bedside table, I believe," Ward said.

"That's right," Millie said. "That's where we were reading last night."

"Thank you," Ian said and retrieved it. He sat back down in the parlor and did what he'd done many times; he just let the book fall open and began to read. It often fell open somewhere in the middle section, which was logical for any book. But this time all the pages seemed to fall away except for one very near the end of the book that seemed to be begging for Ian to read it. He started at the top of the page, even though it was in the middle of a sentence.

Whatsoever thing ye shall ask the Father in my name, which is good, in faith believing that ye shall receive, behold, it shall be done unto you. Wherefore, my beloved brethren, have miracles ceased because Christ hath ascended into heaven, and hath sat down on the right hand of God, to claim of the Father his rights of mercy which he hath upon the children of men? For he hath answered the ends of the law, and he claimeth all those who have faith in him; and they who have faith in him will cleave unto every good thing; wherefore he advocateth the cause of the children of men; and he dwelleth eternally in the heavens. And because he hath done this, my beloved brethren, have miracles ceased? Behold I say unto you, Nay; neither have angels ceased to minister unto the children of men. For behold, they are subject unto him, to minister according to the word of his command, showing themselves unto them of strong faith and a firm mind in every form of godliness. And the office of their ministry is to call men unto repentance, and to fulfil and to do the work of the covenants of the Father, which he hath made unto the children of men, to prepare the way among the children of men, by declaring the word of Christ unto the chosen vessels of the Lord, that they may bear testimony of him.

Ian felt breathless over what he'd just read, and he was certain there was a deeper treasure in its meaning that he needed to go back and search out. The entire paragraph was powerful, certainly, but he felt stuck on that word *angels*. He read that phrase again and again. *Have miracles ceased? Behold I say unto you, Nay; neither have angels ceased to minister unto the children of men.*

"What does that mean?" he whispered aloud.

"Did you say something?" Wren asked.

"No, just . . . thinking out loud," he said and reread the explanation of the office of ministering angels, their purpose, and the very fact that they—meaning angels—did indeed have interaction, and offer assistance, to those here on the earth. *The children of men.* Of course that meant those here on earth. Ian stopped to think about it and had to ask himself if he believed that to be true. If he believed the book was true—and he did—then he had to accept that it *was* true that angels ministered to those on earth. He could not pick and choose which stories and principles in the book he would believe or not believe. Of *course* it was true! Then he recalled the sensation he'd felt at the cemetery, and how it was the very feeling that had spurred him to come home and read from the book—and then how the book had fallen open to *this* page. Was he being guided to understand something? Yes. The answer was obviously *yes!*

Ian was barely starting to take in what it meant when Wren said, "Ian, look."

He looked up to see Gillian leaning back over Wren's arm, staring up at the ceiling in a way that was typical for her—and apparently not typical for other babies her age, according to Shirley's expertise with babies. But Gillian had not engaged in this strange behavior since she'd become ill. For many days she'd been in too much pain to do anything other than fuss when she was awake. But now she was gazing at something above her. Except there was nothing there. At least nothing that anyone else could see. Gillian's eyes shifted as if she were watching movement. Wren said, as she had many times before, "Perhaps it is her mother she sees . . . or her little cousin. Angels are surely with her."

Ian's heart began to pound so hard he had trouble drawing breath.

"Are ye all right?" Wren asked.

"Yes," Ian said. "But . . . I'm certain you're right."

All of the facts came together suddenly in Ian's head, a combination of all that he had felt, and the evidence that was before him now. It was as if Gillian was being shown something that was meant—in that very moment—to prove the truth of what Ian was being taught. The timing could not be coincidence. He knew in his heart that it wasn't, and he silently thanked God for sending a miracle.

"Ian," Wren said, startling him. "What is it, my love? Ye seem . . . lost."

"I was, I suppose," he said. "I need to tell you what happened earlier . . . and what I was just reading. The timing is . . ." He heard himself laugh. "The timing is a miracle."

Ian crossed the room and sat down where he could actually show Wren the passage he'd just read. He read it aloud while she read along silently, as if doing so might make it sink in more deeply. He paused at the mention of miracles and angels, to look into her eyes and share with her the experience he'd had in the cemetery. He was surprised—though he shouldn't have been—to hear her say, "Oh, I'm so grateful, Ian. I know ye've been struggling with yer faith. And I've prayed so hard that ye would know that God was with ye."

Ian took this in. "With all you've had to worry about . . . you were praying for *me?*"

"Of course I was," she said. "I know how hard this has all been for ye."

"No harder for me than for you," he insisted.

"Different, perhaps. But not easier."

"Haven't you been afraid that we would lose Gillian?" he asked.

"Of course I've wondered," she said. "But . . ." tears came to her eyes, "I know that God will carry us through whatever we are called upon t' bear."

Ian felt utterly humbled by her faith and in awe of her courage. When he told her so she brushed it off as nothing and asked him to tell her more about his experience and what he was feeling. Through most of the conversation Gillian continued to look around the room, remaining eerily quiet. Then she looked up at her mother and smiled for the first time in many days. It had been a day of many miracles!

Later it occurred to Ian that perhaps Gillian was seeing angels because her life would be brief and she might soon be required to join them. But Gillian slept better that night than she had since the illness had started, and the following day she was dramatically improved. There was no fever, and her fussing had decreased immensely. She did make it clear, however, that she'd become quite accustomed to being held continually, and she would struggle to maintain that habit. At first Ian and Wren were both thrilled to accommodate her, glad to be holding a happy baby instead of a baby who was miserable. But gradually they had to wean her from this dependence and get her accustomed to occasionally being left on a blanket on the floor to play, or being left in her own little bed to sleep.

Blossoms were beginning to appear on the trees of New York City when a small package arrived, addressed to Ian Brierley, from Nauvoo, Illinois. Ian didn't think at all about his fears or his doubts or his unanswered questions as he tore away the paper while the others looked on. Only Shona was absent, having gone to Shirley's for the day. Inside they found three copies of the Book of Mormon, and they all picked them up and touched them as if they were manna from heaven, a miracle and a wonder with no earthly explanation. Ward fingered a copy intently, then held it against his chest as he asked, "Is there a letter?"

"There is," Ian said, noting the folded papers that had been tucked between copies of the book. He opened the letter and scanned it with his eyes before reporting, "It is a scribe writing on behalf of *Brother Joseph,* as he calls him." Ian read farther down the first written page. "He writes on behalf of him, expressing great joy at receiving our letter." Ian stopped to let out a delighted laugh before he continued. "He wants us to know that Brother Joseph is a very busy man, but he wishes to assure us that when we arrive in Nauvoo, Brother Joseph will personally see to it that we have a place to stay and our needs met until we have time to establish ourselves."

"Oh, how lovely!" Millie said with overt glee. "How gracious these people sound!"

The remainder of the letter gave some details on the best route to travel, suggestions for making the journey as easy as possible, and a little bit about the growing population of Nauvoo. It also stated that the Mormons had only been living in this new community for a short time, and it occurred to Ian that if they'd tried to find them the previous year, they might not have been successful. Ian finished by reading aloud, "'You will find many here who share your beliefs, and we look forward to having you and your family among us. We wish you a safe journey. Know that your brothers and sisters in the gospel will be praying for you.'"

Over the next few days, they made specific plans for the journey to Nauvoo, even though they all felt that they should wait some weeks to begin so that the weather would become less cool; also, they wanted to give Gillian a chance to fully heal from her illness. Nauvoo was not as far into the wilderness areas of America as Ian had first believed. They would actually be able to take hired carriages all the way to Nauvoo. Even so, the journey would take many, many days of difficult travel. They would be able to stay at hotels and inns along the way, and hopefully be comfortable and safe. Of course, they could not predict how the journey would go; they could only pray that they would remain safe and healthy. At least now they knew where they were going. They could finally accomplish what it was God sent them to America to do, to become a part of these people so that their posterity would be blessed. Ian felt hope surge through him like he hadn't felt since he'd left his home in Scotland. Everything was coming together now, and everything was going to be perfect.

* * *

As the time for the planned departure grew closer, Shona seemed especially nervous one morning at the breakfast table, which recalled to Wren's attention that she had been unusually quiet the last day or two. Wren thought that she should make the opportunity to speak later with Shona privately, then Shona cleared her throat in a way that announced her voice was trying to find its way out.

"There's something I need t' tell ye all," she said. "I've been thinking about this ever since we got t' New York, so I'm not doing anything impulsive or . . ."

Ian put his napkin on the table and leaned back as if to state that he wasn't going to eat until she'd said what she needed to say. His expression made clear that he knew it was serious, and he wasn't certain he was going to like it. Wren felt the same way. Shona glanced at Ian, then at Wren, then down at her lap.

"I want t' say how very thankful I am for all that ye've done for me. Being there t' help with Bethia was a joy t' me . . . in spite of the . . . well, ye know what I mean. And I've been glad t' help with the baby, and all. Ye know how I love little Gillian, so . . . this is a hard choice for me t' make, but . . ." Her voice broke and tears moistened her eyes. Wren knew now what was coming, and her heart pounded to think of losing Shona even before she said, "I've got myself a job here in the city. I'm going t' stay here instead of moving on with ye. I'll be living with Ronald and Shirley; they've got room for me, and I feel like such a part of the family. I can help Shirley with the children and still pay my own way and help out and such."

A pall of silence followed her seemingly memorized explanation. Wren was afraid to speak, knowing tears would come with her words. She was relieved when Ian took it upon himself to speak for both of them. "You must do what you feel is right, Shona. I know that you've come this far with us because you *did* feel it was right. We'll be very sad to lose you; you've become like family to us." Wren heard the slightest crack in his voice to indicate that the words came with truth and conviction.

Wren was then able to say, "Because ye're so dear t' us, Shona, we'd never want t' hold ye back from doing what ye feel is best for yer life." The tears she'd feared came forward, but Shona was wiping tears from her own face, and perhaps she needed to know how much Wren and Ian cared for her. "But we'll miss ye dreadfully."

"I'll miss ye, as well. All of ye, but . . . I *do* know this is right for me. I admire yer convictions about finding this religion, but . . . I confess I don't share those convictions. I feel like my place is here."

"We understand," Ian said, barely disguising his disappointment. "And we certainly wish you all the best." He chuckled tensely.

"Perhaps you'll even find the right man here in the city and be able to have a family of your own."

"I can't help hoping," Shona said with a little smile that only lasted a moment. "Of course we'll write. Ronald and Shirley are settled here permanently . . . at least they hope t' be. They would always know where I might be if I'm not with them. So, when ye find where ye'll be settling, ye can write and let me know, and . . . we'll . . . we'll always keep in touch."

"Of course," Ian said and took Wren's hand beneath the table. They exchanged a wan smile, and Wren suspected he was thinking of his family. They'd all promised to write to each other, but it was never the same; it would never *be* the same.

Ian told Wren later that he *had* been thinking about his family, and how the exchange of only a couple of letters in all these months could never ease how much he missed them. The following day, Wren wondered if his mention of it had been some kind of premonition: Ian received a letter from home. As he was tearing it open he said, "I sent a letter weeks ago to let them know we would be moving on as soon as we made a decision about where to settle. They must have known when they sent this that it might not find us."

"Since they *did* send it," Wren said, "it's a good thing we haven't left yet."

"Yes, it is," he said with a smile, and she knew he was anticipating their departure in three days time, but he was also very glad to have received a letter from home.

Wren glanced toward Gillian, who was playing nearby, then she glanced back to Ian just in time to see his countenance falter as he read. He reached blindly for a chair, then sank onto it, his face turning white.

"What is it?" Wren asked, moving toward him.

He hesitated a long moment, as if the words had trouble coming to his lips. "My father is dead," he muttered. Wren went to her knees beside him just as he dropped his head abruptly, as if he feared he might lose consciousness otherwise. He groaned, and the letter fell to the floor.

"I can't believe it," he whispered, his voice raspy. "I just can't believe it. The last letter said he was doing well, and . . . I can't believe it."

Ian slid off the chair to his knees, as if he couldn't even find the strength to sit. He gripped the edge of the table as if it could keep him from drowning in the shock, then he lost his grip, and his hands went to the floor as he hung his head further and the first painful sob leapt out of his throat, followed by another, and another. Wren could only put her arm around him and weep as well. Wren herself had grown close to Ian's father through years of casual association during her youth, but the bonds had deepened following her marriage to Ian and during the time they had lived at Brierley under the same roof as Gavin MacBrier. She thought of the death of her own father, and her empathy for Ian deepened. He had been there that day; in fact, Ian had been the one to discover that her father had died in his bed. He had kept everything under control and he had held her together. Now, with this news, they were too far away to do anything. The funeral was long over, and his loved ones had had weeks to adjust to the news that was freshly painful to Ian.

Ward came out of his room and asked, "What's happened?"

The alarm in his voice drew Wren's attention to him. He was holding to the edge of the door, unable to see anything, but it was impossible not to hear the evidence of Ian's grief. Ian was apparently oblivious to Ward entering the room, so Wren stood and took hold of his arm, saying quietly, "Word has just come that Ian's father has died."

"Oh, it's too much!" Ward muttered. "Guide me to him, please."

Wren led Ward across the room and urged his hand to Ian's shoulder. Ward then went to his knees next to his friend, offering the kind of comfort that Ian would have gotten from his brother had they still been at Brierley.

Later, when Ian was able to face the shock more calmly, he asked Wren to read the entire letter aloud. His mother wrote of details of the sudden, unexpected turn for the worse that her husband had experienced in his chronic breathing difficulties due to emphysema. She wrote of his father's last words, and what the funeral had been like. His mother told Ian who had been in attendance and what the weather had been like. Ian wept while she read, but Wren was glad that his mother had been sensitive enough to know that Ian would want to know how it had been. Then his mother offered a sincere plea for Ian to give up his notions of travel and return home where he belonged. Wren knew that her mother-in-law meant well, but she saw the torment rise into Ian's countenance when he heard his mother's words, and she wondered how he would respond to the situation. She wanted to remind him that their goals were clear, their travel arrangements had been made, and they knew what they had to do. But Wren knew that he was well aware of those things, and it was likely best to just give him time to consider the matter before they talked about it. As much as a part of her longed to go back to Brierley herself, she knew they could never stay there and be content—not with what they'd felt in their hearts, not with what they knew God wanted them to do. The very idea of retracing their steps to sail back across the ocean and return to Scotland almost made her nauseous. Memories of losing her sister during the journey surely emphasized that sick feeling.

After the letter had been read, Ian sat where he was for a few minutes in silence, then he stood up abruptly and declared that he needed some time alone. He grabbed his coat and hurried out, not returning for nearly three hours. Wren suspected he had gone to the cemetery where their little Joy was buried. But she didn't ask him. She simply inquired upon his return whether there was anything she could do for him. He assured her that she was already everything he could possibly need or want. He held her tightly in his arms for longer than a minute, then he went into the bedroom and closed the door, once again declaring the need to be alone. Wren left him to his grief while she endured her own anguish, buoyed up by their dear friends, wondering what they would have ever done without them. She also wondered what would happen now, and prayed that Ian would be comforted and strengthened, and that he would be able to make the right decision.

Chapter Ten
Toward the Horizon

For two days Ian hardly ate and barely slept. Wren stayed close to him, offering compassion and love, knowing that he needed to feel his sorrow in order to move beyond it. But she felt deeply concerned for him in ways that she could not talk to him about; not while he was so consumed with his father's loss. Wren knew he was strong. But she also knew that the loss of their little Joy was still far too close to the tender places of Ian's heart, and the combined losses were weighing heavily on him. Worst of all, Wren feared that his grief would distort his thinking and he might rashly decide to return to Scotland. He went out for a walk with Ward, and when they returned, Ward reported discreetly to Wren that Ian had gone to inquire about ships heading to Liverpool.

"He didn't book passage for us, did he?" Wren asked, her heart pounding with dread.

"No," Ward said quietly so that Ian wouldn't hear them from the other room. "He would never do that without consulting with you."

"But if he's determined t' go back, I could never talk him out of it."

"You might," Ward said. "But I can tell you this. If you are going back to Scotland, we are going with you."

"That's right," Millie said, not even trying to pretend that she wasn't eavesdropping. "You'll never be rid of us."

"Never," Ward repeated, and Wren was glad to know it.

That night Wren put Gillian down for the night and climbed into bed next to Ian. She knew he wasn't asleep, but he didn't move or comment when she put her hand on his arm.

"Are ye all right?" she finally asked.

"I don't know," he admitted. "I feel so torn, Wren."

"Tell me why," she encouraged. When he didn't respond, she prayed for the right words to help him through this. Only one idea seemed stuck in her mind so she said it. "I'm certain yer mother would be so pleased t' see ye, Ian. And yer brother would as well, of course. But then what? After ye were home for a few days, a few weeks, then what? Yer brother is the Earl now. I'm certain he'd appreciate yer help in that, but ye know he can do all he has t' do. Ye both talked about it a great deal before we ever left. What would we do there, Ian?"

Still Ian said nothing, and Wren simply added, "Just give it some thought. I'll be right here if ye need t' talk it through."

A minute later he rolled over and pulled her fiercely into his arms, holding her as if doing so could completely heal his broken heart. "I love you, Wren," he murmured and kissed her. "I love you."

Nothing more was said that night about home or death or being faced with life-altering decisions. The next morning Ian was quiet, but his countenance was heavy and his eyes dark. Wren prayed silently, one prayer after another, that Ian's heart would be comforted and he would make the correct decision. Later that day, another letter arrived from Scotland; this one was from Ian's brother, Donnan. Ian opened it with trepidation, and Wren's heart was pounding. She feared that if Donnan too offered a plea for Ian to return home that he would surely give in and book passage to Liverpool before the day was done. But Donnan's letter proved to be the answer to Wren's prayers. He wrote of the difficulty in losing their father, and his own struggle with taking over all of the responsibilities of being the Earl of Brierley. But he also told Ian that he understood his need to do what he was doing, and that he should not come back out of some kind of pity or concern for the family. He assured Ian that all was well, and that across the distance he was sending his support for Ian in his endeavors.

"*I know you're planning to move on,*" Ian read aloud, "*and I can only hope our letters have reached you before you've left. Either way, I'm certain you'll write again when you're settled, and I will send word that includes all you might have missed should our communication be waylaid. We miss you and your family very much, Ian, as I'm certain you must miss being here, but you are in our hearts and as your brother I would wish you every possible happiness wherever your heart may lead you. I know that Mother feels the same, even if her missing you might make her say otherwise. May God go with you!"*

Ian finished the letter, wiped away a couple of tears, and asked Wren if she would like to go out with him for a while before it got dark.

"Of course," she said, noting the light that had returned to his eyes.

Ian hired a cab that drove them to the cemetery where little Joy was buried. He carried Gillian with one arm and held Wren's hand with the other as they walked between the many stones to the one that held a piece of their hearts.

"We'll be leaving for Nauvoo in the morning," he said, and Wren nearly melted with relief at hearing his statement. "This is the last time we'll likely ever come to this place." His voice cracked when he said it. Wren was not so reserved and couldn't hold back a rush of many tears. "I suppose it's possible we may come through here again one day, but . . ."

"Not very likely," she said, and he nodded.

"I just wanted to come here with you one more time, and . . ." He looked at Wren instead of at the gravestone. "I wanted to thank you . . . formally . . . for the way you stand by me, the way you believe in me when I have trouble believing in myself. We love the same people, we grieve over the same things, we share the same journey. I can't imagine living even a day without you, and I pray that I never have to know what that's like." He kissed her and added, "I pray that it *is* possible to be with the people we love forever, because I can't imagine heaven being heaven without you."

"I would agree with every word," she said and kissed him again.

Ian put his arms around her, noticing that Gillian had become unusually still and quiet. He looked down at the gravestone again, pondering it during a stretch of silence. Then he noticed that it had taken on a pinkish hue. He looked up to see a dazzlingly beautiful sunset, with streaks of pink and orange casting a radiant sheen over the whole sky and everything in sight. The colors and brilliance of the light seemed to beckon to Ian, and it occurred to him that the western horizon had become their goal, and the sunset seemed to be their guiding light. He knew that sunsets were brief, just as the impressive spiritual moments in his life had been. But through long days and dark nights, the memory of such a moment could be resplendent enough to carry him through.

"Oh, it's so lovely!" Wren said, leaning her head against his shoulder.

They stood there together while he did his best to explain what he'd just felt. It didn't take much explaining, because Wren always had a way of seeming to know his thoughts with practically no explanation at all.

They didn't leave the cemetery until the sun had completely gone down and the place became mildly eerie in the gray light of dusk. Together they said good-bye to their little Joy, but reminded each other that she would be with them in spirit, and she was surely an angel in their lives. They returned to the cab that was waiting at the edge of the cemetery, and arrived at their apartment to announce that they all needed to finish up their packing. They were leaving for Nauvoo in the morning—to the beautiful city on the river, where they would stay and find great peace for the remainder of their lives.

* * *

The journey became more tedious with each passing day. Ian could *not* believe how enormous the expanse of America actually was. Looking at a map, the distance between New York City and Illinois had not looked so very long in contrast to the whole expanse of the country. Now he knew that the island on which he'd grown up, which constituted the countries of England and Scotland, was extremely tiny compared to this place that was now their home. He lost track of days, of cities and states, and became utterly weary of the long stretches of land where nothing seemed to exist at all. Gillian came to hate getting into a carriage so thoroughly that the adults all dreaded it simply because of having to deal with the way the baby fussed. At times her mood was tolerable, and at times she slept. Otherwise, she was cranky. But they were all cranky. They were all just mature enough to curb their tongues and keep their opinions quiet in order to not make the situation more difficult for their traveling companions. With four adults sharing the tiny space inside of a carriage, they did their best to make each other comfortable, often passing Gillian around in order to keep her happy. Since Ward was tall and Ian was taller, they often had to come up with ways of shifting the way they were sitting so they could stretch their legs, try to get comfortable, and not be in each other's way.

Ian kept telling himself that every day they were getting closer; every *hour* they were getting closer. But as the time dragged on and the weariness of the journey increased, that sense of doom inside of him that he'd fought so hard against in the past reared its ugly head once again. The long hours became filled with an internal battle while he wondered if he simply had an overactive imagination, or if God was preparing him for the possibility of yet another tragedy. He felt at times as if the devil himself were trying to keep Ian and his loved ones from arriving in Nauvoo safely. But that was simply ridiculous. Wasn't it? He reminded himself that, according to his readings in the Book of Mormon *and* the Bible, he had every reason to believe that God would always be more powerful than any efforts that Satan could throw at mankind. But he'd also read many accounts—and personally felt the effects—of the ugliness of life and how it could tear down the human spirit. The story of Job came to mind. Job never lost his integrity, and he never let go of his faith in his Redeemer. In the end, he was blessed greatly, and all he'd lost had been restored and even doubled. But oh, how Job had suffered! Ian didn't have any trouble looking into the distant future and recognizing that maintaining his integrity and his faith in Christ would surely serve him well in the eternities. But there were times when the possibility—and the probability—of the suffering he and his loved ones might have to pass through to get to that point was daunting and frightening. There were moments when he envied Bethia and his friend Greer, his father, his brother James, and his little deceased daughter. For them, the misery was over. They had moved on to a better place. Of course, Ian would never want to leave those who needed him, and he didn't want to be separated from his loved ones here. His desire to live was stronger than his desire to be free of the possible misery of this life. Still, these were thoughts that managed to find their way into his mind, and he had trouble counteracting them.

To help pass the time, they all tried to come up with word games and guessing games that would keep conversation going. Ian liked the way it kept him from thinking dreadful thoughts he didn't want to be thinking. One of their games was to each say something about what they imagined Nauvoo to be like. They began to get ridiculous in their speculations, creating a description that might be equal to heaven itself. Of course, they were all more realistic than that, but it helped them feel that the goal they were working toward was worth all they were enduring to get there.

Through a particularly long stretch where there was not much of anything but miles and miles of rough road, they knew this was one of those lengths of the journey when there was nowhere suitable to stay the night and they would just have to keep going until a place could be found. The carriage they'd hired had two men who alternated driving so they could go longer distances. It had occurred to Ian that he could have purchased his own carriage or wagon and had more control over the journey. But the fact was that he had absolutely no idea how to handle a team of horses that way, and he was traveling with two women, a baby, and a blind man. He felt more comfortable in the care of men who drove these roads all the time. He was especially grateful for their expertise when the weather became difficult. They had encountered a surge of spring rain that seemed relentless. Ian expressed concern to the drivers over this and suggested that perhaps they should find a place to stay and wait for the storm to run its course. He even offered to pay for their accommodations, but they insisted that they were quite accustomed to it. The warm layers of clothing they wore beneath oiled coats and large-brimmed hats had all been designed to protect them from the weather and they would be fine. Still, with each mile they traveled through the rain, Ian couldn't help thinking about these men up on top of the coach, while they were all tucked safely inside. Their luggage strapped to the top had been covered with a waterproofed canvas to protect it. Once they were settled in Nauvoo, the remainder of their belongings would be delivered by a company that was currently storing them in New York.

Inside the carriage they all attempted to get some sleep since it was the middle of the night. Getting comfortable was nigh to impossible, but they were all utterly exhausted. Again Ian thought of the drivers and couldn't imagine how they were managing. The rain began to pound so hard that the noise itself was almost deafening and added to the impossibility of being able to sleep. Still, they all dozed here and there, unanimously grateful that at least Gillian was sleeping. The sound of the rain and the motion of the carriage were having a magical effect on her after a particularly fussy day. Ian wondered, not for the first time, how they would have managed if Shona had come along. They couldn't have fit another person in here. Or rather, it would have been especially cramped. The only other option would have been to divide their group between two carriages, which could have been very complicated. It wasn't that he felt glad to have Shona absent, because he certainly missed her, and he knew the others did, as well. He could simply see now that it was perhaps best all around. He had a secret hope that things would not work out for her in New York, and she would later join them in Nauvoo. He wondered how she was doing. He thought of her living comfortably—although in crowded quarters—in Ronald and Shirley's home, and he hoped that all they were all doing well.

A sudden swerving of the carriage startled Ian out of a somewhat comfortable position and relaxed state. He knew the others were startled as well by the little gasp that came from Wren and a mild shriek that came from Millie.

"The road is likely just very muddy," Ian said in a voice that was deceptively calm.

The moment he said it, the carriage swerved again, this time pressing them all tightly against one side. Wren slid into Ian, and Ward slid against his mother. Ian had a sudden thought to give the baby to Wren. In his mind he protested initially. If they were in some danger, it was better that *he* have the baby. He was physically bigger and stronger and more capable of protecting Gillian.

Give Wren the baby, he heard again and abruptly did so.

"Take her," Ian said, ignoring her surprise and confusion. There was no time—or need—to explain when everything erupted into chaos. The carriage swerved and slid, then tipped and screeched with thunderous volition while everything went onto its side. Ian instinctively took hold of Millie just before Ward would have landed on top of her. The carriage door flew open at Ian's side, and he barely managed to keep from falling out of it while the carriage was trying to stop and the momentum of the horses protested. In his mind was the flashing image of that door flying open and him tumbling out with Gillian in his arms; or worse, him losing his grip on her and losing the baby completely. He was aware of Wren landing on the side of the carriage, falling onto her back with her arms wrapped tightly around the baby. The carriage swerved again and tipped farther. The women screamed, and Ward called out, "Mother!" as if he could save her simply by calling her name. With a vague perception that Wren and the baby were all right, Ian tightened his hold on Millie just before they went tumbling out the carriage door. Only when they went from the shelter of the carriage into the pelting rain did Ian realize the carriage was dangling off the edge of a bridge. He found himself rolling down some kind of muddy ravine, his arms wrapped tightly around Millie with the hope of protecting her from the worst of it, and with the prayer that they would all survive. Millie clung to him and whimpered fearfully, as any woman would. The drop wasn't as far as Ian had feared it would be, but as he and Millie came to a stop, he heard a sickening thud the same moment that he heard her groan as if all of the air had come out of her lungs in one harsh rush. And then she was frighteningly still. Ian could see nothing except shadows and forms through the thick darkness and the pummeling rain. But as he struggled to orient himself to where they had fallen, his first awareness was Millie lying limp in his arms.

"No!" he muttered. "No, no, no!" He shifted her gently and put a hand to her face. "Millie!" he shouted. "Millie, speak to me!" She made no response, and Ian's chest began to burn as every fear that had been smoldering in him suddenly ignited. He kept shouting her name, kept trying to make her respond. He tried to shield her from the rain, which was an utterly pointless endeavor, but he tried nevertheless. His eyes began to adjust more to the darkness while he thought of how dear this woman had become to him. He thought of his own mother, and how desperately he missed her. He thought of how Millie had helped fill that role in his life since he'd met her. He thought of her love and kindness to him, to Wren, to Gillian—of all she did to help care for them, of her nurturing nature and instinctive goodness. And Ian thought of Ward, who was as good as a brother to him, a friend so very dear. He thought of having to tell Ward that something horrible had happened to his mother, that something had gone terribly wrong. The very idea of having to do such a thing ignited his desperation to get Millie to come around.

"Please God," he shouted into the rain, as if God might not hear him otherwise. "Please don't take her from us. Please, I beg you!"

Ian couldn't think of anything but his longing to have Millie respond. He lost track of minutes and forgot about how this had happened and what might be going on with the others. The flash of a lantern from somewhere above him caught his attention and brought him brutally back to the memory of his wife and daughter and friend who had also been in the carriage. And what of the drivers? The sickening dread of wondering if Millie was truly dead in his arms exploded into wondering if she might not be the only one injured— or worse. A part of him wanted to believe that with a doctor's care Millie would be all right, but the deepest part of him already knew the truth, already knew that nothing could be done for her. Still, he had to get her out of this muddy ravine. He had to get out of here himself. He had to know if the others were all right.

"Ian!" he heard a man call and recognized the voice of one of the drivers. He couldn't be sure whether it was Hank or Fred, but he knew it was the voice of a strong, competent man, and he was inexplicably grateful. "Ian!" he heard again. "Can you hear me?"

"I'm here!" Ian shouted, then he repeated it over and over so that the sound of his voice could guide the glow of that lantern closer.

"I'm coming," the voice called through the rain.

"Be careful!" Ian called back.

Still holding tightly to Millie, Ian looked up to see both Hank *and* Fred standing above him, one of them holding a lantern high. "She's hurt," Ian said and heard a little sob come out of his throat following the words. "She's not moving."

The lantern moved closer to Millie's face as Ian eased to his knees and tried to wipe the rain from his eyes in order to see better. He heard the voice of the man holding the lantern gasp in the same moment that he saw the deep gash on Millie's forehead. Even the continuing downpour hadn't washed away the evidence that it had been bleeding a great deal. But worse than that was the horrible sight of Millie's eyes, frozen half open, clearly declaring that life had been snatched away from her while she'd been wide awake and utterly afraid.

"Oh, heaven be merciful!" Ian muttered, his first thought being gratitude that Ward was blind, and he would never have to see that expression on his mother's face as his final memory of her.

"I'm afraid she's gone," one of the men said, pressing fingers tightly to her throat to check for a pulse, even though they all knew there was no need.

"What about you?" the other one asked. "Are you hurt, Ian?"

"A little bruised perhaps," he said. "I'm fine."

He was given a hand and helped to his feet while he wondered what to do next and how they would ever get out of here with this continuing rain when the mud was already so thick and deep. Only a moment later the rain eased to a slow trickle, and Ian heard the other men comment while he just silently thanked God for a slight reprieve in the midst of this horror. Then he prayed that the others would be safe, and that he would know how to help Ward face this nightmare. He imagined Ward up on the road, also praying and desperately wondering if Ian and his mother were all right. Ian felt sick as he tried to imagine how the rest of the night was going to play out.

Ian was grateful for the gentle efficiency of Hank and Fred as the lantern was handed to Ian and the two men carefully lifted Millie's body and carried it with slow trepidation up and out of the ravine, exercising caution with each step. Somewhere during the ascent, Ian became aware of Gillian crying in the distance, and he breathed some relief. She was alive and well enough to be using those lungs of hers with great gusto. He prayed again that she wasn't hurt, and that neither Wren nor Ward had suffered any injuries. As he came up out of the ravine onto the road, Wren rushed toward him, holding the crying Gillian against her. He let out his breath as if he'd been holding it. *She was all right!*

"Are you hurt?" He demanded to be reassured.

"I'm fine. We're fine. Are ye—"

"And Ward?"

"He's fine. I've guided him t' a safe place t' wait. He's wet; we're all wet. Banged up a bit. But we're fine. Are ye—"

"I'm fine," he said, holding the lamp high for Hank and Fred. "But Millie . . ." He choked on his attempt to finish the sentence, then heard Wren gasp when she realized what was happening.

"Is she . . ." Wren began but seemed equally incapable of finishing the thought.

Ian kept holding the lantern high and cleared his throat in an effort to force away its resistance in wanting to say the words. "She's . . . gone," he muttered, and Wren let out a sharp noise that was a combination of shock and horror. Knowing he needed to offer some explanation, he forced himself to just hurry and say it. "I was . . . holding to her . . . as we went down, but . . . apparently she hit her head, and . . ." As Hank and Fred made those last few steps, Ian moved between them and his wife, muttering quietly, "I don't want you to see her this way. I . . . don't know how to tell Ward."

Wren hurried away, as if to say she *refused* to see Millie this way. He heard her say over her shoulder, "I'll tell him."

The following hour was grueling as it passed so slowly. Millie's body was covered with a wet blanket. Everything was wet. Ward knelt beside his mother on the ground, crying over her the way Ian had cried when he heard of his father's death. It was a pain that Ian understood, but he could do nothing to alleviate it. Wren stayed close to Ward and futilely attempted to keep the baby calm. Gillian had settled down from her initial terror of coming awake to such an intense jolt and the pouring rain that had assaulted them when Hank and Fred had helped them out of the carriage. Now Ian could see that the carriage was practically dangling over the edge of the bridge. It was tipped on its side with more of it *off* the bridge than on. The well-trained horses were standing steady and still, keeping the carriage from moving or becoming damaged any further.

Seeing the reality of the situation, Ian knew it could have been so much worse. The very thought stung as he had to concede that what he meant was that more than one of them could have died, they all could have sustained serious injuries, and the carriage could have been damaged beyond repair. As it was, Hank and Fred had examined the wheels and axles and believed that if the carriage could be turned upright, it could get them to the next town. If not, one of them would take one of the horses and ride on for help. But they would first try to get the carriage upright and functional. They had tools with them to repair minor damages, and they were all hopeful of being back on the road soon.

Ward held the baby while Wren stood in front of the two lead horses, holding their bridles in a way that Hank had shown her, which would keep them from moving. Ian, Hank, and Fred all then situated themselves to the best advantage to push their weight against the carriage with some leverage in their combined positions. It took four tries before the carriage seemed to magically jump into place, as if unseen hands had compensated for the meager abilities of three mortal men. Ian was convinced that angels were assisting them, and he was also grateful beyond words that he had Hank and Fred in charge of this operation, as opposed to being out here in the middle of nowhere by himself, trying to cope with an impossible situation.

Ian sat with Ward while Hank and Fred carefully checked the carriage over to see if it was safe. Wren paced the road with the baby. Ian knew that his wife was crying, and he also knew that she preferred to avoid having the others hear how upset she was.

"I can't believe this has happened," Ward said, holding tightly to Ian's arm the same way he would if they were trying to navigate their way through a crowd. Ian was glad to be his eyes and his strength. He only wished that he could offer him some words of comfort that could make some sense.

"I can't believe it either," Ian said, realizing he was still dazed and in shock. He wondered why, if angels had been there to help put the carriage back on the road, they had not been able to protect Millie as they'd gone down the ravine. Something horrified and raw with pain deep in his spirit wanted to shake his fist toward heaven and demand answers that would soothe the shock of this unspeakable trauma.

"I can't believe it," Ward said again. And again.

"I wish I could change it," Ian admitted, unable to hold back tears. "I wish I could go back and do something to keep it from happening like this."

Ward tightened his grip on Ian. "This is not your fault, Ian. Not in any way. Do you hear me?"

Ian heard him but didn't respond. It wasn't the first time he'd felt responsible for the death of a loved one. He'd felt that way when Greer died—both times. And he'd felt that way when he'd tragically lost his brother, James. And also with the way that Bethia had died. Now, with Millie, he was trying to think it through to a point where he could be convinced of what Ward was saying, but he found it difficult to wade through the muck of the present situation and see *anything* clearly.

As if Ward sensed Ian's thoughts—and the reasons for them—he said with vehemence, "My mother and I chose to make this journey with you, Ian. And even in *this* moment, I do *not* wonder if it was the right thing to do. You did everything you could to keep her safe. This is *not* your fault!"

"Then *why?*" Ian said through clenched teeth, barely managing to not bawl like a baby.

"If we trust in God—and we do—then we must believe it was her time to leave this world, and we must have faith to keep going."

"I fear you have much more faith than I do, my friend," Ian said, marveling that such courageous words could come out of a man's mouth, given the present situation. Ward was sitting in the mud beside his mother's dead body, unable to even see, and he was telling Ian that they trusted in God and they needed to have faith.

"You have more faith than you think you do," he said to Ian. It was a concept that kept coming up, but Ian still had trouble grasping it.

Ian chose to shift the topic and make certain there was no misunderstanding concerning an important point. "Ward, I want you to know that I will always be with you. I know your mother did many little things for you every day to help you. I know she has been your eyes in more ways than I could probably imagine. I'm glad for the privilege I've had to help you here and there, and I'm glad for the privilege to do so even more now. Do you hear me? You will never be left alone in the dark! Never! I will always be there. Do you understand?"

Ward nodded but didn't speak as he was overtaken with emotion. He finally managed to say, "Thank you, my friend. It's very humbling to be in such a position, to know that I cannot exist in this world without help. Your promise means so very much to me. You are truly the greatest friend a man could ever ask for."

"The feeling is mutual, my friend," Ian said and put a brotherly arm around Ward's shoulders while he wept for the tragic loss of his mother.

Ian sat with Ward for many minutes, neither of them speaking, but mutually trying to comprehend the way their lives had been so dramatically altered in the blink of an eye.

Hank declared the carriage safe, and reported that the luggage had all been bound so tightly on top that it was all intact, and even dry. Again Ian felt gratitude to be in the care of such competent men. But Hank spoke quietly to Ian about how to appropriately handle the transportation of the body. He'd not meant for Ward to hear, but he'd underestimated Ward's extra-keen sense of hearing that had compensated for his lack of sight.

"It's all right, Hank," Ward said. "I would like to hold her with me while we move on. If you'd be willing to help me . . ."

"Of course," Hank said with kindness.

Millie was wrapped carefully in blankets, even though they were as wet as everything else. They were *all* wet and cold, but had all become somewhat oblivious to it in light of other more prominent reasons to be upset. Hank and Fred reverently eased the body into the carriage so that Ward could put his arm around his mother one last time and hold her weight against him. It was a pitiful sight for Ian to take in as he and Wren settled themselves onto the opposite seat, but Ian could understand Ward's desire to spend this span of time close to the remains of his mother. He thought of his father's death and wished that he had been able to have personal evidence of that sad event, as opposed to simply receiving a letter. Perhaps then it would feel more real and less like a product of his imagination. He preferred to imagine that his father was still alive and well in Scotland, but he knew it wasn't true. Instead he had to imagine the grief of his loved ones and the certainty that Brierley would feel an emptiness in his father's absence.

They all breathed in deep relief when the carriage moved forward. The rain had stopped now, and they all felt hopeful that they would be able to find a place where they could get warm and dry before too many hours passed. With the motion of the carriage, Wren was able to finally get Gillian to nurse, and she quickly drifted to sleep. With the baby quiet and no one having anything to say, an eerie silence settled over them, accentuated by the presence of a corpse in their midst. It was too gruesome to think about too deeply. Ian preferred to think that Millie was sleeping, but he could only think that if he could block out every grueling detail of his close association to her actual death. And he couldn't stop rethinking those details. He wondered if the memory would ever leave him in peace. He thought of his brother James dying right before his eyes, shot in a duel and helplessly bleeding to death on the ground. Ian had, at one time, been unable to block out the image at all. Now it had become a difficult memory that popped up occasionally. He could only hope that with time, Millie's death would take on that same essence in his memory.

When the carriage stopped, Ian opened his eyes. He hadn't been dozing, but he had been completely distracted from anything going on outside his mind. He realized then that the light of dawn was bringing the hope of a new day, and that they had arrived at some kind of an inn.

"We weren't so very far from civilization," Wren said with more of a positive note in her voice than Ian could have possibly mustered.

Hank and Fred offered, then insisted, that they would take care of getting Millie to the undertaker. They knew this town well, with all of the times they had driven carriages through it and taken rest here. Ward had a difficult moment letting his mother go, but Fred assured him that they would be having some kind of service, and he would have the chance to be with her again before the casket was closed.

"Come along now," Fred said in a way that made Ian realize this wasn't the first time he'd dealt with tragedy and difficult situations. Of course, the same could be said for most people. But not all of them handled it as graciously as these two men, who both felt like angels to Ian, considering the dignified and competent manner in which they had handled all of this. "Hank and me are much dryer than you folks, since we was dressed for the weather. You all need to get inside and get dry so you don't take sick."

Apparently Hank had been speaking to the innkeeper, whom he'd awakened, while Fred had been assuring Ward and Ian that they would take care of everything. The luggage was unloaded and taken to lovely rooms where fires had been lit. Within an hour of their arrival, they were all wearing dry clothes, had a hot breakfast in front of them, and warm beds waiting to be rested in. Ian could think of a thousand things to be grateful for, but the tragedy of this night hovered over them with distinct darkness, and it was difficult to know how they would go on and make peace with such a terrible loss.

Chapter Eleven
The City on the River

Throughout the day, Ian rested here and there in between helping Wren care for Gillian, whose own needs always superseded *anything* going on in the lives of her parents. He also stayed close to Ward and made certain his physical needs were met. There was some awkward adjustment in Ian assuming Millie's role in so many little things that mother and son had become comfortably accustomed to during the many years of Ward's blindness. But Ian and Ward were comfortable enough with each other that Ward wasn't afraid to ask for what he needed, and Ian had no problem doing whatever needed to be done.

Ian tried to imagine—not for the first time—how it might feel if the situation were reversed, and he *couldn't* imagine. He could close his eyes and grope his way around a room, trying to gain a little empathy, but he knew he could *open* his eyes if he got hung up on something, and it was impossible for him to know what life was like for Ward, living continually in the dark. And now he had lost the woman who had given birth to him, nurtured him, and had been his eyes from the time he had lost his sight as a child. They had been as closely connected as a mother and son could be, and the adjustment for Ward would be difficult in ways that Ian could never understand. He could only do his best to be available at any given moment until they developed more of a comfortable routine. Once they were settled in a permanent residence, Ward could have his belongings placed in particular ways so that he could be more self-sufficient. Ian had seen him work his way around in the kitchen and parlor in New York, almost as if he *could* see, simply because he'd become familiar with his surroundings. And those who lived with him knew to always put things back where Ward knew they would be. For now, however, while they were traveling and staying in strange places, Ward needed more assistance with little things. But Ian was more than all right with that. He was reminded of a time when he had helped care for Wren's aging father. He'd been afflicted with severe arthritis, and it had been difficult for him to do many simple things. Ian had found fulfillment in helping Wren's father, and the two men had developed a strong bond through the experience. Ian felt sure that his friendship with Ward would now grow deeper because of these circumstances, but he still would have far preferred that Millie could be alive and well and available to help her son the way she always had. And she'd found such joy in it! Ian hoped that she could find joy now, in spite of being brutally snatched from the earth and from her loved ones. A thought then occurred to Ian that he felt compelled to share.

"You know, Ward, perhaps your parents are together again, after all these years of being apart."

"I would like to think so," Ward said, implying that he too had already had the same thought. "According to most clergymen we've spoken to, such things don't matter on the other side; all those feelings will be forgotten. Isn't that what we've been told?"

"More times than I can count," Ian said with chagrin. "But I still hold to my belief that such a concept simply doesn't feel right. How can it be?"

"Whether or not it's true," Ward said, "I choose to believe that my parents are together again, and I pray that it's so. I think I can feel better about letting her go if I can believe my father can be with her. Perhaps, when you look at it that way, he's done without her for a long time. Perhaps God knew that with such a dear friend as you, I could manage without her now, and she could be with the man she loves."

Ian took in Ward's words, thinking of Greer and Bethia. He imagined them caring for little Joy the way that he and Wren were caring for little Gillian. He then thought of his parents and the separation they were enduring. To think of people who loved each other being reunited in some heavenly realm put an entirely different perspective on death. Ian prayed that his instincts and feelings on that were not deceiving him. Holding to such a belief certainly was more pleasant than the hopelessness that constituted the other alternative.

Ian made certain that Hank and Fred also had comfortable accommodations at the inn so that they could rest while the carriage was being repaired. These men would not be able to take them any farther, since the carriage repairs had set them back, and they needed to return to their city of origin for other obligations. But Hank promised to help make arrangements for them to move on toward Nauvoo.

Later that day, Ian took Ward, Wren, and Gillian to the little funeral parlor in town where Millie's body had been prepared for burial. She looked a lot better than she had when Ian had last seen her, but the evidence of an abrupt and tragic death was still evident on her face. Ian lied to Ward and told him that she looked like she was sleeping, but Ward felt Millie's face and Ian suspected that he knew she didn't. Neither of them said anything to the contrary, but Wren put it all straight when she said, "We know she's in a better place, and that the way she died doesn't matter t' her anymore. We need t' think of that."

"Indeed we do," Ward said.

The following morning a local clergyman met them at the tiny town cemetery where the undertaker was waiting with the closed casket. A few words and a prayer were offered, and the casket was lowered into the ground in a place that they would likely never return to. *Just like our little Joy,* Ian thought, recalling the grave of their baby daughter in New York City. It broke his heart, but there was nothing to be done about it. He held fast to the idea of their loved ones being with them in spirit, rather than imagining their deteriorating bodies lying in the cold ground in obscure places. Surely God would put all of the pieces back together in the end. For now, they just had to keep going.

They stayed one more night in the town where Millie had been buried, then moved on the next day in the care of men that made Ian miss Hank and Fred. These men were obviously competent, but not nearly as gracious. He thought of what they had been through with Hank and Fred and felt sad to think that they'd never see each other again. He didn't even know their surnames. But he would always remember them, and he could pray for their well-being. He did so while they were traveling, and he also prayed very hard that the remainder of their journey would be safe, and that no more unforeseen challenges would rise up to do them harm. The extra space inside the carriage due to Millie's absence was initially filled with another passenger traveling in the same direction, but that person got out at a stop along the way, which made Millie's absence feel more stark, even though it allowed them to stretch out and be more comfortable. The irony was discomfiting and hard to accept.

When they arrived in one more town that would remain nameless in Ian's memory, he learned that through some matter of miscommunication, they had ended up much farther south than they needed to go to get to Nauvoo. It was one of those things that was no one's fault in particular, and there was no one to be angry with. Still, Ian felt angry. He felt inexplicably exhausted, utterly weary, and aimlessly angry. But anger would solve nothing, and he knew there was only one thing to do. He simply had to figure out the shortest, easiest route to Nauvoo now that they were where they were. It turned out that it would be faster and more efficient to go to a little port town on the river, and then take what they called a river boat up the Mississippi to Nauvoo. It was nearly an hour after he'd made the arrangements that the memory of a dream came to him abruptly, taking his breath away. He stopped in his tracks, there on the street, where passersby would believe he'd been struck with the memory that he needed to go back to the general store to get something he'd forgotten. But Ian's mind was far away, vividly back in the dream he'd had of sailing on a huge river, seeing the shore passing by from a distance. And at the end of the journey there had been a beautiful city. In that moment it occurred to him if they had gone the course they'd originally planned, they would have arrived in Nauvoo by carriage, *not* by boat. The next impression that came to his mind took his breath away all over again.

You're exactly where you're supposed to be, Ian.

He reached out to the wall of the building next to him in an effort to steady himself. The journey had been long and difficult and full of mishaps—even deadly ones. But the words in Ian's mind seemed to speak of more than just their present geographical location. It felt to Ian as if it encompassed all they'd endured and experienced, all their losses and sorrows. He repeated the words in his mind. *You're exactly where you're supposed to be, Ian.* It was true. He knew it was true. He was *exactly* where God wanted him to be, and so were those who constituted his family. He walked on to the hotel feeling a little lighter than he had since Millie's death. He hoped that he could adequately express to Ward and Wren what he'd just experienced, but when he sat them down to do so it took hardly any explanation at all before they both got tears in their eyes and declared with equal vehemence that they knew it was true. They *were* where God wanted them to be; they were on the right path, in the right place at the right time, and they would soon achieve their goal and be united with God's people.

It was completely dark when they finally arrived at the port on the river where they would embark on the final stretch of their journey to Nauvoo. From a distance, Ian could see a vague stretch of water, but it was a cloudy night and difficult to see much of anything. The air felt different, however, carrying with it distinct evidence that a large body of water was nearby.

They were able to find accommodations with little difficulty, and settled in comfortably for the night even though they had supper quite late and didn't get to bed until far past their normal time. Ian knew that Wren had fallen asleep quickly. She was so deeply exhausted that any time her head came into contact with a pillow, she would almost immediately succumb to sleep. She had to be awake when Gillian needed to be fed, and therefore cherished sleep when Gillian slept—especially at night. Wren's regularly falling asleep so quickly had prevented much of the comfortable and intimate conversation they used to share during that quiet time of day when they were relaxing. But Ian was fine with that. He didn't necessarily feel like talking these days.

The baby was resting peacefully, and there was no reason why Ian shouldn't have fallen asleep as easily as Wren. His exhaustion had become an integral part of his human existence. The fact that tomorrow they would embark on the riverboat that would take them to Nauvoo should have eased his anxiety and concerns; it should have given him tangible hope that the nightmare of this journey was almost over. But the nightmare itself seemed to have damaged his faith. All of the illness, the injuries, and the hardships lined up and marched through his mind, taunting him with the belief that there could not possibly be anything good and peaceful at the end of this journey. And worst of all was the loss of the baby. He wondered now how he might have felt about taking this journey if he'd known that by the time it was over he would have lost his sister-in-law and his daughter to death. He wanted to think that he would have had the faith to leave his home regardless, but he couldn't be sure. The very fact of his doubt seemed to imply that he didn't have nearly as much faith as he should have had, and that only fed his belief that he didn't deserve to have this nightmare end.

When his thoughts became so maddening that he felt his brain would slide into some form of insanity, Ian finally prayed with a desperation that came from the depths of his soul. He asked God to forgive him for his lack of faith, and to preserve and protect his loved ones in *spite* of his own shortcomings. *Whatever frailties I might have, Lord,* he prayed silently so as not to disturb Wren, *I ask that thou would overlook them and help me to guide these people in my care to a place where they can live in peace.* Ian prayed for a long time before he started to feel just a little bit better. Perhaps Nauvoo *would* be the end of the journey, as they had reason to believe. Perhaps his fears were simply distorted and magnified because of his prior experiences. Holding on to that flicker of hope, he finally slept and didn't wake until Gillian demanded to be fed. He drifted right back to sleep and woke again to find Wren beside him in the bed with the baby at her breast. And again he went right back to sleep, trying to imagine what life might be like in Nauvoo for him and his loved ones.

* * *

"Oh, it's magnificent!" Wren declared when she saw the Mississippi River in the gleaming light of day.

Ian agreed that it was a remarkable sight, and he enjoyed hearing her try to describe it to Ward, but he was still caught beneath a cloud of discouragement that made it difficult for him to fully appreciate its actual beauty. Ian looked at the riverboat that would take them through this stretch of the journey and wondered what might go wrong. He was wondering if Nauvoo even really existed as they'd been told, or if they would arrive and find new disappointments. He chided himself for being so cynical, but he just couldn't force his thoughts into brighter places, as Wren seemed to do. He did give himself credit for managing to keep his thoughts to himself. He suspected that Wren could see past his efforts to be cheerful and positive, but she didn't comment. She likely knew that she couldn't talk him out of feeling the way he felt, any more than he could force himself to feel any differently than he did.

After they'd embarked on the boat and had their luggage all settled, Wren *did* say to him, "I know ye wonder if ye have sufficient faith, Ian."

He wanted to demand to know how she knew any such thing, then immediately realized what a preposterous question that would be. He'd certainly shared his feelings with her, even if he hadn't spoken of them recently. And she certainly knew him better than anyone. For all of their lack of conversation of late, she surely knew his heart and his thoughts—the majority of them, anyway.

Ian could neither confirm nor deny her statement. He looked out across the river toward the distant bank and waited for her to continue.

"Ye have a lot more faith than ye think ye do," she said. "Ye didn't turn around and go back t' Scotland, now did ye." It was not a question. "Ye could have declared long ago that we would stay where we were, find a comfortable home, and forget about this quest of ours. But ye didn't. Ye haven't cursed God or stopped praying t' Him."

"I've been tempted," he admitted.

"I know," she said, putting a gentle hand on his arm. "But ye haven't given int' the temptation, and that shows the strength of yer character, Ian Brierley. The very fact that ye're on this boat, heading once again int' the unknown shows the kind of man ye are. God knows yer heart, Ian, and we will be blessed. I know we will."

Ian thought about that for a minute and had to say, "Your faith inspires me, Wren. It also humbles me. A part of me could feel that given my own struggle with faith, I'm simply not deserving of such a fine woman, but—"

"Don't be ridiculous!" she said. "Ye're the finest man I've ever known, and if anything, it's the other way—"

"Let me finish, please," he said. "But I'm more prone to just thank God that he gave me such a fine woman, and I hope that it's all right if I lean on *your* faith when mine is not so strong."

"It's more than all right," she said and put her head against his shoulder. "Heaven knows it's been the other way around at times, and it will surely be again. That's why we have each other, Ian; t' help each other through the rough times . . . and t' share the joy when it comes." She smiled up at him. "And surely we will find joy at the end of this journey. I know we will!"

"You keep telling me that, Mrs. Brierley, and I'll keep doing my best to hold on to that thought."

"Ye see," she said with triumph, "ye have a lot more faith than ye think ye do . . . like Peter in the Bible."

"Peter?" he said with an incredulous chuckle.

"Ye know the story where he walked on the water t' come out t' meet the Savior?"

"Of course I know it. His faith faltered and he fell. Is that what you're referring to?" As much as he knew he was struggling with his faith, he almost felt insulted by the comparison.

"But ye're missing the important parts, Ian. Ye have t' remember that when he *did* falter, the Savior reached out t' rescue him . . . *immediately*, it says. We only need t' have faith in Christ and He'll surely help us in our time of need. But ye also have t' remember that Peter was *walking on water*, Ian. What about the other disciples? What were they doing? They were still in the boat. Watching it all from a distance, they were. Peter got out of that boat and *walked on water*. Ye're more like Peter than ye think ye are, Ian. Ye're not back in Scotland, are ye? God told ye t' take yer family t' America, and here ye are. He told ye t' find these people and become a part of them, and ye've done everything ye could do t' make that happen. It's the same as having the courage and the faith t' get out of the boat."

Ian fell silent at the end of her explanation. He felt humbled, but he also felt a little better. Maybe he *did* have more faith than he believed he did. Wren conveniently and graciously wrapped up the conversation when she said, "Whatever happens, Ian, we'll all be together."

Ian silently agreed, but his mind added of its own accord, *Except for our sweet baby.* He didn't say it aloud, not wanting to remind Wren of something she was surely trying so hard to forget. It just felt so wrong for their baby to not be a part of their lives, and he couldn't find faith enough to accept that her death was a part of God's plan.

Perhaps that was the truest crux of the problem. And he wasn't sure if such a wound could ever be healed in this lifetime. He felt hypocritical for even thinking such a thought, when he'd experienced remarkable healing over the deaths of his dear friend and his brother. But this felt different, and he couldn't imagine ever making peace with it. He forced the issue completely out of his mind and focused instead on their destination, praying that it would be all they were hoping for. If not, he wasn't sure that he could go anywhere but back to Scotland, and then Wren would know for certain that he didn't have as much faith as she believed he did.

* * *

As the river took them closer to their destination at an even, lazy pace, Ian felt a growing combination of hope and dread. He didn't fully understand why he felt the way he did; therefore, it would be pointless to try to explain it. He kept doing his best to keep up the appearance of being pleased with their progress—as the others were— but his spirit was struggling, and he knew that Wren knew it. She seemed to be finished with trying to talk him into mustering up some outward evidence of *having more faith than he believed he did.* So they talked about other things and tried to find things to do to occupy their time. They were all reminded of their journey across the ocean, except that instead of sails, this vessel had an enormous paddle at the back that propelled it forward. And Ian liked being able to see land on either side as they journeyed along the center of the wide river. Through the course of their river journey, Gillian entered a new phase where she was more contented and happy. She frequently smiled and made happy noises, and for the first time ever she slept through the night, which Wren declared was a great blessing. With a good night's sleep, and the hope of getting the same more frequently, she was as pleased as a sleep-deprived mother could be.

The announcement that they would soon be arriving in Nauvoo took Ian off guard. He'd known how long the journey would take, and he'd certainly not lost track of the time, but he felt surprisingly unprepared to step off of this boat into the city he'd been searching for. He wasn't sure of the reasons; he only knew that he didn't feel ready. But there wasn't time to analyze the reasons. He just gathered up the family and the luggage and stepped onto the pier of the place he'd often imagined to be much like heaven on earth. With time, he'd taken on a more realistic perspective, and he was ready to find out for himself what this place was like. *Nauvoo.* They had finally arrived. He breathed in the May air and pondered how many months it had been since they had left their precious Scotland. Seasons had come and gone, life had changed in many ways, but the warmth of late spring was strong in the air, and with it came a sense of indefinable hope.

Ian wondered if all newcomers just stood there in a little huddle the way they were, surrounded by their luggage and not quite knowing what to think or what to do. A kind gentleman approached Ian and said, "Might I help you find your way, sir? I've got a wagon for hire, or if you can't afford to pay I can still help you out, I'm sure."

"We can afford to pay for your services," Ian said. "Thank you, but . . . we were hoping to speak with Joseph Smith."

The man erupted with a good-natured chuckle. "You and everyone else who comes here. Those who don't want to kill him just want to shake his hand and see what it's like to be in the presence of a prophet."

"A prophet?" Ian echoed, his tone of voice betraying how the word had made his heart pound.

The man repeated that hearty chuckle. "I take it you don't know too much about Brother Joseph if you've not heard of that."

"We've read the Book of Mormon," Ian said, liking this man's candor. "And we sent a letter and got this response." He took the letter he'd received out of his pocket and handed it to the man.

"Ah," the man said, looking it over, "it looks as though I'd do well to take you to see Brother Joseph, then. I'm Brother Moore. And you are?" He extended a hand and Ian took it, receiving a firm handshake that reminded him of the missionary he'd spoken to in London.

"Ian Brierley," he said and motioned to the others. "My wife Wren, and our daughter Gillian. Our dear friend Ward Mickel."

"A pleasure to meet you all," Brother Moore said and helped Ian load the luggage into his wagon. With the luggage in place, the kind gentleman helped Wren step up to be seated on one of two wide seats at the front of the wagon. Ian guided Ward to where he needed to sit, then he sat himself next to Wren. Brother Moore unlatched the wagon brake and took the reins into his hands as he said, "You don't look nearly as bedraggled as most folks when they step off the boat, or some who have just walked here from one direction or the other."

Ian didn't comment, and neither did any of the others. He *felt* bedraggled; he knew they all did. But obviously others had come here under much worse circumstances, and with much more sacrifice. Knowing what he knew, he could understand why. He simply felt too humbled to speak. When the silence became awkward, he quietly stated, "We've been very blessed, all things considered."

"That's good; very good," Brother Moore said.

Ian took in the reality of the community of Nauvoo with both awe and trepidation. Its newness was evident, but so was its growing beauty. There were pretty little houses and industrious-looking business, many with an appearance of being recently built. Only an occasional structure looked older, as if it had been here before these people had arrived the previous year.

"Speaking of . . ." Brother Moore went on, "it's a blessing you didn't come *last* summer. We were all just trying to settle in here then, and the swamp was threatening to swallow us. The bugs were something terrible, and so many of us folks got sick, me included. But you'll find we're a pretty hardy stock, and we find a way to keep going no matter what. Those of us who have been with Brother Joseph since Ohio have stories to tell, but that should wait for another day, I think."

"I would love t' hear yer stories, Brother Moore," Wren said.

"So would I," Ward said.

"Then I'll have to be sure and check in on all of you and see how you're coming along, but we're here now."

"Where?" Ian asked.

"This is where you should find Brother Joseph," he announced.

"Did you say people were trying to kill him?" Wren asked as if she'd just remembered him saying that back at the pier.

Brother Moore chuckled. "It happens now and then," he said as if it were commonplace. The very idea sent a chill up Ian's spine.

"Why?" Ward asked, but Ian noticed a woman with dark hair coming out of the front door of the rough-looking home they'd stopped in front of. She was taller than Wren but equally pretty. And she was significantly pregnant.

While wiping her hands on a long apron the woman called, "Hello, Brother Moore. What can I do for you?"

"Good day, Sister Emma. I've brought newcomers." Brother Moore jumped down from the wagon, and Ian did the same. "They got a letter from Brother Joseph . . . all the way in New York City."

"Then you must be exhausted," the woman called Sister Emma said to Ian, her glance taking in Ward, Wren, and the baby. She said more to Brother Moore, "Joseph isn't here." Her eyes shifted again to Ian. "He's gone . . . on Church business, as usual. But you're more than welcome to stay until we can figure out something more permanent."

"We don't want to impose, Sister Emma," Ian said, following Brother Moore's example of the usage of her name. Apparently the usage of *brother* and *sister* had to do with this being a religious community, and he liked it. But he couldn't figure why some people had their given name attached to the prefix, and others their surnames. He supposed he would get used to it. "We can certainly pay for accommodations, and—"

"There's no need for that," Sister Emma said with a warm smile. "At least not tonight."

It occurred to Ian who this woman was but he needed to say it aloud. "You're Brother Joseph's wife."

"That's right," she said and added with a soft chuckle, "Not that I ever see him." She nodded at Brother Moore. "Let's get their things inside, shall we?"

Brother Moore nodded in return and let out a delighted chuckle, as if doing so would be nothing but a pleasure. Ian settled with Brother Moore, but had to talk hard to get him to take the money. "You have to make a living, I'm sure," Ian said. "We're very glad for your assistance."

"Thank you, Brother Brierley," he said and was soon off.

Once inside the house, Ian found it humble but very cozy. In the first few minutes, he realized that this Emma had a daughter, and at least a few sons, and her pregnancy became more evident as he observed her awkwardness in getting around. There were also a couple of children living there who did not belong to Emma. She mentioned the extra children casually, as if caring for them were nothing out of the ordinary, offering in simple explanation, "Many were left without family after the hardships in Missouri." Ian wanted to ask her to expound on that, but she was busy attempting to make them feel at home. When Ian realized she intended to have Ian and Wren sleep in the bed she normally shared with Joseph, he strongly protested.

"We'll not have you giving up your own bed," he insisted. The fact that she was pregnant made the situation seem all the more ludicrous. "We will be fine with anything, and—"

Emma's protest was at least as strong as his own. "Joseph's not even here tonight, and if he were, he would insist on nothing less. I can assure you it's far from the first time it's happened." She smiled kindly. "When people come here they're weary from traveling, and I'm just glad to *not* be traveling. As blessed as I am to have a roof over my head, I'm glad to share those blessings." She shrugged. "I'll sleep in with Julia," she added, referring to her daughter. "I do sometimes anyway when Joseph is gone."

When it had been firmly decided who would sleep where, Emma invited them to supper, declaring that she always made enough for company because there usually *was* company, in one form or another. While they enjoyed a simple meal, Ian tried to figure out the names of the boys but he couldn't be sure if he had it right. There was one thing he absolutely knew for certain, however, long before the meal was over. He felt as if he'd come home. Being here in this house, with these people, felt much the same as when he'd returned to Brierley following nearly two years of senseless wandering. Being here felt as he had imagined it would feel to return to Brierley now, and it was a blessed relief to simply know that he'd come to where he belonged. But he knew now more than ever that returning to Brierley would not bring any such feeling; not anymore. He didn't belong at Brierley; he belonged here. What he felt now was *more* than he'd ever felt in coming home; it was deeper and stronger and impossible to define. But he knew it was the solution to every feeling of unrest he'd experienced for as long as he could remember. The instinct to wander had seemed to be planted in him from his very infancy, and those feelings had eventually led him to the decision to come to America and to find this place. It was not how he'd imagined it to be—not in actuality at least. But the warmth that filled his being was far more than he'd ever imagined or hoped for. He was exactly where God wanted him to be, and he knew it with all his soul.

Ian became so caught up in the examination of his own feelings that he was startled to realize the table was being cleared. He got up to help but realized that he was needed more by Ward, who was in unfamiliar surroundings. Ian guided Ward to a comfortable place by the fire, where the little boys gathered around him, apparently fascinated by his blindness. Ian left Ward long enough to go and get Gillian so that Wren could help Emma in the kitchen without needing to care for the baby. He returned and set Gillian on the rug to play. One of the boys became fascinated with the baby and said to Ian, "My mama's going to have a baby."

"I know she is," Ian said in an animated tone he used with small children. "Do you think it's a brother or a sister?"

"Just a baby," the boy said, and Ian chuckled. He then turned his attention to watching Ward answer questions about his blindness, and then he started telling the boys a funny story about a silly old man he'd met on the ship while crossing the ocean to come to America.

* * *

Wren was glad for an opportunity to be alone with Emma Smith. Only her daughter Julia was in the room with them. Emma took on a slow pace at cleaning the dishes, and Wren matched her pace in rinsing them, then Julia dried them and put them away. When Julia got behind, Wren found a clean towel and helped her dry. They had only been in the kitchen together for a minute or two when Wren couldn't keep herself from forcing the conversation past small talk.

"Is it true?" Wren asked. "About your husband?"

Emma chuckled comfortably. "That question could apply to a great many things. I don't know what you've heard exactly, so perhaps you should tell me what you *do* know, and where you've come from to get here. Everyone who comes here has a story to tell, and it's usually a very difficult one."

"It is?" Wren asked, feeling a sense of belonging just from hearing that one statement.

"Oh, it is!" Emma said. "Satan is very busy in opposing the work of the Lord, and it seems he finds his way into the lives of good people more often than any of us like to say." Emma paused, and a look that gave Wren a chill came briefly over Emma's countenance. She wanted to ask Emma what *her* story might be, what difficulties *she* had endured. All in good time, Wren thought. Emma smiled, and the darkness in her eyes vanished as she repeated, "Tell me what you know."

"I know the Book of Mormon t' be true," Wren said. "We all know it. That's what brought us here. My husband got the book from missionaries in London some years ago, but he didn't speak to them, and we didn't know where t' even find these people that believed the same as us. But God has guided us here."

"And that's all?" Emma asked, astonished.

"Ian wrote t' yer husband once we found out ye were all gathered in Nauvoo. Then he wrote back and invited us t' come. It says in the book that yer husband translated the record that is the Book of Mormon. Is it true?"

"It is," Emma said. "I never actually saw the gold plates on which the record was written, but I felt them, and I was his scribe some of the time. It was truly a miracle."

"How did he find the record?" Wren asked. "And how did he know how t' translate it?" Emma looked so astonished that Wren wondered if her questions were inappropriate. "Forgive me," she added. "Perhaps it's not right for me t' ask, but . . . I've wondered."

"Of course it's fine if you ask, and I'm happy to explain all that I can. I think there are some things you should hear from Joseph himself, or at least you should hear his version, but . . . for now, I think once the dishes are washed and the children are put to bed, we should perhaps all talk about these things."

"Oh, that would be grand!" Wren said.

"In the meantime," Emma said, handing Wren another clean plate to rinse, which she handed to Julia to dry, "tell me where you've come from."

"Scotland," she said.

"I thought that was the source of the accent," Emma said, "but I wasn't sure. Your journey has been long, then."

"Yes, we stayed in New York City through the winter."

"Very wise," Emma said with a vague hint of that shadow in her eyes again. But it passed quickly.

Wren didn't want to talk about the hardships they'd endured to get here, even though Emma had suggested she should. Instead she took notice of this sweet girl helping with the dishes. She wondered what Gillian might be like by the time she reached this age.

"Ye're a very beautiful girl, Julia. Yer mother is very beautiful as well," Wren added with a wink.

Julia and Emma exchanged a glance that seemed somewhat conspiratorial, as if they shared a great secret that they both found pleasure in thinking about. Again Wren wondered if she'd said something wrong, but Emma said, "Julia *is* very beautiful, but I'm afraid she bears no resemblance to me. She is very much our daughter, but I did not give birth to her."

"My mama died when she had me," Julia said. "Me and my twin brother."

Wren had such an abrupt rush of unexpected emotion that she wasn't sure what to do with it.

"Whatever is wrong?" Emma asked, picking up on it immediately. "Are you unwell?"

"No, no," Wren said, wiping at her tears with her sleeve. "I . . . just . . ." Emma guided her to a chair and sat as well. Julia hovered nearby but kept drying dishes.

"What is it, my dear?" Emma asked with perfect compassion.

"It's just that . . . I was looking at yer sweet Julia and thinking of my own Gillian, but ye see . . . Gillian is my sister's daughter. My sister died . . . during the crossing, and then . . . our own little girl died the day she was born." Wren wiped more tears and realized she was sharing her struggles even though she'd not intended to. "Little Gillian was with a wet nurse at the time, but . . . I needed her and she needed me, and . . . when ye said what ye did, it just . . . all came back t' me for a moment. I'm fine, really. We've been very blessed."

Emma put a hand over Wren's. "So you have. And so have we." Emma turned to look at Julia. "My sweet daughter is one of the greatest blessings in my life."

"Ye have a twin brother, ye say?" Wren asked Julia, not recalling a boy at the table who had looked so near to Julia's age.

That dark cloud appeared momentarily again in Emma's countenance, but it was Julia who explained, as if the story was very important to her. "His name was Joseph, and he died before he was one year old. He had the measles. I had the measles too, but he got such a bad chill when those men came into the house, wanting to hurt Papa, and—"

"I think we should save that story for another time, Julia," Emma said, hurrying back to the sink to continue washing dishes.

Chapter Twelve
Visions

"I'm sorry for your loss, Wren," Emma said. "We have much in common. Joseph and I lost our first baby, our little Alvin, on the day he was born. And then we had twins, a boy and a girl, who also died right away. But Julia and her brother were born near the same time, and they lost their mother. God gave me those beautiful babies to care for, just as he gave you your Gillian. She's a beautiful girl, by the way."

"She is," Wren said, back at Emma's side, rinsing cups. Her mind was stuck on what Julia had begun to say about her father, but Emma obviously didn't want to talk about it. She also remembered Brother Moore saying something about people trying to kill Joseph. It seemed there were at least a hundred things she wanted to know, but she would be patient and wait until the adults could all talk later, and then if she had other questions, perhaps the opportunity to have them answered would come up at another time. Instead, she thought about what Emma had just said about their babies. They *did* have much in common. But she had to say, "I don't know how ye could bear t' lose so many children. Just losing one has been so hard on a mother's heart."

"It *is* hard on a mother's heart," Emma said with a heaviness in her tone, but still she turned and smiled at Wren. "But God soothes the pain and gives you strength enough to move on."

"I would agree with that," Wren said.

"And you lost your sister since you've left Scotland," Emma said. "You've suffered much."

"Not just me," Wren said. "We lost Ward's mother not very long ago; a carriage mishap in the rain." Again Emma stopped what she was doing to watch Wren more closely, her expression radiating compassion.

"Because of Ward's blindness, his mother assisted him a great deal. Now Ian has tried to take her place that way, but . . . it's been difficult t' lose her." Now that Wren had some momentum, it was easy to keep going. "And news came from Scotland just before we left New York that Ian's father had passed. I know his heart is heavy with that, but I also know he is very glad t' be here. We've all known that we needed t' come here. We've known it for a long time. We're so glad that we've finally arrived."

"And I'm glad for it too," Emma said. "Surely things will be better for all of us now."

Wren heard the implication as Emma went back to washing dishes, and she couldn't resist asking, "Have things been difficult for ye, then? Ye say things will be better now. Do ye mean that—"

"We lived in Missouri before we came here," Emma said, focusing very intently on the dishes. "It was *very* difficult there, but we're all here now . . . and safe. And we are very grateful." She shook the soapy water off her hands and said, "I think that about does it for tonight. Let's finish up and get the boys to bed, shall we, Julia?"

"Yes, Mama," Julia said.

After a few minutes making certain the kitchen was in order, the women joined the men and children around the fire, where Emma initiated reading from the Book of Mormon together, as if it were a regular habit. Then they all knelt together to pray. Emma offered the prayer herself, expressing gratitude that "these wonderful people have arrived safely and that we have the privilege of enjoying their company in our home, and feeling of their faith and their strength." She also prayed that Joseph would remain safe and be successful in his endeavors. She prayed for many people they did not know, and asked that the Saints be protected in this beautiful city. Once the amen was spoken, Emma asked to be excused long enough to help the children to bed, and then she would return and they could visit. She invited them to make themselves at home and hoped they would be comfortable.

When she was alone with Ward, Ian, and Gillian, Wren quietly told them the things Emma had said in the kitchen. Ian was deeply touched to realize that Julia's situation was very much like Gillian's. He then commented, "There is a wonderful feeling in this house."

"Indeed there is," Ward said. "I feel more at home here than I've ever felt in my life, and we've only been here a matter of hours."

"Exactly!" Ian said, and Wren felt tears burn her eyes as if in agreement with what had been said.

It was nearly half an hour before Emma returned. She sat down and subconsciously placed a hand over her pregnant belly. "Now," she said, glancing back and forth between Ward and Ian, "I've been told that you know very little about my husband's history, and how all of this came to be. I must admit," she said, laughing softly, "it's not very often that *I* get to tell this story to someone who's never heard it before. And I consider it to be a privilege. Since you already know the Book of Mormon to be true . . . I assume Wren told me correctly."

"That's right," Ian said, and Ward added, "We absolutely know it."

"Then it should not be too difficult for you to accept that the means by which it came about are also true. It's a challenge for some people to accept the truth of what happened to Joseph, but if you pray about it, you can know the truth for yourselves, just as you've come to know the book is true."

Wren wondered what fantastic thing might require such a statement to preface it. Emma got a faraway look in her eyes and began, "When I first met Joseph Smith, there were rumors circulating about him that had caused quite a stir. My father was not happy about my seeing him at all, mostly *because* of those rumors. Eventually Joseph told me his story, and I soon came to know for myself that it was true. I married him because I loved him *and* because I knew it was true—in spite of what my father thought."

Wren could hardly bear waiting to hear *what* she knew was true, and she could see equal anticipation on the faces of the men. Gillian started to fuss, but Wren nursed her and she settled right down.

"When Joseph was a young man, living in New York," Emma began, "there was a great stir over the matter of religion. He was very troubled, wondering which church to join, and after much prayer and pondering over the matter, he went one morning into the woods to pray. This is the part that you must surely hear from Joseph when he returns, therefore I'll tell you the brief version and I'll personally make certain he tells you the details at some future date."

"We'll look forward to it," Ian said, even though none of them had any idea what she was going to say.

"Joseph's prayer was answered in a way he never would have imagined. He actually saw two heavenly beings." She paused as if she expected them to need a moment to take that in before she clarified, "He saw God the Father, and His Son, Jesus Christ."

"Face-to-face?" Wren asked, incredulous.

"Yes, exactly," Emma said. "He was told not to join any of these churches, for none of them were true. In short, that was the beginning of the *true* gospel of Jesus Christ being restored to the earth."

"Restored?" Ian asked. "I don't understand."

"When Christ was on the earth, he established His gospel in its complete form. Over time, a great apostasy occurred and the religions of the world have become lost, so to speak, only knowing partial truths, and lacking the proper authority to act on God's behalf."

"I could certainly agree with that," Ian said. His experience with other religions had not left a good impression on him.

"Through Joseph," Emma went on, "these truths *and* the proper authority have gradually been restored."

"Remarkable!" Ward said. Wren was impressed that he could actually speak, and actually come up with a word to describe what he felt. Wren felt utterly speechless to imagine what Emma was telling them, but her spirit didn't feel at all resistant to it. She could already feel the truth of it, and knew that Ward and Ian did as well. She could see it in their faces.

"And what of the record that he translated?" Ian asked. "How did that come about?"

"Some time after Joseph's first vision, he was visited by an angel named Moroni."

"The prophet in the book?" Ward asked.

"The very same," Emma said. "It was he who completed the record his father Mormon had abridged. He buried the record, and appeared to Joseph multiple times as an angel to instruct him. Eventually, Moroni allowed Joseph to retrieve the record, and the translation began. Of course, there has always been hardship and persecution in regard to this work. But in spite of all that, the translation was completed in a miraculous amount of time—especially for a man like Joseph who has so very little education."

"How *was* it translated?" Ian asked.

"As Joseph would say, 'by the gift and power of God,'" Emma said. "As long as you know it's true, the specific details of the method really don't matter, now do they."

"No, I suppose they don't," Ian conceded.

"I know it's a lot to take in," Emma said. "Angels, visions, ancient records. I myself was once hearing it for the first time. But I can tell you that I know beyond any doubt it is true, and if you ask God, He will let you know for yourselves that it is."

Emma slid gently into talking about the gathering of the Saints—as she called the people here—to Nauvoo, and how the previous spring and summer in this place had been very difficult; but the people were settling in more easily now, and they had the hope of this summer being much better.

That night Gillian was settled comfortably into a cradle that Emma had asked Ian to carry in from another room for their use. Wren lay staring at the ceiling, with Ian doing the same beside her. They were holding hands beneath the covers, while Wren tried to take in everything that had happened in the few hours since they had in Nauvoo—all she had seen, and heard, and felt. And she knew without asking that Ian was doing the same. There was so much she wanted to talk about, expound on, and analyze, but she didn't know where to begin. She was relieved when Ian broke the silence.

"It's true, Wren; I know it's true." He laughed softly. "I can't say how I know, and it's so . . . *incredulous* . . . that I can't begin to accept it on any logical level, but . . . I know it's true."

"I couldn't have said it better myself," she muttered and shifted her head to his shoulder as he eased his arm around her.

"We must find a place t' stay that will not be a burden for Emma," Wren said.

"I agree."

"But I don't want t' leave her home; there's such a grand feeling here."

"I agree with that, as well," Ian said. "But the more we learn about these things, the better able we will be to have a home with this same feeling."

Wren thought about that and laughed softly.

"Is something funny?"

"Not funny," she said. "I was just imagining how it might be for your family t' travel *here* and t' find us with such a feeling in our home. How would that be?"

"It would be . . . heavenly," Ian said. "But I doubt they will ever make the journey, and I'm not certain I would want them to. There are too many risks involved; it's too far to travel. I would far prefer imagining them safe and sound at home. Now that we're here, we can send letters and look forward to getting some in return."

"That is also a delightful thought," Wren said. "I love ye, Ian Brierley. I love ye with all my heart."

"I love you too, Wren Brierley."

"There's something I need t' tell ye."

"Yes," he drawled and leaned up on his elbow. A sliver of moonlight made it possible for her to see his face.

"I think I'm pregnant again, Ian."

He was silent for a long moment, and she felt nervous. "I thought it couldn't happen while you were nursing a baby."

"Maybe for some women, but . . . I do believe I am. Just the last couple of days I've started t' feel ill in the morning . . . just like before, and . . . there are other symptoms." She paused in anticipation of a reaction. When she didn't get one, she asked, "Are ye not happy about this, Ian?"

"I *am* happy about it," he said with fervency. "To think of having more children is wondrous! Little in life could make me happier than that. I only worry for your well-being, and . . . it's hard not to be afraid that . . ."

"I know," she said, "and ye don't need t' say it. But surely it will be all right this time."

"You said that Emma told you she lost a baby, and then twins the next time. We can't know for certain that it will be all right."

"No, but we have t' keep trying and trust in God," Wren said. "It's got us this far."

"Yes, I suppose it has," Ian said. "I wonder sometimes about my faith, however. I struggle, Wren, with too much fear, I think."

"And I'll say what I've said a hundred times: ye've got more faith than ye think ye do. We're here in Nauvoo. I'm certain life will be better for us now."

"I'm certain you're right," Ian said and relaxed his head on the pillow again, wondering if this was the pillow where a prophet of God usually laid his head. The thought caused him wonder, and a deep contentment. He knew Joseph *was* a prophet, and he'd not even had the opportunity to see his face. Still, he knew it. And he looked forward to when he *could* meet the man face-to-face. The very fact that they were here in the city where he lived was a miracle comprised of many miracles, and it was easier now for Ian to see the good that had occurred since they'd left Scotland rather than the heartache. He felt certain that with time it would continue to fall into perspective. He thought of Ward and hoped that he would feel the same way about losing his mother and all he'd given up to be here.

Ian thought of what Wren had just told him and placed a hand gently on her belly. She placed her hand over his and it was still there when he fell asleep, pondering what it would be like to raise a family here in Nauvoo.

* * *

They stayed in the Smith home for a few more days, but Emma remained very busy and there was little time for conversation. Ian chopped some wood for her and did a few minor repairs to the house when he insisted that he would do something to earn their keep or leave immediately. Her kindness was readily remarkable, and yet it came across in such an unassuming and natural way.

They all hoped that Joseph would return before they left the house, but on the other hand, it would be best if he had a bed to sleep in when he came home. Emma helped make arrangements for them to live in the home of some Church members who had more space than the Smith family. They were wonderful people, and glad to take in newcomers. Ian insisted on paying room and board, and he knew these people were grateful to receive the money, but it was also evident that they would have opened their home to Ian and his family with or without any compensation. Brother and Sister Harsden were moving into their older years in the respect that all of their children were grown, but they didn't seem old at all. They made the bulk of their living from the barn full of dairy cows they had. Brother Harsden cared for the animals and milked them twice a day. Sister Harsden made butter and cheese and sold it either to individuals or to the store in the center of town.

They hated saying good-bye to Emma, but of course she assured them they were not very far away and they would cross paths frequently. She promised to invite them over for dinner when Joseph returned, and they would all have a splendid visit.

Within a couple of days they had settled into the Harsden household with their own comfortable rooms and the opportunity to share meals with this kind couple. They made it easy for Wren and Ian to help with the necessary chores and to feel at home, and they also took easily to Ward and his limitations, gracefully finding things that he could do to help as well. They were glad to comply with making a few adjustments in their home to accommodate Ward so that he could find things more easily on his own, and so he could move from room to room by feeling his way around and not bumping into things that were left out of place.

The Harsdens wanted to hear every detail of life in Scotland and of the journey they had taken to come to Nauvoo. The Harsdens shared their own story of finding the gospel. They had been living in Ohio when word had come to them of a new religious movement taking place in the city of Kirtland. They talked of good times there, being among people who shared their beliefs, people who were working together for the promise of great eternal blessings. And they talked of the sacrifices made by the people to build a temple. Ian didn't understand the significance of a temple, but it was obviously very important. Not wanting to stop the momentum of Brother and Sister Harsden going back and forth in telling their story, he didn't interrupt. Their moods darkened as they talked of growing hardships that had forced them to leave Ohio, and their temple, behind.

"What *kind* of hardships?" Ward asked. It was a question Ian had wanted to ask himself, but a part of him had hesitated, not certain if he really wanted to know. He felt Wren's hand tighten in his as they were told of the persecution of the Saints by evil mobs who didn't want the Mormons in their communities. They spoke briefly but clearly of being driven out of their homes, stories of violence, exposure, and all kinds of injustice. They'd gone to Missouri where a portion of the Saints had been gathered, and they'd hoped to band together there in order to make things better. But Missouri had only been a worse version of the hatred they'd been exposed to in Ohio. Eventually they had been driven from there as well, and the people had flocked to Illinois, where they were just now settling into peace and prosperity once again.

Ian was already feeling stunned and horrified when Sister Harsden said, "And the situation in Missouri was made worse with the prophet being in prison for so long."

"Prison?" Wren echoed as if she was certain she'd not heard correctly.

"You *would* think that in the United States of America," Brother Harsden said with a subtle trace of anger that had not been evidenced thus far, even with all of the maltreatment that had been discussed, "that a people could worship how they choose. But our poor, dear Brother Joseph has been falsely accused of ridiculous crimes more than any of us have fingers and toes to count. And there in Far West he was betrayed by his friends. By *his friends* . . ." Brother Harsden actually wiped a tear from his face. "He was in that horrible prison for months, waiting for a trial that never came, while the people suffered so very, very much."

"We all came here," Sister Harsden said, "or very near here, while the prophet was still in that wretched place. The people here were very good to us, and when Joseph was finally able to escape with those who had been in prison with him, he arranged for the Church to have this land, and now we hope to be able to live in peace . . . once and for all."

Ian hoped so too. He still couldn't comment. He was too disturbed by what he'd just learned. He didn't even have to ask himself *why* such things would happen. He'd long ago accepted and understood the principle in regard to some of the hardships faced in their own lives. Satan would always oppose good things. Still, it was difficult to imagine such harsh and cruel treatment being allowed in a supposedly free country. Ian didn't have to wonder whether learning that such things had happened would affect his feelings about joining with these people. He even asked himself if knowing that it was possible for it to happen again would make him change his mind. He knew what he knew, and he could never deny it. He thought of the conviction he was seeing in these people, and others they'd met in the short time they'd been here. The faith of these people was inspiring in and of itself. If so many people remained banded together in spite of all they'd suffered, there surely had to be power and meaning in their reasons for believing what they believed.

Later that evening Ian had a long talk with Ward about the things they were learning and the perspective it had given them. He and Ward were very much in agreement concerning their beliefs, and they both reiterated their gratitude for the bond of friendship they shared, especially as they were embracing such remarkable beliefs that they knew could bring on further testing of their faith.

Once Ian had made certain Ward had everything he needed, he snuggled up with Wren and shared a similar conversation. He deeply admired the faith of this woman that he loved so very much. They didn't know what the future would bring, but they both knew beyond any doubt that they were where God wanted them to be, and nothing was more important than that.

On Sunday they attended church service with the Harsdens. Ian couldn't believe how many people were there. They actually met outside, since there was no structure large enough for a common gathering in Nauvoo, and at this point in time the people were more concerned with establishing homes and businesses. Although there *was* talk of once again building a temple. Ian sensed excitement over the prospect, and he wanted to understand what it meant and why the people had such convictions regarding it. He had so many questions he wanted answered, but reminded himself that there was no hurry. They weren't going anywhere, and if they did, it would be *with* these people.

Ian, Wren, and Ward all agreed after the service that it was a wonderful experience to actually share Sunday worship with people who all believed the same things. They were all full of excitement at having heard scriptures quoted from the Book of Mormon. And even though there were many things they didn't yet understand, they were all eager to learn and were looking forward to the wonders that would yet be unfolded. They had also been unanimously pleased with the hymns they had sung, some of which had been specifically written in regard to this religion. They learned after church from Sister Harsden that the hymns had actually been compiled by Emma Smith, back when they had lived in Ohio. She was obviously an amazing woman in many respects.

As a new week began in their new life, Wren became absolutely certain she was pregnant due to the sudden worsening of her illness. Sister Harsden was wonderful to help make her feel comfortable, and Ian did all he could to help with Gillian, especially in the morning when Wren felt the worst. By evening Wren was also feeling especially tired, and Ian didn't want her health to be at risk in any way. Memories of her illness, followed by the ordeal of childbirth, still haunted him.

Ian became comfortably accustomed to helping Brother Harsden with his chores and always being certain Ward had what he needed. He was also guided to the right people to help him arrange to have a home built for his family so that they could settle in Nauvoo permanently. Ward was eager to contribute financially to the home, since it was a home he would live in as well, hopefully for the rest of his life. Ian worked out a fair arrangement with him and they talked together about plans for the house and how there could be living quarters for Ward that were separate but not too much so.

May eased toward June as Ian and his wife and friend got to know more people in the community. They learned that Mormons were generally good people, but certainly human in their frailties like anyone else. They all had to let go of some of the idealism they'd brought with them to Nauvoo, but on the other hand, they were still thrilled to be joined with a people who shared their beliefs. Evidences of a common bond of charity and respect abounded. There were also indications of something else that was difficult to define but impossible to ignore. Ian and Wren both agreed wholeheartedly that the trauma these people had experienced was readily apparent. There was hardly a person who hadn't personally endured terrible losses—in their families if not personally. Lives had been lost, people abused and mistreated, and unspeakable horrors suffered. The people shared a bond of hardship that had strengthened their unity and their faith—except in a few rare cases where some had become crusty and embittered. But for the most part, people reaffirmed their closeness to God through their trials as well as their belief that enduring well would bring eternal blessings. In a strange way, it made Ian grateful that they *had* experienced some severe losses and hardship during their journey to Nauvoo. He would feel terribly out of place to be among these people and have nothing but an easy life behind him. Before he had even known the hardship the Saints were experiencing, he had been growing closer to them, and he felt strangely grateful.

Nearly two weeks after their arrival in Nauvoo, a note came from Emma Smith stating that Joseph had returned and they were invited over for supper the following evening, if they were able to attend.

Wren sent back a note stating that they would love to come and to plan on them being there. The Harsdens had spoken about Brother Joseph with familiarity, and even though the community of Nauvoo consisted of thousands of Saints, it seemed that everyone knew Joseph Smith, or knew of him well enough to say they'd had some kind of personal interaction with him. He was clearly a legend in his own time and among this people, but then being a prophet of God who was living in their midst certainly made him that. Having a testimony of the truthfulness of Joseph's visions seemed to be integrated irrevocably into knowing that the Book of Mormon was true, and therefore knowing that this was indeed God's true church on the earth. Therefore, associating with Joseph Smith himself held a certain mystique, and yet it was also regarded by the people as very normal and commonplace. Ian, Wren, and Ward had shared many conversations about the prophet, speculating over what he might be like, and putting together the pieces of all they'd learned—about the man *and* his great spiritual experiences. They had analyzed and wondered, and now they would actually get to meet him. They'd heard many different opinions and versions of what he was like, and had decided that they simply had to find out for themselves. They considered it a great privilege that they had actually stayed in the Smith home, and that they now had a personal invitation to dinner.

"It's something we can tell our grandchildren about," Wren told Ian, and he heartily agreed.

* * *

Ian found it difficult to sleep as he pondered what it would be like to meet a prophet of God. In truth, he'd not gotten nearly enough sleep since he'd come to Nauvoo. The stories he'd heard had rambled around in his head over and over while he'd tried to make sense of them and find his place in the midst of all he'd learned. The experiences of the Mormons spanned a spectrum of extremes that Ian had never imagined possible. Visions and revelations glowed on one side of the scale, and on the other were unspeakable persecutions and hardships. Joseph Smith himself had surely experienced both the best and the worst of it. Brother Harsden told Ian while they were feeding the cows that Joseph had once been dragged from his bed, then tarred and feathered from head to foot. Ian had felt so sick when he heard the story that he'd feared losing the breakfast he'd just eaten. He felt that same sick feeling to think of it now. Apparently that was the night Julia's twin brother had gotten a dreadful chill as a result of the invasion, and his measles had taken a turn for the worse, taking his life only days later. Experiencing such horror seemed unimaginable!

Ian thought of his own personal experiences where he'd felt God speaking to his heart. He thought of the unspeakable joy and peace he'd felt, and how such moments put everything else in life into perspective. He thought of his own personal suffering in losing loved ones and fearing for their safety. He could see now that he knew *nothing* about hardship; not in comparison to a man like Joseph Smith. He wondered if the glory of Joseph's visions felt worth it to him when placed on the other side of the scale with all he had suffered. Ian thought of a phrase from the Book of Mormon that had always fascinated him. He'd read it many, many times.

For it must needs be, that there is an opposition in all things. If not so . . . righteousness could not be brought to pass, neither wickedness, neither holiness nor misery, neither good nor bad . . . having no life neither death, nor corruption nor incorruption, happiness nor misery, neither sense nor insensibility.

Ian felt like an infant in understanding such things, but he felt eager to learn and to become a better man. He was surprised at how deeply he understood the reasons these people had endured so much and remained faithful. When real truth existed in the human heart, there was no worldly suffering that could erase it. Ian knew that well enough, but he also knew that he didn't *really* know *anything*.

While Ian pondered what he *did* know, his mind went back to that day he'd encountered those missionaries in London. He'd been at the lowest place in his life that he'd ever been, and he could look back now and see that a force beyond himself had guided him to the square where the missionaries had been preaching. He'd listened for a few minutes, and he'd felt obsessively compelled to buy that book. Later he'd actually wondered *why* he'd purchased the book, until months later when it had called to him from the bottom of a dark closet. Seeking it out and allowing its message into his life had *changed* his life. Little by little, step by step, that book had led him here. Wren's convictions about it, and then Ward's, had joined with his own as they'd been able to strengthen each other and remain united in their quest. Ian recounted the entire story in his memory, as if it were happening all over again. It was as if he saw his own life in the form of a vision, and the significant points that had brought him to this day were illuminated brightly, as if to remind him once again that *God* had brought him here, and God would continue to guide his life.

Ian recalled then an impression that had come clearly to his mind when he'd first received his own powerful and undeniable witness that the book was true, and that God was truly with him in his life. It was also the moment when all of his previous feelings had come together and he'd known beyond any doubt that he needed to go to America. The memory of those thoughts and feelings came so clearly to his memory that he felt chilled and warmed at the same time. He'd been born to wander, but he knew with every fragment of his body and spirit combined that at the end of the journey was a destiny that would bless his posterity for generations to come. And he knew that as long as he remained true to the undeniable witness of the power of Jesus Christ, he would be guided and strengthened to face whatever challenge might arise. And now Ian knew all over again that it was true. Their coming here *would* bless their posterity for generations to come. And he was willing to do whatever God required of him in order to ensure those blessings for his children and his children's children. It was his mission, his reason for being in this world. He knew it and he could never deny it. And with that knowledge he experienced a gentle comfort that finally lulled him to sleep.

Chapter Thirteen
Horizon to Horizon

It was little Julia Smith who answered the door and invited the guests inside, graciously offering to take their coats and inviting them to sit down.

"Mama's in the kitchen," Julia reported, "and Papa will be here in a minute."

"Thank you," Ian said.

"Might I help yer mother?" Wren asked.

"She said she'd be in soon," Julia said and left the room.

Ian guided Ward to a chair and was about to sit down himself when they heard a bit of a ruckus somewhere in the distance—the sound of children running, then their laughter, and mixed into it was the deep, rich laughter of a man who appeared a moment later with a boy over each shoulder, as if they were bags of potatoes, with a third one clasped onto his leg. He laughed again and deposited his giggling burdens onto the floor before he said, "You must be Ian Brierley."

It took Ian a moment to respond as his eyes met those of Joseph Smith's across the room. He wasn't what Ian had expected, but now that he was seeing the man, he wasn't certain exactly *what* he had expected.

Ian stepped forward with an outstretched hand. "I am. And you must be Joseph Smith."

There was nothing unusual about the handshake beyond it being firm and steady, but in the brief moment that their hands were connected, Joseph looked into Ian's eyes with a gaze as firm and steady as his handshake. Through the span of a long moment, Ian felt an hour's worth of thoughts come into his mind. This man had spoken to

God face-to-face. He had seen visions and conversed with angels. He was here in this time and place to do a great work that no other man in the world could be capable of doing. Ian knew it was true. He knew it was *all* true. He'd known it was true before this moment, but the striking intensity of the moment cemented his knowledge irrevocably.

While Ian was thinking he should let go and not make a fool of himself, Joseph put his other hand over Ian's and said, his eyes sparkling and a remarkable smile lighting his face, "It is such a great pleasure to have you in our home, Brother Ian." His eyes shifted, and he let go of Ian's hand to step closer to Ward, who seemed to sense it and stood, holding out a hand. Joseph took it into both of his and said, "And this must be your dear friend, Ward. Emma's told me all about you."

"A pleasure to meet you," Ward said with awe in his expression and the subtlest hint of a crack in his voice.

Joseph then greeted Wren with kind respect and genuine joy, as if she were family and not a stranger. He made a fuss over how adorable Gillian was, then expressed compassion for the losses they had experienced during their journey, saying that Emma had told him of the deaths of their loved ones. It seemed Joseph had intended to say something more on the matter, and Ian felt as if his words might be magical. Then Emma appeared, announcing that dinner was ready. While they shared a lovely meal, Joseph asked his guests many questions about their homeland, the family they had left behind, and the people they'd lost to death. He made it easy for them to ask him questions, and he spoke casually of his own experiences of persecution and hardship as if they were nothing more or less than insignificant and unpleasant memories. When the meal was finished the adults remained around the table and continued to visit, Joseph *did* tell his version of his vision in the woods, and Ian knew there could never be a moment in his future or past more powerful than what he was experiencing right now as he looked into the eyes of Joseph Smith, who said with conviction, "I saw God the Father and His Son, Jesus Christ. For all that I have been persecuted and tormented, I cannot deny it. I *will* not deny it!"

A reverent hush followed his statement, which ended with Joseph sharing a loving glance with his wife across the table. He then stood and said, "Let's get these dishes washed, Sister Smith, then we'll have some of those cookies you baked." He winked at Emma as he added, "No one makes cookies like my Emma."

A while later adults and children were all gathered near the fire, talking and laughing. Ian held Wren's hand while he observed the pleasantries and tried to absorb all he was feeling. They watched as Joseph sat in the middle of the floor and the little boys all piled on top of him, screaming and giggling as they simultaneously engaged in some kind of wrestling match with the apparent belief that the boys united could overpower their father. It wasn't Joseph's strength and size that outdid them, but his ability to tickle more than one boy at once. They all eventually fell into a heap of giggles that made the adults laugh boisterously. It was tender to see how Joseph lovingly included the boys who were not his own in their play. Joseph and Emma were both clearly accustomed to caring for others in need, in many situations.

"Oh!" Joseph groaned and laid down flat on his back as if he'd just fought a fierce battle and would likely never recover. "You boys are just getting too big. I don't think I can keep fighting off such a ferocious lot."

The boys apparently took his statement as a challenge and all heaped themselves on top of him again. He laughed, and the wrestling and tickling commenced again while the onlookers thoroughly enjoyed the entertainment. Even Ward was laughing a great deal. He couldn't see the ruckus, but he could certainly hear it, and even *that* was very funny.

Too soon it was time to leave, but not until they all knelt together for prayer at Joseph's insistence. It was much like when they had prayed with Emma and the children while they had stayed here, but this time Joseph spoke the prayer. It was simple, but it was profound in its simplicity and certainly impressive.

When the boys were on their way up the stairs and Julia had gone to get the guests' coats, Joseph said with alarm, "Oh, wait! You can't leave yet. There's something very important we need to talk about."

Emma sighed and smiled at her husband. "I'll put the children to bed," she said, and he gave her a kind smile and a squeeze of the hand in appreciation. It seemed she understood the need for people to have important conversations with her husband. Ian wondered if such things were a part of their everyday lives. Most likely they were. Feeling greedy himself to be in the presence of this man and take in any words of wisdom he might offer, Ian also felt a deep gratitude for Emma's support and patience in regard to her husband's work.

Julia brought the coats, but they were set aside before she kissed her father and went off to bed. Joseph made himself comfortable, as they all did, and Ian wondered what he might consider so important. He was surprised, as he knew Wren and Ward were, when Joseph said, "I think you have a question you want to ask me, Brother Ian, and I'm relatively certain that I have the answer you've been looking for." Following a long moment of stunned silence, Joseph chuckled and added, "No, I cannot read your minds. I'm partially assuming, simply because I know you've lost loved ones to death, and I know from vast experience—my own and that of many of the Saints—the most pressing question that comes to people in these situations. I also just . . . had the thought that it was important for us to talk about it tonight. I admit that I'm a very busy man. Perhaps another opportunity will not present itself for quite some time. So, ask me, Brother Ian."

Ian swallowed carefully, amazed at how clear the question was in his mind, and how much time it had spent hovering there in the months preceding this moment. He cleared his throat and said it. "Will we be with our loved ones again after we die?"

Joseph smiled, as if Ian had not disappointed him. "The answer is yes, my friend. Through the restored gospel of Jesus Christ, marriage can be eternal, and families can be united forever. In time the Lord will reveal all that is necessary to make this possible."

Ian wanted to ask how it was possible that *he* knew the answer to that question—and knew it so firmly—when no other clergyman Ian had ever encountered knew the answer. But Ian didn't have to ask. He already knew. Joseph Smith had been chosen by God to restore the full truths of the gospel to the earth. He knew things that *no one* else knew. But his mission was to share such glorious truths with the world, and Ian had the privilege of sitting across the room from him while he spoke of eternal truths on behalf of people both living and dead, so that they could all be united for eternity. That sparkle in Joseph's eyes became brighter as he spoke of his personal knowledge that this work would go forth throughout the world. Ian held tightly to Wren's hand, trying to take it all in. The information was overwhelming, and some of it was difficult to understand. But he realized he didn't have to understand it all right now. Joseph understood it, and he knew what he was doing. And Ian could trust in him as a prophet to know that he was speaking the truth.

Emma returned to the room and sat beside Joseph. It was readily evident that her pregnancy was drawing very close to its fruition. He held her hand in his while he continued to talk of glorious and wonderful things. When he had apparently said all that he felt he needed to say, he asked if they had any other questions for him. Ian felt as if he already had far too much to think about. When Ward and Wren remained silent, Ian spoke for all of them, saying, "Nothing at the moment. We thank you for your time." Ian stood up, which seemed appropriate. It was getting late.

At the door, Ian shook Joseph's hand again, saying, "Thank you. We *did* need the answer to that question. There is great peace and joy in knowing this glorious truth."

"Yes, there certainly is," Joseph said, then he tipped his head as if an idea had come to him. Without letting go of Ian's hand he said, "Have you people been baptized?"

"Baptized?" Wren asked, as if it were a foreign word.

Joseph chuckled. "How long have you been in Nauvoo?" He chuckled again. "The people around you are falling behind in their work. I'll send someone over to make the arrangements right away."

Ian figured that whoever Joseph sent would be able to answer their questions, so it was left at that and they all thanked Joseph and Emma for a wonderful evening; they had been spiritually fed as well as enjoying a good meal and good company. Ian felt sure that as long as he lived *this* night would be one of the highlights of his life. On the way home he broke the pronounced silence by saying, "We knelt and prayed with a prophet of God."

"So we did," Ward said. "I would say that makes the journey to Nauvoo more than worth it."

"Yes, I would say so," Ian agreed and continued to take it all into his heart and his spirit.

"And it's true, Ian," Wren said. "It's really true! Death is *not* the end. We knew it in our hearts, but now we know how it's possible."

"That *certainly* makes the journey worth it," Ian said and squeezed Wren's hand. He'd never imagined feeling such peace.

* * *

The following afternoon Ian heard a knock at the door. Brother and Sister Harsden had gone into town to do some errands. Wren was lying down while the baby was napping. So Ian answered the door, certain it would be someone looking for the official residents of the house and he would simply pass a message along. He was surprised to see Joseph Smith, dressed as if he'd been working in the garden and had barely washed up enough to be presentable for a visit.

"Good morning, Brother!" he said brightly. "You're just the man I want to see."

"You're in luck then," Ian said, "since I was the only one available to answer the door."

"The Lord works in mysterious ways," Joseph said in a joking tone, then he chuckled.

"He does indeed," Ian said and showed him into the parlor where they both sat down. "What can I do for you, Brother Joseph?" Ian asked.

"I've had a thought that has stayed with me, and it makes me wonder if you might be able to help with a sensitive situation I've become aware of. There is a young lady who is very much in need of something meaningful to do with her time." Joseph's countenance became very grave. "She endured the worst kind of persecution in Far West," he said. Ian's stomach knotted up, and he knew what Joseph was implying. He didn't need to say any more. "She also lost all of her family there; some died in a fire, some of illness."

Ian had to put a hand over his mouth to keep from groaning aloud as the picture became very clear. He waited silently for Joseph to finish explaining his purpose.

"This young lady—Patricia is her name—has been living with a very kind family. She has a great deal of faith and she's very devoted to the gospel. She works hard and has a giving heart, but . . . she has been deeply affected by these events in her life, and . . . it's my belief that if she could have some other purpose . . . something to offer her some fulfillment, that she might find healing through the giving of charitable service to someone in need."

"And you have someone in mind?" Ian asked, not seeing how he or anyone in his care was in need.

"It's been my thought," Joseph said with a sparkle appearing in his eyes, "that our friend Brother Ward could use some company; someone to read to him perhaps. Do you think he would agree to that?"

"I think he would be very pleased."

"I must clarify that if Patricia believes that he truly *needs* the companionship, she will be eager to help. If she believes that we're trying to help *her*, she will have no interest in the situation. It is . . . sensitive."

"I understand," Ian said. "We can certainly be . . . sensitive. I'll get Ward and we can speak to him about it."

"Superb!" Joseph said with jubilance.

Ward could hardly contain his excitement when Ian told him that Joseph was here to speak with him. He guided Ward into the room and observed a warm and tender greeting between the two men, as if Ward were the most important person in the world to Joseph. He had a way of making *everyone* feel that way. Ward was eager to meet Patricia and said in a mildly facetious tone that he'd become very discouraged and was very much in need of some company and someone to read to him. "And I'm certain," Ward said in the same tone, "that Ian could surely use a break now and then from having to get every little thing for me, especially with his wife ailing with her pregnancy."

"My thoughts exactly!" Joseph said and chuckled. "Emma and I will come by later and bring Patricia to meet you, if that's all right."

"That would be fine," Ward said. "I'm not going anywhere." He turned to Ian. "Am I?"

"*I'm* not going anywhere," Ian said, "and *you* can't go anywhere without *me*."

"That might change," Ward said, "if I can convince this sweet Patricia to take me for a walk now and then."

"Excellent!" Joseph said and was quickly off to make the arrangements. Ian could imagine him having a sincere conversation with this Patricia about the poor blind man who had recently arrived in Nauvoo and had lost his mother—a mother who had done so well at caring for him and keeping him company.

Not an hour later, a knock came at the door again. Gillian was still asleep, but Wren, Ian, and Ward were all sitting in the parlor visiting, waiting to meet Patricia. Wren went with Ian to the door. He opened it to see Joseph and Emma, and huddled just behind and somewhat between them, was a young woman, slight of build with brown hair and a wounded look in her eyes. She was in her mid-twenties Ian guessed, and the majority of one side of her face bore a dark red splotch.

"Good day," Joseph said. "This is our dear Sister Patricia."

"Hello," Ian said. "I'm Ian Brierley, and this is my wife, Wren."

"It's so good t' meet ye," Wren said with her usual kindness.

"It's a birthmark," Patricia said, "so you don't have to ask." She didn't say it unkindly or defensively, but her words also lacked any kindness; in fact they lacked any emotion at all.

Wren clearly didn't know how to respond, so Ian did his best to handle this graciously. "I wasn't going to ask," he said. "There's a very distinct birthmark that runs in my family, actually." He left it at that and added, "Please come in and sit down."

"Thank you," Emma said and put a hand on Patricia's arm to guide her into the parlor.

It only took a moment for Ian to assess all of the aspects of the situation now that he'd met Patricia—her age, her appearance, her circumstances. He leaned close to Joseph as he closed the door and whispered, "Match making?"

Joseph gave a barely perceptible smile with a hint of conspiracy in it. "Perhaps," was all he said. "The Lord works in mysterious ways," he added, exactly as he'd said it earlier.

"Indeed He does," Ian said and observed the mysterious ways unfolding as Joseph introduced Ward and Patricia to each other. Then Joseph hurried away with Emma, saying they had another obligation to see to.

Ian sat down next to Wren after all the introductions had been completed and Patricia sat awkwardly next to Ward on the opposite sofa.

"Should we read or something, then?" Patricia asked Ward, again in that toneless, emotionless voice.

"That would be grand," Ward said. "But we should be *properly* introduced first, don't you think?"

"What do you mean?" Patricia asked.

Ian and Wren exchanged a knowing glance. *They* knew what he meant.

"May I touch your face?" Ward asked. "It's the only way that I can know what someone looks like, and I very much want to know."

Patricia hesitated and was thinking about it when Wren said, "She's very beautiful, Ward. I can attest t' that."

"I'm *not* beautiful," Patricia said, "and you don't have to lie to me to make me feel better." She said more to Ward, "I have a dreadful red birthmark on my face."

"Should that matter to me?" Ward asked, which seemed to take Patricia off guard. "May I touch your face?" he asked again.

"I suppose you can," Patricia said.

Ward lifted his hand toward her, and she hesitated only a moment before she took his fingers and guided them to her face. Ward leaned closer to Patricia and used *both* of his hands to gently explore every contour of her face. He took his time about it, as if he didn't want to stop. Ian leaned closer to Wren and took her hand. He heard her gasp softly, which echoed his own sentiment as they both observed something indescribably magic taking place through the passing of one or two tender minutes. Patricia's expression softened as if ice were melting with the touch of the sun. It was as if the physical contact between them, so perfect and pure and innocent, had created a connection that had visibly altered both their countenances.

Ward finally spoke in a voice that cracked with the same kind of emotion Ian had heard when he'd spoken of the truthfulness of the gospel and other tender experiences in his life. "Oh, you *are* beautiful!" he said, and tears rose to glisten in Patricia's wounded eyes.

Ian was startled when Wren stood abruptly and took Ian's hand so he would do the same. "We've some things t' take care of," she said, but Ward and Patricia didn't seem to hear her. "We'll be nearby if ye need anything."

"Thank you," Ward said, and Wren hurried Ian out of the room.

She whispered in the hall, "I do believe Ward can handle the situation from here."

"I dare say you're right," Ian said and chuckled, following her into the kitchen. He chuckled again to think of Joseph's very inspired conspiracy. But of course, Joseph would always give credit where credit was due, and Ian did the same. "The Lord works in mysterious ways," he said and put his arm around Wren as they walked down the hall.

* * *

Within a few days, Patricia had developed a habit of spending the afternoons with Ward, reading to him and seeing that he had what he needed. Even though Ian and Wren had not known her previously, it was evident even from the few minutes they'd interacted with her before she'd met Ward, that the change in her had been miraculous. It seemed they were immensely compatible in ways that no one who knew them could have imagined—except perhaps for Joseph Smith, who had obviously been inspired.

A few weeks later, arrangements finally came together for Ian, Wren, and Ward to be baptized in the Mississippi River, just as the sun was coming up over the east horizon. Everything warm and hopeful that Ian had ever felt in his life culminated in that experience with a peaceful joy beyond all description. Joseph and Emma were there with their new infant son, and their joy over the event further inspired Ian's own happiness.

That very day Ian sat down to compose a letter to his family. He found great pleasure in telling them that they had settled well into the community of Nauvoo and would be staying here indefinitely. Then he took great care in explaining more fully than he ever had his reasons for coming to America, his feelings about the gospel, and his convictions that had brought him and his family to this place. He was able to state with confidence that his feelings had guided him well, since he had found exactly what he'd been looking for, and he was truly happy. He sent the letter off with hope and a prayer that his loved ones in Scotland might have some interest in knowing more about these dramatic and wonderful changes in Ian's life. He included with the letter a copy of the Book of Mormon, hoping that *someone* in his family might actually have the desire and motivation to read it.

Later that summer, Ward and Patricia were married. They had quickly become inseparable, and they were both happier than they'd ever been. The love they shared seemed to be a glowing manifestation of the healing power of Christ in their lives. No one who had known Patricia before could look at her now and not attest to the miraculous changes. And Ward had healed as well. He'd never been an *un*happy man, but now his happiness was all-encompassing, in spite of the losses he'd experienced.

The house that Ward and Ian were having built as a joint project was coming along beautifully. In spite of Ward marrying, they had decided that it would still be good for the two families to share a home, even though they would have separate kitchens and living areas. This way, Ian could always be close by if Ward needed more help than Patricia could give him. They all got along so well that it was easy to think of living under the same roof, given the practical provisions they had all mutually decided on. In the meantime, the Harsdens were more than happy to allow them to continue staying on until the house was completed.

On a clear morning with the first hint of autumn in the air, Ian felt the sudden need to take a walk, as if the earth and the sky were calling to him. Since Wren was half awake, feeding the baby, he whispered to her that he was leaving and he'd be back in time for breakfast. She smiled up at him, and he touched her face, then kissed her, savoring a simple, common moment that represented all that was most important to him. He kissed her again for good measure, then quietly left the house, taking in the light of dawn that illuminated his surroundings in a soft glow, with no direct light that brought with it beams and shadows of light and dark that collided with each other and distorted the scenery.

Ian felt drawn to that place by the river where they had been baptized. He stood there for a long while, recalling the magnificence of the experience, purposely searing it firmly into his memory as a light that would carry him through whatever the future might bring.

Watching the sun come up over the east horizon, he felt a clear recollection of standing in the cemetery in New York City, watching the sun go down, knowing that he needed to leave that place and continue in his quest. He now saw the rising sun as a symbol of the beginning of a new life, and he knew in his heart that everything he had left behind, everything that had been lost, had all been worth it.

He knew that in the end, God would make up his losses. He knew it because Joseph had told him so, and he knew Joseph to be a prophet of God. And surely that knowledge would see him through whatever lay ahead.

About the Author

Anita Stansfield began writing at the age of sixteen, and her first novel was published sixteen years later. Her novels range from historical to contemporary and cover a wide gamut of social and emotional issues that explore the human experience through memorable characters and unpredictable plots. She has received many awards, including a special award for pioneering new ground in LDS fiction, and the Lifetime Achievement Award from the Whitney Academy for LDS Literature. Anita is the mother of five and has two adorable grandsons. Her husband, Vince, is her greatest hero.

To receive regular updates from Anita, go to anitastansfield.com and subscribe.